VENOM&
VANILLA

ALSO BY AUTHOR

The Rylee Adamson Series

Priceless (Book 1)
Immune (Book 2)
Raising Innocence (Book 3)
Shadowed Threads (Book 4)
Blind Salvage (Book 5)
Tracker (Book 6)
Veiled Threat (Book 7)
Wounded (Book 8)
Rising Darkness (Book 9)
Blood of the Lost (Book 10)
Elementally Priceless (A Rylee Adamson Novella 0.5)
Alex (A Rylee Adamson Short Story)
Tracking Magic (A Rylee Adamson Novella)
Guardian (A Rylee Adamson Novella 6.5)
Stitched (A Rylee Adamson Novella 8.5)

The Elemental Series

Recurve (Book 1)
Breakwater (Book 2)
Firestorm (Book 3)
Windburn (Book 4)
Rootbound (Book 5)

The Blood Borne Series

(coauthored with Denise Grover Swank)
Recombinant
Replica

The Nevermore Trilogy

Sundered
Bound
Dauntless

A Celtic Legacy

Dark Waters
Dark Isle
Dark Fae

Contemporary Romance

High Risk Love
Of the Heart

VENOM&
VANILLA

THE VENOM TRILOGY

SHANNON
MAYER

Published by 47North, Seattle

www.apub.com

Amazon, the Amazon logo, and 47North are trademarks of Amazon.com, Inc., or its affiliates.

ISBN-13: 9781503938359
ISBN-10: 1503938352

Cover design by Damonza

Printed in the United States of America

For all those who have stood by me from the very beginning—the ones who took a chance on an author they've never heard of before and have been with me and my characters ever since. Family members, friends, readers. Believers.
This one is for you.

AUTHOR'S NOTE

CHAPTER 1

"Alena, do you remember the conversation we had about what I should do after you die?" Roger's voice was distorted behind the mask and full-body protective suit. Every time he took a breath, the air wheezed in and out as though he were Darth Vader having a particularly bad day. I half expected him to pull out a lightsaber and point it at me, demanding that I reveal the rebel base. Then again, maybe that was the painkillers making me delusional. It surely would not be the first time I'd gotten loopy on the drugs.

I blinked up at my husband from the hospital bed. "What do you mean? That was only last week."

"Well, I know. But . . . the doctors said this Aegrus disease would move fast. I . . . didn't want to assume anything day-to-day. I want to talk to you while I still can, and while you still understand me. You know?"

I ran my hands across the overstarched sheet, finding the tiny hole I'd been picking at for the last few hours. The loose threads were about the only amusement I had. Our ward wasn't allowed any technology, not even a TV. I don't know what they thought we were going to do, looking at a TV. Maybe get excited and press our nurse buttons repeatedly?

"Roger, I'm not going to lose my mind, honey. That isn't how this works." I thought for a moment. "It's more like a cake that falls in the middle of baking. I'm going to just puff out of existence."

He turned his head away, and the biohazard suit crinkled like parchment paper being shoved into a baking pan.

I wanted to think about anything but dying, anything that would take me away from the brutal reality in front of me for at least a few minutes. I would take Roger away from it too, if I could. We'd both suffered so much already, and we had very little time left to us. I wanted to make it memorable in the best way—to go out on a high note, as it were, and to make him forget that I was contagious. To make him remember that I was his beloved wife no matter how horrendous the disease made me look. "Do you remember when we met?"

Roger turned back to face me, his eyes wide. "You want to talk about that?"

I smiled up at him but kept my lips closed. No need to show him how many teeth had fallen out. "Yes. Because that was the day I fell for you, and I want to hold that to me right now. Even if I can't hold you, I can remember, and know that what we had was meant to be. No matter how it ends."

I closed my eyes, the scene as vivid to me as if we were there again, at the edge of Kerry Park. All around me, the summer rose up like a slow-moving dream in full bloom. The smell of green living things and sweet floral fragrances heavy in the air taunted me to shed my shoes and run wild through the forest as I'd done as a child. The rush of wind through the few stray hairs that had slipped my tight, conservative braid, the tickle of grass against my ankles, even through the nylons—all of it imprinted in my brain. All of it was a part of the day my life changed.

I'd gone with my mother to preach the good word, and Roger had been there in the park playing Frisbee with a small group of his friends. They'd laughed at us as we strode toward them. Pamphlets in hand,

I'd walked with confidence, knowing what I did was right, that if they would listen, they would be so much happier. Of course, we'd talked to the whole group about sinning right off the bat. The shorts they wore showed off their legs, and some of them even had taken off their shirts, including Roger. He was the first man I'd seen topless, besides the occasional glimpse of my father or brother, and I'd struggled to focus on anything but the sight of his trim body.

Like a knife through hot butter, he'd cut through the words I'd been raised to believe without question.

Pointed out the inconsistencies.

The hypocrisy.

I'd followed him to a coffee shop to set him straight, my mother urging me to save his soul, which I'd completely agreed with her about. In the end, we'd stayed for hours. We'd argued philosophy while he drank coffee and I drank decaffeinated tea, no sugar, no cream.

"I'll save you yet," I'd told him, staring into those eyes that so fascinated me. He had such a different view on the world, and I couldn't help but want to know more.

"Not if I save you first." He'd kissed me then, my first real kiss, and my fate was sealed. My knight in shining armor, he'd been the one to open my eyes to the truth of the world.

"Do you remember yelling at my mom, telling her she was blind as a bat when it came to understanding the world? That if she was too stupid to see what was right in front of her, it wasn't worth arguing about?"

He grunted. "Didn't exactly endear her to me, did it?"

I laughed, the sound odd in the small room. "No, but then, she might have forgiven you someday if you hadn't blurted out—in the middle of Thanksgiving dinner no less—that you'd taken my virginity before we were married."

He laughed and his helmet wobbled, tipping precariously to one side. His hand snaked up and grabbed it before the clips came apart. "Wow. That was close. Would suck to . . ."

He stared at me and I stared right back, unable to even blink for fear I'd lose control of myself. I gathered my words, like scooping out a measure of flour, counting it off in my head.

"Get sick? Yes, rather," I murmured, doing my best to keep the sting out of my words.

As hard as dying was on me, I knew my fate. His was far more uncertain, and I wasn't sure I could watch him break down again. The first few weeks had been rough: crying jags over the phone late at night when I was still allowed that much contact. You only were allowed to use the phone up until the final stage of the disease. At that point, you were completely cut off from the outside world. The phone calls were brutal. All I could do was listen to Roger weep. I couldn't even cry with him, because my tear ducts dried up within days of my diagnosis.

That was before I was shipped to the End Stage Ward, here on Whidbey Island. The hospital was one of only four in North America that was designed for dealing with the Aegrus virus. Which really only meant it was set up to help people die at a rapid, pain-filled pace.

Really, people died from the virus so fast it wasn't a surprise that beds opened up at the rate they did. I'd only had to wait in the lockdown ward in Virginia Mason Hospital for a little less than a week.

So now, either someone saw me in person or they didn't talk to me at all. There weren't very many people who would take the chance of stepping into an End Stage Ward and take the risk of catching the deadly virus. Besides, they all knew the outcome. We humans all did.

Roger laughed again, but there was a birdlike twitter to it that made me cringe. His nerves were showing again. I let out a sigh. How was it that I was the one in bed dying, fading away at a pace the doctors didn't understand and couldn't stop, yet he was the one who needed handling with kid gloves? My lips curled up at the edges; he was my sensitive guy. The artistic one who wore his heart on his sleeve. Which was part of the reason I fell for him in the first place: the way he'd spoken with such passion, defending his beliefs. Then there were his romantic gestures, the over-the-top dates, the candles, the flowers, and the complete wooing.

I was the business-minded one; I was the grounded one. I'd built my bakery on the back of hard work and the school of hard knocks. Developing my own recipes so I stood out in the midst of all the cafés around me had taken years. Trying new combinations of ingredients, tweaking them, learning from my mistakes; every burn, every late night was worth it.

Roger, on the other hand, could make the same mistake ten times and still insist he'd get it right the next time. Stubborn fool. I smiled, my heart aching with the thought of not seeing him ever make another mistake.

"Rog, sit with me."

"No, I can't. I can't stay."

With effort, I lifted my hand up to him. "Please, just hold my hand. Even through the suit . . . it's better than nothing at all."

He fidgeted, then twisted to look at the closed door. A face popped up in the window, and the woman waved her hands in a shooing motion. Long blond hair and brilliant red lipstick were all I saw before she was gone. Maybe she was one of the new nurses? They didn't like me to have many visitors. The chance of infection was too great among other humans. Which is why they sent us all to this facility on Whidbey Island to keep us contained. Or as my roommate called it, the Super Duper Hospital.

Supes were immune to the Aegrus virus. At worst, they got the sniffles. With humans, though . . . we weren't so lucky. It killed within weeks, sucking the life out of the body at a lightning pace.

"You sit with your wife," the woman in the bed next to me spit out. She was a little younger than me, twenty-five years old and on the same deathbed as me, if a bit further along.

"Dahlia, don't pressure him." I rolled so I could look her in the eyes. We didn't need mirrors in our ward; the disease stripped us all down the same way. Dahlia had been a redhead, according to her. Now there wasn't a single hair on her scalp, eyebrows, or eyelids. Several of her teeth had fallen out, and she had only a single fingernail left. Her body was wasted to the point of being a mere skeleton with skin stretched taut over the bony edges, like a macabre attempt at a tent by some tiny little devils who'd set up a home inside her.

Her sunken green eyes stared into mine. "You're dying. Least he could do is man up, find his balls, and hold your hand."

Roger grunted as if she'd punched him in the gut.

A tentative hand wrapped around my fingers. I smiled as I turned. "Roger. You're so brave. I know how much this scares you."

His fingers tightened on mine until they were squashed together in a rather intense embrace. I didn't say anything, though. At least he was holding my hand.

Through the barrier of the mask, I could see that sweat clearly dripped down the sides of his face. "We talked about what I would do. With the money your dad's parents left you, and what I should do with my career." The words tumbled out of him in a rush. "I've made some decisions."

"I don't think there's a rush, Rog." I tried to squeeze his hand. "I mean . . . you have your whole life ahead of you. We both know that snap decisions aren't your forte. Take your time."

He reached to the back of his head protection as if to scratch at his neck. "I'm going to sell your grandparents' house. Your mom and dad are going to buy it back from me. At a good price, mind you."

I stared up at him, a slow curl of horror starting in the pit of my stomach. The house was worth over two million dollars; there was no way my parents could afford that. "You're selling the house . . . to my . . . parents? Why?"

Apparently he didn't pick up on the nuances of my question. "Yeah, it's great. They're actually paying me over market value to keep it in the family, not that your mom wanted to. I'm going to put that money in with the life insurance money after you die, and start up a new business. I even have a business partner lined up."

My hold on his hand slipped, and I dropped my fingers to the bed. Whatever heat I'd imagined through the suit from his touch was gone.

"What kind of business?" There was no way he could run a business. I'd tried to get him to help in the bakery, and he'd bungled even the simplest tasks. He couldn't even man the cash register without fouling the entire day's transactions, a position I normally hired a teenager to do.

I stared at him, trying to understand what had happened in the space of minutes.

"Dog grooming. It's a booming industry." His words echoed in my ears, bouncing around like kids in a ball pit, screaming and laughing at my shock.

I had to be dreaming. Because this was the sort of weird twist that occurred only when I slept and the painkillers were heavy in my system. This was not reality.

There was no way Roger would start a dog-grooming business. No way he would sell the house that meant so much to me.

"You hate dogs," I managed to get out. "You always said we couldn't have one because they were too stupid to exist. They stink. And bark incessantly on top of being too needy. You chased Mrs. Whitmore's poodle with a shovel, threatening to brain it because it peed on our lawn."

He took his hands and clasped them behind his back. "That was then. I'm a changed man, and, well, I've changed my mind. We'll be grooming cats too."

I stared at him with my mouth open, unable to fully process the speed at which the conversation had begun to tank. What the fricky dicky was going on? Had he smacked his head on something and gone off the deep end?

I pinched the bridge of my nose as I struggled to get hold of the conversation and myself. I had to steer this the right way, or Roger would never pull himself out of the mess I could see him sinking into. And in not too many weeks I'd be gone and unable to help him.

"Okay, let's assume you really do this. Cats hate water, they have claws and teeth they aren't afraid to use. And if I may remind you, the last cat I had, I caught you dancing a jig when she got hit by a car."

"I wasn't dancing, I was upset." His eyes lowered and he sniffed loudly.

"What, you just decided at that moment to see if you could still do the Robot?" I snapped. This was ridiculous. Dying I might be, but I wasn't going to let him throw his life away on some harebrained—no pun intended—scheme. Sitting up was no small effort, but I pushed my deflated body upright and leaned back against the metal-tubed head-board. "Roger, this is ridiculous. You're being stupid, and there isn't time to mince words."

"Tell him how you really feel, Alena," Dahlia said with a snicker.

"That's why I can't come here. I told her you would be like this. The needle to my hot-air balloon." Roger spoke as though his business partner actually had some say in this conversation.

"You got that right, you're a hot-air balloon." I took a slow breath and tried to contain my emotions. "Roger. You hate animals. You know nothing about running a business; the bakery was all me. You couldn't even take the garbage out without spilling it all over my kitchen. Three times in a row." I paused, summoning the courage to tell him the truth. "Roger, my love, someone has seen that you have money, and they're taking you for a ride. They're using you. Whoever this business partner is, they—"

He stepped back, his whole body shaking inside his suit. "That's exactly what she said you'd say. I told her you loved me and would want me to be happy. I guess I was wrong. There is something else too."

I put a hand to my head, my whole body trembling. Whether it was with fatigue from sitting up, or from what Roger was spitting out, I wasn't sure. "Who is this 'she' you are talking about?" Oh, God, the blonde in the doorway. "Your business partner came with you? Wait, what else have you got to tell me?"

He drew himself up, and I knew in my belly what he was going to say. I held a hand out. "Don't you dare sell *my* bakery to *that* woman. Don't you dare!" If he sold my bakery to Colleen Vanderhoven, I might die on the spot and be glad of it. She'd been the bane of my existence from the day I set my shop up. The closest thing to an archnemesis I'd had in my entire life. She'd done everything she could to sink my business, from setting up her bakery a street over, to attempting to steal my recipes, to actually stealing some of my employees.

"We're signing the papers next week." The words started out of his mouth strong and ended on a sigh.

My bakery. I leaned back against the headboard, eyes aching as though tears fell from them. I loved Vanilla and Honey almost as much as I loved the house my grandparents had left me. Shaking, holding back the gulping sobs that leapt up to escape me, I managed another question. "Tell me about this business partner. Who is she?"

What if he was partnering with Colleen in more than one capacity? Burn my sugar biscuits! If he partnered with fat-nosed, mean-as-a-badger Colleen in the dog-grooming business, I would strangle him myself.

Roger nodded, "I don't know why you're surprised. You were the one who said I should move on with my life. To find love again so I wouldn't be alone."

What was he going on about now? I opened my eyes and stared at him as his words settled around me.

Dahlia let out a low groan from her side of the room. "Oh, you didn't, you dumb schmuck. Tell me you didn't."

He acted like he hadn't heard her. As he leaned close, his helmet moved like a bobble-head doll on the dashboard of a car, giving the illusion that his head wasn't quite attached the way it should have been. Which in that moment I could believe. "I love her, Alena. I know you understand because, really, this was your idea. But Barbie doesn't want me coming back to see you anymore. She's afraid I might get sick, and she has a point. Not to mention the cost of the ferry back and forth all the time. I have my whole life ahead of me. You said it yourself. So I'm getting on with it."

"But I'm not dead yet," I whispered, horror making my voice soft. Or maybe that was the growing anger that wrapped itself around my throat, cutting my words in half.

His suit crinkled as he backed away, and he lifted a hand in a feck-less, offhand farewell. "A part of me will always love you, Alena. Take care of yourself. I mean . . . as much as you can now. You know." He shrugged, cleared his throat, and left the room.

The door whooshed shut behind him, the click of the latch signaling it was closed tight. I stared at the metal panel with the square window as I attempted to process the last ten minutes of my life. A week? It took him a week to find someone new and decide he would leave his dying wife in her hospital bed alone because some woman named *Barbie* told him it was a good idea?

"Tell me you didn't hear that, Dahlia. Tell me I was dreaming."

She sucked in a slow breath. "I'm sorry, honey. That totally happened. He's a dickwad."

There were no tears, of course, but the sobs in my chest were real enough and my bones creaked with the force of the shaking.

"Don't cry over him, he doesn't deserve it. Alena, don't cry. You'll hurt yourself," Dahlia said, her voice soft and gentle.

"Take care of myself? What does he think is going to happen in the next few weeks? A magic damn cure? The doctors are going to come in here and wave a wand over us and that's it, we'll be all better?" The words exploded out of me, and while they hurt my throat, it was better than holding them in, letting them fester along with the pain in my heart.

Silence fell between us, or at least as silent as a hospital got. Outside our room the slap of feet on the cheap tile and the hum of voices drifted through the thick auto-closing door. Here the quiet was never real, rather an approximation of the big sleep that would soon come for us both.

Dahlia shifted and her bed creaked under her. "There is a magic cure. If you can afford it, you know."

Again, I wondered if I was hearing things. "What?"

"It's expensive, but if you've got the money . . . a warlock can help you." Dahlia's dark-green eyes locked with mine as they had so often over the last week.

"Dahlia, those are urban legends. I heard the rumors before I got sick too. I even saw that special exposé on TV. *The Supe Conspiracy*. That magic is the cure, and it's only a matter of time before the world knows. But there is no way our government would allow so many people to die if they could help."

She smiled, her pink gums shining between the few teeth she had left. "Really? Do you not pay attention at all? They're trying to corral all the Super Dupers above the forty-ninth parallel. Keep them contained. The fewer there are south of the border, the better. They did the same thing in Europe and Asia, put up walls to keep the Supes contained in the middle, away from the humans. Every time someone is found to be a Supe, they ship them. My house isn't far from the Wall, I've seen large vehicles cross the border more than once in the middle of the night."

She leaned closer and I tried not to sigh. Dahlia was a confirmed conspiracy theorist. Aliens, monsters, government. You name it, she had a reason it wasn't the way people thought.

Her green eyes locked on mine. "That Wall isn't what they say it is. It isn't protection for the Super Dupers. It's confinement, like an oversized zoo. I'd think living so close to it, you'd know that too."

My mind wandered. Maybe this time she was right. Seattle was close enough to the newly built Wall that I really should have known what it was all about. But Vanilla and Honey had taken all my time and attention. I'd barely seen outside my bakery for the last two years.

Between the setup, launch, and day-to-day running of the bakery, I'd worked seven days a week, easily sixteen hours a day for almost my whole marriage. There was a reason my shop had been booming before I got sick; I'd given it everything I had.

Maybe I should have given more to Roger too? I didn't want to think about it. He'd barely worked the last two years, happy to live off what I was doing. Happy to be at home and let me cook for him when I left the bakery. Happy.

I thought he'd been happy.

I sank into the thin pillow at my back. "Dahlia, I know what you're doing."

"What?"

"You're a good friend, but you don't have to distract me from what just happened. Roger . . . I was going to have to say good-bye anyway. Maybe this is better." Those were the words I said, but they weren't honest. I wanted to scream and rail against the injustice in life. To have my dream home, no financial burdens, running my own business, life had been too good. I should have known it would crash down around my ears. That the fates would deem my dreams and me a necessary casualty in the war of life.

My mother had been telling me for the last year that I was doing too well. That life would find a way to humble me. I plucked at the hole in my sheet. Humble. I'd never thought of myself as prideful, yet it looked like Mom was right.

Talk about hitting the bottom of the barrel and crashing on through to the other side.

"Listen," Dahlia said, "I've got a warlock coming tomorrow. My parents thought they could get the money into my bank by then. You'll see. You talk to him about the cure. You have the money. You said so yourself."

I closed my eyes and leaned back in my bed. What was the point in discussing this with her? *Hope* was a dangerous word as close to death as we were, and I knew it would eat her up. I thought about my bakery, of the different recipes I'd been perfecting. Like the vanilla-mousse cupcakes I'd developed right before I got sick. I whispered the recipe to myself, trying to push away what I really wanted to think about. After ten minutes of mumbling recipes and messing them all up, I rolled to my side and looked at Dahlia. I had to ask her one more question. Just out of curiosity, of course.

"How much does this supposed cure cost, exactly?"

"I don't know. The fee is different for everyone. I've heard as low as fifty, as high as two fifty."

I was pretty sure she didn't mean only fifty dollars. Fifty thousand was a big number, but we did have it in the bank. I'd put every bit of profit into savings and built up a great nest egg even before my inheritance. We had more than fifty thousand in the bank—a lot more with the addition of the inheritance from my grandparents on my dad's side. I clutched the edges of my sheets and allowed myself a thin measure of hope. To believe maybe there was a way out of this that didn't involve a pine box, hearse, off-key choir, and questionable meat platter.

As long as it didn't involve breaking my moral code, I was willing to listen to the warlock. Who was I kidding? Just interacting with a warlock was enough to send me straight to hell, according to Pastor Wrightway. And yes, that was his name. Rather convenient for a pastor.

"I see it in your eyes, Alena. You know I'm right."

I settled deeper into the bed. "I'll talk to him, if for nothing else than to show you that you would be wasting your parents' money. I've seen my share of charlatans, Dahlia. They'd come into the bakery with their miracle tool that would save me time and money, the tool that would do the work of three people and ten machines. The spinning whisker. The fancy chopper. The silly egg cookers. All garbage." I blew a raspberry.

Dahlia went off on a tangent that I listened to with only half an ear.

"Hey, I asked if you have any siblings?"

Her question sent a shot of pain through me. Five years ago we'd lost my only sibling, and it was a loss I felt daily. Since childhood when I'd been picked on for having crooked teeth and glasses, he'd been my defender and my best friend. There had been no one I trusted more. No one I thought of as often.

I smoothed a hand over the sheet. "I did. A brother named Tad. He . . . he caught the Aegrus virus about five years ago."

"Shit, I'm sorry."

"Yeah."

"Your poor parents."

I bit my lip, wanting to blurt out that they were anything but poor; oh, poop on it. "They think it's punishment from God. The virus, that is, and since he left the church, they said it was justice."

"Oh, man." She sucked in a slow breath. "They're Firstamentalists, then?"

I didn't want to correct her that it wasn't just my parents who'd gone to the Church of the Firsts. I'd attended with them every week since as long as I could remember. My big mistake? Marrying outside the church. Roger had been my one rebellion, and it had gotten me kicked out of the congregation. Since then, the fact that my parents spoke to me at all was a wonder.

Yet the faith was still the way I'd been raised, and I had believed. Even if I wasn't allowed to attend anymore. There were things I'd grown up with that were so firmly ingrained I couldn't let them go, even now that I'd turned away from the faith. I didn't drink, I didn't swear. But I wore shorts that came above my knees and let my hair go unbraided. I was a real rebel as far as my parents were concerned.

The church forbade anyone from within its congregation to interact and befriend people outside the Walls and was rather strict with the rules. My family had followed the way of the Firstamentalist beliefs for longer than I'd been alive.

Even my grandmother on my mother's side, my yaya, went to services. Though her attendance was rather erratic and she was likely to spout off when she shouldn't, she got away with it because of her age. Pastor Wrightway tolerated her since she didn't really do anything wrong. He said she was crazy. Some days I thought he was right. Most days I just enjoyed the way she saw the world. Yaya had been the one to start my love of baking. She saw me take to it and encouraged me from a young age to pursue my passion.

"That's why your parents haven't come to see you?" Dahlia asked. Her parents had tried at least, and they lived on the East Coast. Maybe that was why they hadn't made it: to save money for her supposed cure?

I cleared my throat. "Yeah. They think they'll go to hell if they show me compassion, since I obviously deserve to be sick and die."

"Shit, that's rough."

I shrugged. "I knew it would be this way the second I was diagnosed." Not that knowing the way things would fall out made it any easier. Compassion wasn't something Firstamentalists understood. One of the reasons, outside of Roger, I pulled away from them. I could believe some things the Firstamentalists taught, but not everything. In other words, I was a mess of contradictions and I knew it.

"I'm tired," I said.

"Me too."

Apparently, though, the day wasn't done with me yet, because it got even stranger when my grandmother pushed her way through my door.

Without a hazmat suit on.

CHAPTER 2

"Yaya!" I couldn't believe what I was seeing; her wrinkled face and sparkling green eyes were a balm to my aching heart even while her presence terrified me. The last thing I wanted was for her to get sick. If me getting sick weren't bad enough, to infect my own grandmother, who was the sweetest and probably the sassiest woman I knew, would surely send my soul to hell.

"Yaya, what are you doing here?"

She closed the door behind her and went on her tiptoes to peer out the square piece of glass.

"Have they stuck a tracking device in you yet?" Her words were muffled as she turned side to side, as if trying to see farther down the hall.

"What is a yaya exactly?" Dahlia rattled the rail of her bed to get my attention.

"It's Greek for *grandmother*," I said absently, not even looking at my roommate.

Yaya stared at me. "I came to see if you were really sick. Your parents keep telling me you're on vacation. But that asshat you married, you know I saw him out in the parking lot kissing a blonde with huge fake boobies? I think if I poked one, it would pop like a balloon."

I pulled my blanket up over my mouth and nose. "Yaya, I don't want you to get sick. You'll die, and I couldn't bear knowing that I was the cause of it."

She waved a hand at me. "I'm old. And everyone dies, Alena. You know that. I came to make sure you weren't doing anything you shouldn't. Getting into trouble runs in our blood, you know."

If I'd had hair on my eyebrows, I'd have raised them. "I'm lying in bed, slowly dying. What kind of thing could I be doing?"

She spread her hands wide. "The magical kind of things. Things your mother always told you not to even think about. I want you to be very sure of your decision when the time comes."

Oh dear. Maybe she'd been listening in on our conversation? Time to play it innocent.

"Yaya . . . *what* exactly are you talking about?"

She smiled, the skin around her deep-green eyes crinkling up. "Your mother got into the wine last night. Several bottles, to be fair."

I was going to get whiplash from the way she moved from topic to topic. "Wait, Mom doesn't drink. Are you sure she was drinking? Maybe it was that sparkling apple juice she likes. She keeps several bottles in the pantry for when Pastor Wrightway visits. Between the sugar and the bubbles, she gets a bit silly; we've all seen her crack a knock-knock joke after a glass of Martinelli's."

Yaya clapped her hands together, just once, then pointed a finger at me. "That's what you think. You should have seen her. She stood up on the table and wailed at the top of her lungs some song I didn't know. Something about having faith, you gotta have faith. She didn't know all the words, but she kept singing that damn chorus over and over. It's stuck in my head like Krazy Glue now."

The thought of my straitlaced, prudish, ultraconservative mother getting drunk and standing on the kitchen table was impossible to conceive. Especially singing a George Michael song. "No, she didn't."

"She did!" Yaya slapped her hands on her thighs as she laughed. "That blonde out there, Roger's boinking her now?"

Dahlia choked on a laugh. "Oh, God. Boinking. That's one I haven't heard in a while."

"Yaya. Please don't make me laugh." I couldn't help myself; it *was* funny. Maybe there was something wrong with me that the thought of my husband boinking some girl named Barbie was enough to send me into hysterics. Or at least something more wrong with me than the Aegrus virus. The laughter's edge curled tight to the edge of dry tears, and I struggled not to break down again.

The three of us settled, the laughter slowly dying out like a record fading into nothing. Yaya patted my leg. "Alena, there are things you don't know about our family. I'll tell you someday. Okay? But for now, will you trust me? Don't do anything . . . *super* stupid. Got it?" Her eyes darted around and she hunched her back. "Be careful. Will you do that? Just be careful. Whatever you do, don't believe everything you hear. We'll talk soon. I can't say more, I'm being watched." She blew me a kiss and backed out of the door. As she turned, my last glimpse of her was a side profile, the shape of her jaw and the fluffy salt-and-pepper curls that fell to her chin.

She pointed as she left the room. "Roger, get your hand out of there. You don't know where that girl's been or who she's been playing with! She could have rabies for all you know, you idiot."

The door slowly shut on Yaya giving Roger hell. I could easily imagine him cringing as she put him in place, and I didn't try to stop the smile. What was Roger doing back in the hospital?

The truth circled around me. Probably he was trying to find out how long I had left. Maybe Barbie had put him up to it.

"Oh my God," Dahlia said. "That's your grandma? She's a riot. I wish I'd known her before."

The two visits back to back had drained me, and I rolled onto my side. "Good night, Dahlia."

"It's only five."

"I'm tired."

Except I didn't fall asleep. I lay there, my heart hurting. Roger had been my first love, my first in so many ways. He'd been the hand I'd needed to cling to in order to leave everything I'd ever believed was true. I'd already seen that I didn't want to be a Firstamentalist, but I didn't know how to cut my ties on my own.

"I can hear you sniffling." Dahlia's voice was groggy with sleep. I closed my eyes tight, squeezing them to block out the light from the doorway. The recipe for macaroons should help. I could envision them fluffing up as they baked.

"Two-thirds cup ground almonds; one and a half cups powdered sugar; three large egg whites, room temperature; five tablespoons granulated sugar; one teaspoon vanilla extract. Preheat the oven to two hundred eighty degrees. Line two rimmed baking sheets with parchment paper. Draw one-inch circles on the back of each sheet, spacing the circles at least a half inch apart. Grind the almond meal with the powdered sugar in a food processor until fine. Sift the almond-sugar mixture twice through a mesh sieve . . ."

The words tumbled off my lips like powdered sugar dusting a fresh batch of cookies, and sleep finally rocked me in its dark embrace.

An unfamiliar man's voice jerked me out of scrambled dreams of a Barbie doll grooming dogs while cats chewed on Roger's face and he twittered like a bird.

"Jesus, you two look like death warmed over, baked, fried, and set out on the curb for the crows."

I rolled to one side, my bed creaking. The man who'd woken me sat on the edge of Dahlia's bed. His dark-brown hair was slicked back, tight to his skull and curled up at his shoulders. Of average build, he didn't seem all that menacing. Nice profile, clean cut, wearing a well-fitted suit. He looked like the last salesman who'd tried to hawk his wares to me: an instant whipping device for eggs that had broken as he'd given me the demo. The man on the edge of Dahlia's bed tipped his head, and I got a glimpse of the marks on his neck: two perfect puncture marks.

Bite marks.

Vampire bite marks. We'd been warned about them in Sunday school, and the teacher had shown us pictures so we knew what we were looking for when out in the "real" world. Two tiny holes with bruising around them, spaced an inch and a half apart on average.

"Merlin, are you going to help me or not?" Dahlia breathed out, her voice raspier than just a few hours before. I craned my head to look past him to her.

"You got the money?" He rubbed the first two fingers of one hand over his thumb in a slow circle.

The skin above her left eye lifted. "How much exactly are we talking?"

"For you, a deal. Seventy-five."

This *was* the warlock, then. A warlock who played with vampires. A shudder rippled through me, and I pulled my sheets up closer to my chin. The movement seemed to draw his eyes to me.

Dark eyes with a hint of blue around the edge that was so faint I almost missed it locked onto mine. "Your roommate looks only marginally better than you. She got any money?" His eyes never left me as he spoke, and I slumped farther down into my bed. My heart rate kicked up, and perspiration tried to pop up all over my body. No more sweat for me, though.

He grinned at me, but that did nothing to soothe the growing anxiety in my gut. "She's scared of me. I can smell it on her."

He could smell me? What kind of freak show was he?

"Leave her alone, Merlin. She's a Firstamentalist," Dahlia said.

His grin widened, and I could see he was far from perfect. His front teeth were slightly crooked, turning east and west respectively. "Really? Firstamentalists are so much fun to play with, with all their gasping about going to hell and how every supernatural should be burned at the stake. You know, they were huge supporters of all four Walls that separate humans from Supes."

Four Walls. I knew there were two in Eurasia, one here in North America, and there was a proposed Wall—

"That's right, they are building a Wall in South America now, cutting the continent in half. No one thought the numbers of Supes would be near as high as they ended up being."

He stepped away from Dahlia's bed as he spoke. There was nowhere for me to go, nowhere for me to get away.

So I closed my eyes.

A laugh burst out of him. "Oh, goddess, bang me, baby. She closed her eyes. Does she think I'm a bogeyman?"

Dahlia sighed. "Merlin. I said to leave her alone."

"In a minute. I'm enjoying myself."

My bed creaked as he leaned his weight onto the edge, and I squeaked, "Go away."

"Tell me your name."

"No."

"Why not?"

"The devil needs a name to call you by, and I'm not giving you mine."

His laugh was deeper this time, darker if that was possible, and the tone in it made me shiver. "I'm not the devil. I've met him, mind you. He really is an ass, but hardly anyone to worry about."

I couldn't help it; my eyes flew open. Merlin's face was only a few inches from mine. "You have *not* met Lucifer."

His lips twitched. "It really wasn't all that memorable. He's quite the sloth. Lazing about in bed, eating, belching, telling terrible jokes and expecting people to laugh. Boring as . . . well, hell." He winked as though I wouldn't get his stupid joke without his prompt.

I pushed myself farther into my bed, close enough to the far edge that another inch and I'd fall out. "Why aren't you going away again? I don't have money, and I'm not interested in whatever it is you're hawking."

Merlin tipped his head to one side, and his eyes narrowed ever so slightly. "You are human. You're dying. Yet you're more afraid of me than death. That's rare. It's intriguing."

"I don't want to intrigue you."

He shrugged and backed off the bed. "Too late . . . Alena."

"You told him my name!" I snapped.

"I didn't," Dahlia breathed. "I swear I didn't. I knew he was the real deal. I knew it."

My charts, he had to have read it from my charts. Except I knew my charts were at the nursing station under lock and key. Everyone who contracted the Aegrus virus had his or her information kept that way.

"Dahlia, you have your price. Can you afford it?" He didn't look at her, but instead continued to stare at my face.

She chewed her lower lip. "Is there anything . . . cheaper?"

Merlin blew out a low grunt. "You said you didn't want to howl at the moon every month."

"I don't."

"That's the only cheaper option."

Good God. Understanding hit me like a frying pan to the back of the skull. "You're going to turn her into a Super Duper?"

Dahlia choked on a laugh as Merlin slowly turned to face me once more. "I'm sorry, what?"

I wasn't sure I had the blood flow for my face to burn red with embarrassment, but it sure felt like it. "I mean, that's what . . . we call—"

"You call supernaturals"—he paused, closed his eyes, and pinched the bridge of his nose—"Super . . . Dupers?"

He was going to kill me. I knew it without a shadow of a doubt. He was going to strike me down with his fearsome rage—

Merlin clapped his hands together and let out a laugh that echoed in the room. Not like his earlier laugh; this one was full-bellied, like he couldn't control himself. Tears streamed down his face as he roared. I looked at Dahlia. Her eyes were wide and she shrugged. "At least he didn't kill us."

"He hasn't left yet," I pointed out.

She grimaced. "If he kills us, he can't get paid, now can he?"

Slowly, in tiny increments, he got control of himself. He brushed his hands over his face. "Good goddess, I have not laughed like that in decades."

Decades? Just how old was he? Not more than thirty by the looks of it.

He pointed a finger at me and I flinched. "Alena, you stay there. We're going to speak more in a minute."

Ridiculousness. "Just where am I supposed to go, exactly?"

"Don't die. We have business, you and I."

I swallowed hard but didn't move. Business I understood all too well. That he thought I had any with him was more than a little unnerving. I braced myself; if there was one thing I was good at, it was business. There was no way he could outbusiness me.

Not that there was any way I was doing any such thing with him.

Merlin leaned over Dahlia and handed her a cell phone. "Here. Transfer the money."

We weren't allowed cell phones in our ward—too much chance of telling people what the Aegrus virus really did to us, I guess. It made me ache all the more for Tad, that he had been through this alone. I'd snuck away to the ferry and made it to Whidbey Island only once. Tad had been sick when I saw him, but he was nowhere near as bad as I was now.

"Sis, you shouldn't have come."

I wore the suit they gave me. I squeezed his hand, clutching it between both of mine as I sobbed, fogging up the plastic of my helmet. "I couldn't not come. You can't die, Tad. You can't."

"Not really my choice now, is it?" He grinned, his face a mask for what I knew had to be an immense amount of fear. His dark-brown hair was the same color as mine, and his eyes the same brown as well. As close as we were in age, we'd passed for twins more than once. But his eyes didn't look afraid. They were nothing but calm. He had always been stronger than me, leaving the church when he was only sixteen, living on his own, standing up to Mom and Dad no matter what.

He pushed my hand away. "Go home, little Lena. I'll be okay here on my own. I promise."

I fell on him, wrapped my arms around his neck even though the suit kept us apart. "I love you, Tad."

"Love you too."

The memory hurt, knowing that if he hadn't had a roommate like I'd gotten in Dahlia, his last days would have been completely cut off from the world.

I itched to get my fingers on the tiny phone and lose myself in the technology, to pretend I was still a part of the world I knew.

Dahlia gulped. "Okay, give me the phone."

With trembling hands she took it from Merlin, and her fingers skimmed over the keyboard. The room was bloated with silence between the three of us. Less than a minute later she handed it back to him. "The money's gone. My parents were taken by someone saying that they had a cure. They were scammed." A sob hitched in her throat. "I don't understand. They told me they were going to leave it there until today. That I had until today to use it before—"

I didn't want to point out that Merlin was scamming them too. Either way, there was no cure. I knew it.

"Well, that's too bad." Merlin tucked the phone into his back pocket. "Good luck on the other side, Dahlia."

He turned and faced me with a wide grin. "Alena. You're paid for. What would you like to be? Carte blanche for you."

What was he saying? Paid for? Me? No, that wasn't possible.

"Roger paid for me to be . . . turned into a Super Duper?"

Merlin shrugged. "No name attached to the cash. Just your name as the recipient."

There was no way it was Roger; he would have said something. He would have waited for me instead of moving on to his Barbie doll with the bleached blond hair and penchant for dogs. Which of course explained why she liked Roger. I pulled my thoughts away from my husband with some difficulty.

"Well?" Merlin prompted. "What do you want to be?"

"I don't understand what you're talking about." I frowned up at him, putting my best Yaya face on. The one my brother and I had seen when we'd been caught red-handed in her cookie stash.

Merlin smiled. "Ah, let me explain. As a Firstamentalist you wouldn't know, I suppose. The Aegrus virus can be cured very simply. I will turn you into the . . . Super Duper"—he chuckled, and his eyes sparkled—"of your choice. Vampire. Werewolf. Witch. Whatever you'd like." He paused. "So what will it be, Alena? Which monster do you want to become?"

CHAPTER 3

Dahlia gasped. "Alena, why didn't you tell me?"

"I didn't know any of this. I mean, I don't even know who would pay for me." I picked at the hole in my sheet as my mind raced. "Did my parents pay for this?" That was almost as ridiculous as thinking Roger had paid for me to be cured. No, not cured, turned. The cure was as bad as the disease. I believed that. I did. Really. I didn't want to go to hell, my soul burning in fire and brimstone while a lazy Lucifer laughed. This was one of those things I couldn't let go of, a belief I knew was true all the way to the tips of my toes no matter how far I strayed from the church.

Maybe.

I shook my head. What was I thinking? I wasn't going to do this. Yet a teeny-tiny part of me screamed to listen to him. To take the chance.

Merlin sat on the edge of my bed again, the mattress bending under his weight, inadvertently rolling me toward him. "You have your pick. The money covers any number of possibilities, really. You want to be a mermaid? I haven't done that in a while, but here in the Pacific Northwest you're dealing with nipple-screaming cold water if you go that route."

I slapped a hand over my mouth to keep from laughing. I had to be dreaming still. First Roger with his Barbie doll and dog-grooming scheme, and now Merlin's offer. There was no other answer to this strange, surreal, ridiculous moment.

But my soul was on the line if this really *was* happening. Merlin kept his eyes on mine but didn't ask again. I knew the question. I might not have attended church in a long time, but I knew the consequences of taking him up on his offer, of saying yes to living. And I knew in my heart that I couldn't risk it.

"No. I don't . . . I don't want it."

I should have felt relieved at making the right moral choice. My mother would have been proud of me. Yet all I felt was a sense of defeat so sure I thought I would pass out.

Dahlia gasped. "You can't turn this down, Lena! One of us has to make it out of this crap hole of a ward."

"You take it, then. If the money is there, and you really want to do this, Dahlia." I looked at Merlin. His eyebrows shot up, but he nodded.

"Yes, the money is there. They didn't say you couldn't transfer the goods."

"Then cure Dahlia. That's what she wants. I don't." I smiled at my friend while a part of me screamed inside to tell Merlin yes.

Lies, lies, lies. I was lying to myself. I didn't want to die. I wanted to live. But I'd believed too long that being a Super Duper, a supernatural, was beyond evil. That even if you were turned by accident, your soul was stripped from you. And you'd never be the person you had been before. You'd be of the devil. You'd be a horrible beast, a monster that was violent and dangerous. You'd never go to heaven, blocked from being with your family forever.

I couldn't make myself do it. Tad was already there on the other side; I couldn't bear never seeing him again. Never hearing his voice because I made a selfish choice out of fear.

Dahlia reached a hand out for me. "Maybe there's enough money for us both?"

Merlin grunted. "If you both want to be werewolves, sure. The money's there."

Dahlia cringed. "I'd do it. If that means we both survive. We could howl at the moon together. Help each other get the excess hair off our backs."

My eyes welled, and my lips trembled. "You're a good friend, Dahlia. I'm sorry to have met you here and not before."

"Truly touching, ladies." Merlin clapped slowly. "What is the decision?"

"Help Dahlia," I said.

He kept his eyes on me. "You sure? No backsies."

I raised a hairless eyebrow at him. "Backsies? What kind of warlock are you? Were you in a boy band in a prior life?"

His eyes twinkled. "Firstamentalists don't believe in past lives. Or are you not as hard-core as you make yourself out to be? Perhaps you'd like to change your mind?" Why was he pushing me so hard? He had his money, what else did he need? Why did I get the feeling this was personal for him?

"Manner of speaking," I mumbled as I pressed my arms into the bed. Mostly to keep from flipping him the bird. He winked at me, as if he could read my mind, before he turned back to Dahlia.

He bent over her and she let out a moan. "Don't hurt her!" I jerked upright, and my chest protested the sudden movement. A low crack vibrated through me. One of my ribs was my guess.

He turned with Dahlia in his arms, the sheet wound about her skeletal frame. "She's not the one to worry about, Alena dear. She's going to survive. You, on the other hand, are going to die here alone, without even your friend now to hold your hand."

In a few quick strides he was at the door and pushing through it. Dahlia reached back for me, her eyes wide with fear . . . and hope.

"You'll never get past the nurses," I whispered. With bated breath I waited for the alarm to go off, though I hoped for Dahlia's sake they made it out.

I counted to one hundred. Nothing happened. The minutes ticked by, and I finally had to admit to myself that somehow Merlin—if that was even his real name, which I seriously doubted—had gotten them out of the ward.

So why wasn't I happy for her? I was. Of course I was. But I was sad too. Dahlia had been my only source of comfort and human companionship for the last few weeks, and really, I'd thought we'd die within days of each other. A friend who'd be with me to the literal end. Merlin was right about that. I was going to die alone now.

I lay down, easing back into the fluffy pillow, and surprised myself by drifting back to sleep without a single dream to mar the bliss of escaping the world for a few hours.

The next several days were so quiet I might as well have been entombed already. The nurses—all of them some form or other of Super Duper so they were not at risk of infection—checked on me regularly. They brought me meals, asked me how I felt. None asked where Dahlia had gone. They cleaned her clothes and items out, changed the bedsheets, and said nothing about her absence.

The second day, I stopped my nurse from leaving right away. "Can I ask you a question about being . . . a supernatural?"

The nurse, a slim lady with slightly pointed ears and long flowing hair, paused as she tucked in the sheet at the foot of my bed. "What would you like to know?"

Merlin's words about the Walls being created had continued to reverberate through me, long after he left. I picked at the hole in my sheet as I formed the question.

"Do you think the Wall is a good thing?"

She shrugged as she smoothed out my top sheet, her voice low and soothing though the words were anything but.

"My family is scattered on both sides of the Wall. Some are human, some are supernatural. Others are half-breeds." Her hands slowed. "I'll never get to see my little sister again. My family adopted her, she's full human." A tear dripped down her face, just one. It plopped onto the bed, leaving a tiny wet spot. "I'll never get to be an auntie to her babies. She had a little boy last year. I'm not even allowed to see pictures of him. Even having a picture is enough to land me into trouble." From her uniform she pulled a tiny, folded photo and handed it to me.

I took it, surprised she would trust me.

"Who are you going to tell?" she asked, not unkindly. She had a point.

I unfolded the image. A little boy grinned up at me. He had blond hair and bright-blue eyes, and his nose crinkled up with captured laughter. "He's beautiful." I handed the picture back to her and took her hand. "Firstamentalists, they helped fund the Wall. Do you . . . hate them?"

She snorted. "They did help, but it was the government, Alena. They're afraid of us."

"I didn't ever meet a supernatural before I came here. I mean, not that I know," I confessed.

"We aren't allowed across the Wall. Unless you've got a lot of power, or a specific job like us here on Whidbey, there's no reason to let us out. We are causing the virus to spread. That much is true."

She put my hand down. "Do you hate supernaturals?"

I realized then she knew that at some point I'd been a Firstamentalist. It would have been in my chart to indicate that as a minor I wasn't allowed certain procedures. Like having a gynecological exam for fear of my virginity being lost.

"No," I whispered, and I realized it was true. I didn't hate the Super Dupers. I didn't want to be one, but I didn't hate them either.

She smiled, bent, and kissed my forehead. "You're a better person than most, Alena. Don't forget it."

My heart swelled, her words meaning more to me than I would have thought.

On the third day I asked another question that had been tumbling through my head. The nurse on duty this time was part gargoyle, part something else. I wasn't sure of the mix; I knew only that as gentle as she tried to be, her hands were rough like granite stone on my tender and easily torn skin.

"Nurse Polli."

"Yes?" She didn't look up from changing a dressing on a bedsore that had rapidly spread up and over the bone of my hip. I bit my lip through the sharp pain as her knuckles brushed against the raw wound.

"Why does no one talk about the real cure to the virus? Merlin was in here and he just walked out with Dahlia, and now everyone acts like she was never even here."

Nurse Polli froze in place, and her eyes slowly rose to mine, a flicker of fear behind them. "There is no cure for the virus. Dahlia died three days ago. I took her body out myself."

I frowned. "No, Merlin took her out."

Her eyes darted away from mine. "Merlin is a fictional character, honey."

I rolled my head back. "Well, I'm not entirely sure it was his real name. I think it was like a pen name. You know, like how authors do sometimes because they don't want their prudish friends to know they write erotic fan fiction of their favorite sparkling vampires."

Her eyebrows rose incrementally as I spoke. "Really."

"Yes, but that's just from what I've heard. Where are you going? Are we done already?"

She nodded as she backed away and out the door, her gray eyes never leaving mine. Like I was going to suddenly reach up and grab her. I mean, she outweighed me by at least two hundred pounds, and I was weak as a newborn kitten. Yet she looked at me as if I were raving mad.

The door swooshed shut behind her, and I checked my dressing. It wasn't even finished. She'd left it unbound and open to the air. Maybe I'd get an infection and die faster. The laugh that escaped my lips turned into a sob.

I didn't want to die. But I'd thrown my chance away. And if I were being honest, even if Merlin showed back up right that moment, I would have turned him down. I'd been raised to do the right thing. Even when it hurt me.

Maybe most especially then. Because suffering was a part of life, and without it you grew prideful and full of ego.

I'd only flouted the rules with Roger, and look where that had gotten me: a cheating husband who couldn't wait for me to die so he could have all my money. Yaya was right. He was an asshat. Even if I never said the word out loud, it was true.

Dignity, that was all I wanted now: to die with dignity. But how could I do that when I was trapped in this tiny hospital room with nurses who acted like I was already dead?

Then there was Roger. He deserved a special place in hell for not standing by me. Even if he'd just waited till I was dead. He could have pretended that he cared a little longer.

"Pig-brained clodhopper." I pushed myself into a sitting position, my arms trembling with the effort. Even if I could move, I was tied to the catheter that allowed me to not have to use the bathroom. I checked the bag that hung off the edge of my bed. It was maybe a quarter full.

A thought formed, slowly at first, then faster as I latched onto it, a final plan put together with a definite goal in mind. The rooftop was only a floor above me. We were in the middle of January. The icy-wet cold would do me in faster than if I lay in my bed and continued to waste away.

"It'll be like going to sleep," I whispered to myself. I'd be breaking a big rule, a major belief. Suicide was a big no-no in the Church of the Firsts. But . . . I wanted to see the city lights before I died. The hospital was west of Seattle; maybe I could even see the Space Needle one last time. The best way to do that was to get to the roof. I'd sit awhile, and if I fell asleep, that wasn't my fault. Right?

I pressed the call button, and a nurse, not Nurse Polli but one I didn't recognize, poked her head in. "What's up, darling?" Her southern accent was soft and soothing. I liked her immediately.

"My catheter is bothering me, itching like mad. Could we take it out? Maybe just for a few hours even?"

Her deep-violet eyes softened as she stepped into the room. With her willowy height and light-brown hair she was probably elfin in background. "For a little while, I suppose. Might be hard to get it back in, you know."

"Not like I'm going much anyway." I pointed at the bag. She nodded, and within minutes the catheter was out.

I gave an exaggerated sigh of relief. "Thank you so much. I think I'm just going to snooze a bit."

She patted my shoulder. "You do that, darling. Just relax."

I closed my eyes most of the way, peering at her as she slipped out of the room. This was it. I sat up and swung—painfully slowly, mind you—my legs off the edge of the bed. Clutching the metal bed railing for support, I put weight on my legs, waiting for my knees to buckle.

But they never did. "Dang, I guess there is an upside to all that weight loss."

With a shuffling walk, I moved from the bed to the bathroom door, and from there to the main door. The muscles I had left trembled but kept me upright. I put a hand on the cold metal door handle. Here was going to be the real test. The door was heavy so it would shut behind people going in and out, lowering the chance of infection to the outside world. Good for them, not so much for me.

I pushed down on the lever handle and threw my body weight backward. The door creaked up as I scrabbled and panted for oxygen, my feet slipping on the floor as I fought to get a hand around and into the small opening. The door was open only a foot at the most and already sliding shut, taking me with it.

My breath came in a gulping draw as I slipped my right arm and leg around the edge so I ended up hugging the door. It continued its slow arc, coming to rest finally, trapping me in the doorframe.

"Well thought out, twit," I muttered. "Dang it all." I was stuck, pinned at the sternum on one side, spine on the other. Pursing my lips, I looked, or tried to anyway, down the hall toward the nursing desk. So much for my grand plan. "Um. Can someone help me?"

No one answered. In fact, it was rather quiet, even for the middle of the night. Where was the soft-spoken nurse who'd just checked on me? I took a breath, and as I breathed out, the door closed more, trapping my chest even tighter.

"Oh no," I gasped. The struggle to breathe became a real and terrifying thing. Yet the only thought in my mind was that I was going to die, not on the rooftop breathing in the cold, clean winter air. No, Alena Budrene was going to die in an escape attempt gone terribly wrong when she couldn't outwrestle the door to her own room.

I put both hands on the edge of the door and shoved with everything I had left. Two fingernails popped off as I slipped from my self-made trap and fell to the floor with a resounding slap of bare skin on cheap linoleum tile. I sucked wind hard, grateful I could breathe again, and surprised I hadn't broken any bones in the process.

I forced myself to my knees. "Keep moving. Someone will come and find you if you don't. They'll know what you're doing, and you can't have that."

"And just what is it that you're doing, exactly?"

I snapped my head up and was sure I gave myself whiplash. Merlin stood in front of me, his hands on his hips and one leg cocked to the side. He wore the same clothes as when he'd come to talk to Dahlia, with the exception of one thing. He'd added a bright-red tie. His dark-brown hair was still slicked back to his skull, and his eyes still looked at me with an equal amount of humor and curiosity. He ran a hand down his tie.

"What are you doing on the floor, Alena?"

"Exploring my local environment. What are you doing here?" I tucked my gown around me so my backside was covered. I might be dying, but I was going to do so with dignity. Right. That was my thought as I crawled on hands and knees, moving toward the door that would take me to the stairwell.

Honey puffs, I hadn't thought about another door.

"I came back to see you, of course. You're the only one who could use my services. I have to ask, are you trying to escape?"

I kept my eyes on the prize and the bright-red "Exit" sign that beckoned to me. One way or another I was going to do just that. One last grand exit.

"Is Dahlia okay?" I breathed out past the heaving to keep my lungs and heart working.

"Wonderful. She took the full package. But your benefactor was not pleased you turned me down."

I paused but didn't stop. If I lost momentum, I'd never get going again. But my gown was slipping, and I would have to stop to tuck it tight again so my bare bum was not exposed to Merlin and the rest of the world.

"Go away. I told you I don't want your help."

"Well, here's the thing. I didn't get to plead my case properly the other day; I think I can do better this time." He held the door open for me.

"Thank you," I said without thinking.

"Oh, you're very welcome." He laughed the words, as if I'd cracked some ridiculous joke.

I faced the stairs; one flight, right to the roof. The hand railing was above my head, but Merlin didn't offer to help again so I was on my own. On my knees I reached over my head and gripped the metal bar.

With my legs and arms working in concert I pulled myself to my feet inch by inch.

Triumphant, I smiled at Merlin while I panted for breath. "See? Exploring."

"Sure thing, sugar. You know, I saw your husband with his new girl. Blond, blue eyes, big bazookas."

"She had a gun?" I couldn't stop myself from asking.

"A pair, actually."

I whipped my head around only to find him grinning at me. "I like you, Alena. And considering your past, that's saying something. I quite hate the Firstamentalists I've dealt with. True assholes in their condemnation of anything they deem less than them."

I flushed, knowing he spoke the truth. "I'm not really—"

"I know. I looked you up." He took a step. "You left them. Very unusual, you know. They have such an iron grasp on their people. But I shouldn't be surprised. You're sharp. Quick-witted. And I'll admit, giving Dahlia your funds was somewhat of a surprise."

My mouth was dry, and all I could think about was a big ice-cold glass of water to ease the desert that was my tongue. "She's my friend."

"Let's try another tactic." He paused and took another step so his face filled my vision. "Wouldn't it be rather apropos to show up on Roger's, pardon me, your own doorstep, alive and more beautiful than ever? To shove it in his face that he walked away from you and if he'd been more faithful, he could have had the most amazingly beautiful woman in town?" There was a tone in his voice that called to me. Begged me to listen.

I shook my head. "I don't care about him."

"He's going to live off your inheritance, your grandparents' home, and waste it on a piece of ass who is using him for his money, and you don't care? You don't care he's selling your bakery to fat-nosed Colleen?"

Good grief, it was as if he were inside my head.

I didn't want to feel his words, yet they burrowed under my skin like tiny biting ants that wouldn't let me be. They climbed to my brain and whispered that I should at least listen to him. I could do that much while I made my way to the roof. Not like I had a choice anyway.

One step after the other, I climbed the stairs while Merlin made point after point.

"You could take him for every penny. Open your business again. Start fresh. Have a life. Find love. Be everything you ever dreamed of and maybe a few things you didn't even know you wanted. I could help you do that."

We were at the top of the stairs, and I was back on my knees. "You don't understand. I had what I dreamed of. I wanted to be a wife. A baker. A mother."

"You could still be a mother."

"Not if I'm a vampire. And that's what you want me to be, isn't it?"

He crouched in front of me. "What do you want, Alena? How can I convince you to come with me?" His dark eyes sucked me in, and his words made me believe he was really there for me. If he was a huckster, he was the best I'd ever met.

"I want to be human," I whispered.

"I can make you look so human, no one will ever know you're a supernatural under the skin. I can make you fit in like no other," he sighed, and I leaned into him, putting my head on his shoulder.

The fight slipped out of me. I wanted what he offered: a life and a second chance. I didn't want to die. I thought of Tad and wavered, knowing I was giving up on any belief I had of going to heaven. Maybe my brother would be able to visit me in hell. Maybe if I lived my life well as a supernatural, I wouldn't go to hell.

"No werewolf. No vampire. No witch. No mermaid."

"Something special, then? A one-of-a-kind supernatural no one has seen before?"

I lifted my head. We were close enough to kiss, but I doubted he had that on his mind any more than I did.

"Special?"

"Beautiful. Powerful. Exotic. Cured. And no one will ever know what you are by looking at you." He smiled, and there was so much sincerity in it I couldn't help but believe him.

I swallowed hard, feeling the weight of the moment on me. This was it. A cold blast of air swirled in from under the rooftop door. Outside lay my death; it might take a few hours, but it would happen. Inside lay my death if I went back to my room. I was caught between the two possibilities, never truly believing there was a third option. I could tell him to take me back to my bed, and I'd waste away over the next few weeks until I was gone, as if I'd never been.

But if I went with Merlin . . . I'd have a third possibility: a second chance at life. And if I was honest, I would relish the chance to rub it in Roger's face. Show him he was a fool to have walked away from me when I'd needed him most. I could take my bakery back from stupid Colleen and her crappy, ripped-off recipes.

I clutched at Merlin's arms and slowly nodded.

"Yes. I want that. Make me special."

CHAPTER 4

Merlin shifted me into his arms, and I fell asleep as if he'd put a spell on me. Which, looking back, I'm sure was the case. My dreams were of the world I'd left and all the things I'd seen; like viewing a history show locked on every channel I'd ever watched, I couldn't get away from it.

First was the outing of the supernatural community, right around the time I was born. The various world governments had botched things trying to keep the Super Dupers out of their countries, yet it was impossible because there were so many of them, and they were everywhere. Every community, every family—there was nowhere that supernaturals weren't. So many stayed hidden, afraid of what was happening. Worse were those who'd come out and tried to take over because they were stronger than the humans. I saw again the way the world had sat on the edge of war for years, riots and rallies on both sides.

Finally treaties were put together, a judicial and penal system that would apply specifically to supernaturals. The Super Dupers had signed it, a member from every sect of supernaturals speaking for their entire species in North America. For a space of time, a little over two years, the Supes lived side by side with humans. I remembered going to the grocery store with my mom and asking about the man behind the butcher counter. His eyes were enormous, bug eyes, and his mouth was wide with two extra canines on either side. I still have no idea what he was, only that at the time he was terrifyingly different. My mom had grabbed my hand and dragged me from the store, her face flushed as she yelled at any who would listen.

"Supernaturals, they will be the death of us. You wait and see!"

Looking back, her words were rather prophetic.

The Firstamentalists had protested and petitioned to have all supernaturals wiped out; their rallies were epic, according to my mother. The rise of the Aegrus virus in the early 2000s had served them well, producing enough fear that in the end it had enabled them to get a Wall built along the forty-ninth parallel, mimicking the two Walls in Eurasia. The supernaturals were asked nicely to stay on their side of the border while the humans stayed on the other. For the most part, it worked.

I'd always lived on the southern side, of course, in Seattle, and while there was some crossover, it was not so much that I'd ever noticed. Like the nurse in Whidbey had said, there were only a few reasons supernaturals were allowed to cross the Wall. Specific jobs being one of them. They weren't allowed to just roam into town to grab a coffee from Starbucks and then head back on over the Wall by lunch.

As far as I knew, no one in my life was a Super Duper.

Until the old man who started sitting outside my bakery. Every morning he was there, his eyes reminding me of my brother, the deep, dark brown so soft and gentle. Even the clothes he wore with his hoodie and torn-up jeans reminded me of Tad. So every morning I gave him the leftovers of my baking from the day before. I didn't know he was a Super Duper; I learned that later in the worst way possible.

The last time I'd seen him, he'd clutched at my hand. "Bless you. You are an angel in disguise. A merciful angel. I wish—" He'd coughed and slid back to his spot holding up the wall. I'd waved him off with a smile, feeling like I'd done my charitable duty, more than I would have ever done as a Firstamentalist. I handed him the bagels I'd brought out for him and went back into the warmth of my shop. Of course I'd washed, but the virus . . . it worked so fast it was already in me just from that small contact. It had been too late for me the moment I'd handed him the bagels.

My dreams shifted and faded, grew in intensity and color until it felt like I was inside a rainbow, swimming through the colors as they washed over my bare skin. Waves of pleasure rolled through me, and I arched toward the sensation, the warmth trickling over my limbs like fingers plucking at a harp. Roger, was I with Roger? No, sex had never been this good with Roger; this thought-numbing sensuality was like nothing I'd ever experienced. I went with it, let it flow through me, embracing it for all it was worth.

I wanted to clutch the sensation to me, and a low, deep laugh rumbled from nearby. "Alena, you are going to be my finest work. A goddess in disguise. Beautiful and luscious in every way. Submissive, malleable. Sheer perfection."

The man's voice slipped away and I slid back into my dreamland, fading in and out. Perhaps this was death? Had I died and not realized it? Consciousness slowly grasped hold of me and pulled me out of the fog. Not dead, then. I'd been sleeping. My skin was hot and flushed from the wild sensations, and I ran a hand down my side, the skin as soft and smooth as whipped butter.

Naked. I was naked. I groaned and slid the same hand up and over my chest.

Flesh and muscle twitched under my fingers, and I opened an eye. Above me a ceiling fan swirled lazily enough that a few flies played dodge the blade with it. I sat up and my sheet fell to my waist. I glanced down and my jaw dropped.

"Oh, my." I had a waist again. I had breasts again and they were stunning: at least a C cup with gravity-defying perkiness that I'd only ever dreamed about.

Merlin hadn't been kidding. Perfectly formed, I skimmed my hand over my body, reveling in being able to move, to feel my skin without worrying it might tear or hurt. I tipped my head, and a swath—yes, an actual swath—of straight blue-black hair slid over my back and shoulder. A shiver of pleasure cascaded through me on the heels of the hair. I'd been a brunette before, a dark brunette, but I'd never dyed my hair despite always wanting that perfect midnight tone.

My mother would have had a fit of epic proportions if I'd—

I lifted a leg and the sheet fell the rest of the way off. My legs were longer. How was that possible? Longer, muscular yet still unbelievably feminine. I pointed my toes and let out a soft sigh. I was going to look fabulous in heels.

I'd always wanted to wear heels. Another no-no taboo I was about to break. Even after I was kicked out of the church, I'd tried to live the tenets. Just in case they let me back in.

I caught my lower lip with my teeth. Maybe this was it. This was the slide into a den of depravity I'd always been warned about. First I'd dye my hair, then I'd wear heels. The next thing you know, I'd be shooting people and taking their money while I whored myself on the street corner and kicked puppies as they ran by.

"Stop it, you know that's ridiculous," I said out loud. I slapped a hand over my mouth. My voice wasn't even my own. I pulled my hand off and cleared my throat. "Alena."

Saying my name didn't sound right. My tone was huskier, and sensual, like my voice should have been whispering naughty things into the confessional closet at church. Things that would make Pastor Wrightway want to renounce his vow of celibacy.

"I'm going to hell," I purred.

I sat like that for a few minutes, not thinking. Just breathing and taking the fact in that I'd actually allowed myself to be turned. That I was one of the monsters now. Tears prickled at the corners of my eyes and dripped down my nose.

"What have I done?"

The whoosh of a door opening, reminding me far too much of my hospital room, brought my head up. Merlin stood in the door, deep-brown hair slicked back as before. No suit jacket, though, just the white shirt and bright-red tie. The throat of his shirt was open, showing a little of his skin, and the tie was loose as though he'd just gotten off work. I realized I sat there naked as the day I'd been born. That is, if I'd been born a fully grown and rather well-endowed woman.

An undignified "Eeeek" escaped me as I lunged for the sheet on the floor, yanking it up to my neck.

Merlin smiled. "I've seen it all. Some of my best work, I believe."

"You've seen me naked?" The words were a strangled squawk of disbelief and horror. "I'm a married woman!"

"Well, not really. You see, there is a fine point of the law." He stepped farther into the room and began a slow pace back and forth. "Even though you didn't die, the government can't acknowledge you are still alive. If they did, they'd have to acknowledge there is a cure for the Aegrus virus. Which is why part of the deal when I turn someone is I have to make them look different enough that they won't be recognizable. To those who know you well, they'll know you. But to the world, you are no longer Alena Budrene. Just Alena now."

Merlin stopped and held a hand out to me. "But that's not really the point. The point is by law you are now a widow. Even though you were the one who died."

Widow. "But I'm not dead. So my marriage vows still count."

He shrugged. "Not in the eyes of the law. And now, you don't own your house. Or your bakery. Or the bank account with all your money in it."

I put a hand over my mouth while still clutching the sheet to my chest. Oh my word. What had I done? I didn't even know what the judicial and penal system held for me as a Super Duper. A small part of me protested that Merlin had lied to me. He'd told me I could have my bakery. But now he'd just said that I didn't even own it anymore.

Merlin walked across the room to a small door and flung it open. "Much as I personally love the look you have going on with the Greek goddess and a mere toga, you can't go out like that. You'll cause a ten-car pileup. Pick something out here." He pointed at a closet. "It's part of the deal, and we'll get your starter package ready for you at the door."

I slipped off the bed and wobbled a little as I walked to his side. He was a couple of inches taller than me, but I had no idea just how tall I was anymore. Maybe five ten, maybe taller. Closer to six feet actually, if where my head came to the closet door was any indication.

Inside the closet was an array of clothes in every color and kind of material. I reached out and brushed a hand over them: satin and silk, brushed cotton and leather. The selection of colors was big, but not the styles. "They're all shirts. How am I going to make that work, exactly, without any bottoms?"

"They're all dresses," he corrected.

My jaw dropped and I spluttered, "I can't wear these. I'll be showing all my bits!"

He chuckled. "Buy what you want when you get out of here. But you have to wear something in order to leave. Unless you want to go naked?"

I reached out and touched the first dress that caught my eye. A tan color my mother would have chosen for me because of my brown hair and eyes.

"Not that." Merlin pushed my hand away. "You have green eyes now, that color is far too bland for you." He rifled through the closet a moment before pulling out a dress and shoving it at me. "Just try it on."

I clutched the material to me and stared as he walked out of the room. At the door he paused. "And put on heels too. You've got a great ass, show it off."

The door closed behind him, and I stood there clutching the frilly concoction he'd shoved into my hands. I dropped the sheet and pulled the dress on, moving on autopilot, doing as I was told. Strapless, the bodice was tight enough to push my new breasts into perfect cleavage. But it was the bottom that had me smiling.

Sure, it was too short and stopped above the middle of my thigh, but the skirt was fabulous. Black crinoline held the green material of the dress out just enough to accentuate how tiny my waist was now above the swell of my hips. The skeletal image I'd been only a short time before was replaced with a soft hourglass. I smoothed the dress along my new curves and peeked into the closet. At the back was a pair of four-inch green heels that sparkled with glitter.

"Oh my heck, Mom would flip out if she saw me in these." I grinned. "Fricky dicky, why not?" I grabbed the shoes and slipped them on. With only the slightest of wobbles, I walked to the door and took a breath. "New life, Alena. New life, new you. You can do this."

Right, as if it could be that easy.

I put my hand on the doorknob, turned it, and pushed it open. I stood in a long wood-paneled hallway. The ceiling was easily ten feet tall, and from it hung a skinny chandelier with mismatched gems that cast light here and there. As the only light source it didn't actually illuminate the entire hallway, only the center. I stepped forward, my heels clicking on the wood.

The steady thump of music and distant sounds of laughter and voices tugged at my ears and reverberated in my chest. A pulse of life that called to me, even though the music was anything but proper. The words were low and seductive, the rhythm that of things done in the darkest of the night between sheets of silk. My whole body flushed with the imagery that ran through my head.

Focus on something else. Anything to stop hearing the music so clearly. To my right hung several old paintings of men in black robes with severe faces and Merlin's nose.

Where was this place? Was it his house?

The hall ended in another door, this one with no knob. On the other side, the music played and the voices were clearer. A party, then? I put my palms against the door and pushed.

The door flicked open, and several faces turned toward me. All men, all Super Dupers by the teeth, eyes, and claws I caught glimpses of. A fricky-dicky den of iniquity.

I was going to hell in a handbasket woven with my own fingers.

Eyes widened, and two of the men grinned as they stepped in my direction. The door swung shut and I let it. I took several steps back into the hall before I forced myself to stand still.

That was the old Alena. The one who would have run from any Super Duper for fear of what it would do to her soul. "You get out there. You're one of them now," I whispered.

The words didn't really help.

Like diving into the coldest part of the river, I stepped forward and pushed my way through the door. Several of the men whistled.

A hand grabbed my wrist. "Beautiful, where the fuck have you been all my life?"

"Don't you use that language with me." I jerked my hand out of his. That was what I thought I was doing. But he hung on to me, his fingers digging into my arm. Taller than me by a foot, he was easily the biggest man in the room. Or not so much a man. A faint, musky odor permeated the air, and I breathed it in. A picture flickered in my mind.

Thick fur, big paws, rounded ears, sharp claws and teeth.

Maybe some sort of bear shifter then, because obviously he wasn't only a bear. Even I knew that much.

"Now, now. Don't get sassy. Merlin said you're a good girl. Obedient. Well trained. He said you would be as submissive as they came—"

I jerked my hand again, this time putting my weight into it, flexing my new muscles for all I was worth. Bear Boy gripped me, but that did him no good as he sailed through the air, all the way across the room and into the wall. He hit a picture about five feet in the air and slid down in a groaning crumple.

The room went silent and I swallowed hard. Time to make myself clear. "I said, don't use that language with me and don't touch me."

The men backed up a step. Except for one.

Merlin. He grinned at me. "What did I tell you? Beautiful, exotic, and they all think you're human."

"Shit, you didn't tell us she was one of us." A blond man grumped. His blue eyes roved over me as he put a tongue to a fang. Vampire. I couldn't stop the gasp.

"I'm leaving. And I am *not* one of you."

Laughter followed me as I strode across the room to the only door I could see. Of course it was locked. I looked over my shoulder at Merlin. "Either open it, or I'll open it for you."

"Look at her, getting all tough chick. Two minutes as a Supe and she's bossing us all around."

Merlin walked toward me, a key hanging from his finger. "Your benefactor isn't going to like you leaving before he can say hello. And don't you want your welcome package?"

That did stop me. "You aren't going to tell me who it is?"

"No." He grinned. "Which means if you want to meet him, you need to stay here."

A slow, low hiss slipped out of me, a noise that came out of nowhere and sounded a great deal like . . . no. That wasn't possible, because there was no Super Duper that was reptile, not that I knew anyway. I put a hand to my throat.

"What did you do to me?"

Merlin took a step back. "You are my special snowflake, Alena. One of a kind. Or close to it."

Behind us the door opened. "That wasn't the deal, Merlin. You were supposed to make her a naga, like me."

I knew that voice. Five years, a hundred years, it wouldn't matter. I knew him.

CHAPTER 5

I spun around and stared. His hair was jet black and his eyes green; his facial structure was different, as was his voice, but I would know him anywhere. My best friend was alive and standing right in front of me. I flung myself into his arms. "You're alive."

"That's what they tell me." Tad patted my back and then set me away from him. "Damn, sis, Merlin did good on you."

I frowned. "You saying I was ugly before?"

The men behind us laughed, and Tad shook his head, his hands raised in surrender. "I meant I wouldn't recognize you. Even your voice is different. But we still look like siblings."

He was right. His voice was familiar to me, but he had the same shift in coloring that I'd had. Brown hair and eyes had slid into black hair and green eyes. He grinned, showing off a pair of tiny fangs. Oh dear, that wasn't going to be good. Fear clutched at me, and I fought to keep myself from cringing away from him.

"You're a vampire?"

"No. A naga. Different species altogether."

I blinked stupidly up at him. "A what?"

"A snake man. Same as Merlin made you, right, Merlin?"

Merlin nodded, but I thought I caught a twinkle in his eyes. "Of course. You asked for her to be a snake girl like you. That's what I did."

Tad patted me on the arm. "Listen, it's a pretty good deal. I can shift, don't have to drink blood, and am somewhat long-lived." He slid an arm over my bare shoulders and tugged me tight to his side. "Thanks, Merlin."

"You know the deal," Merlin said. "You owe me."

I pushed away from Tad. "Wait. Stop." I turned and pointed a finger at Merlin as my questions tumbled out of my mouth. "You paid for this? How? Where did you get that much money? Why didn't you come home? Where's Dahlia?"

Merlin shook his head. "She's not your friend anymore, Alena. She's a bloodsucker, and they stick to their own kind. You can't talk to her."

"Why not?" That was stupid; what reason could he possibly have for me not talking to her?

The blond vampire leaned back in his chair and put his legs on the round table in front of him. "Because every supernatural group sticks to their own kind. Vamps to vamps, wolves to wolves, witches to witches. There is no crossover. Except here when Merlin has his poker nights."

The men in the group all nodded in unison. Poker night. I looked closer at the scene in front of me. The chips on the table, the cards, the drinks.

I backed up, bumping into Tad. He put a hand on my shoulder and steered me to the door. "Come on, I'll explain everything."

I let him lead me out of the room, through the door, and into the street. The house we stepped out of was tall and narrow, painted a deep red with a black door. The windows were shuttered and nailed closed. On the lawn was a sign: "Merlin for Hire."

My brother dragged me down the street as Merlin waved from the doorway. "You forgot your welcome package." From inside the house the men laughed, a rolling sound I knew I shouldn't have been able to hear from that far away. "Come back when you want it. We can discuss things then."

"What could I want to discuss with him?" Dang, it was like I couldn't stop with the questions. And no one was answering me. "Tad, stop, I want to know just what is going on. What did he turn me into? Back there I . . . hissed. Like a snake. Am I a naga thing like you? That's what I am?"

Tad didn't slow. He checked the street and dragged me across. I hurried as best as I could in my heels and fluffy skirt, but I've got to be honest. Four-inch heels are made for slinking and wiggling hips, not jogging.

He hurried to a big black Harley-Davidson. "We've got to go, before the Supe Squad finds us." He didn't hand me a helmet, nor did he put one on himself.

"Tad, this isn't safe. Where are the helmets?"

"We aren't going to die, Lena. This isn't as unsafe as you think." He swung a long leg over the bike and looked back at me.

"But I don't want to crack my skull open when you tip us over. I remember the ATV incident all too well."

He frowned at me, brows dropping low over his bright-green eyes. "Lena. We. Will. Be. Fine. Even if there's a wreck. We aren't human anymore, we can take a licking and keep on ticking. Get on. We have to go. And the ATV flipping over was not my fault. There was a bump in the trail I didn't see."

Lips pursed, I stepped up, put my hands on his shoulders, and swung a leg over. My skirt bunched up between us, which exposed even more of my new long legs. I wrapped my arms around his waist, and he kicked the starter stand thingy once. The engine roared to life, and behind us, the sound of a diesel engine revving caught my ear.

Except it wasn't what I was hearing, it was what I was feeling along my skin, the vibration of sound in the air caressing my skin like an oversized cat purring.

"Shit, they're on us already," Tad bit out.

He twisted the throttle and the bike leapt forward. I squeaked and clung tighter to my brother while my skirt flipped and flapped in the wind. My hair pulled out behind me, and I buried my face against his back.

"Tad, not so fast!"

"Don't hold me so tight!"

I tried to loosen my grip, but fear kept me clinging to him. He took a hard left, and the bike tipped precariously close to the ground. My knee was only inches above the asphalt.

"Stop screaming, you crazy woman!" he shouted at me. I couldn't help it. This was all happening so fast—in every sense of the word. The wind tore at me. Tiny pellets of water raining down from the sky hit my skin, and I knew they would make the road slick as slug snot.

We were on a straight stretch, and Tad pulled the throttle again. The bike shot forward as the diesel engine behind us roared again. I dared to look back, twisting my head to the side.

The diesel engine belonged to a large square truck—a semitruck with chrome stacks and a large cage on the back of it on top of a flat deck. "That will never catch us."

"It doesn't have to," Tad yelled back to me. "Runners."

Runners? From behind the black semi to either side two motorbikes—crotch rockets was what Dad called them—raced toward us. "Oh dear."

"No shit." Tad hunched his back, and I realized he intended to go faster. I didn't want to go faster. All I could see was us hitting a pothole, wiping out on the asphalt, and watching all my skin peel away like wet toilet paper in the wind.

"What do we do?"

"Go faster than them," Tad said. "And if all else fails—" He reached to his waist and handed something back to me. I took it without thinking, the shape familiar to me even though I'd never handled one before.

"A gun? Are you out of your ever-loving mind? What's wrong with you? I can't shoot at them!"

"You have to. They'll take us downtown, and you don't want to be chipped, sis."

Chipped. What had Yaya said? "With a tracking device?"

"Exactly."

"Honey puffs," I whispered more to myself than Tad, but he heard me anyway.

"That the best you got?"

The two bikes roared up beside us, flanking us. Their helmets were completely dark, hiding any indication of a face.

"Shoot them, Lena!" Tad yelled, and the bikes wavered back. I held the gun but didn't know what to do. I didn't want a tracking device put in me. I didn't want to hurt anyone.

I didn't want to be a Super Duper; I just didn't want to die. This was ridiculous. "I can't."

Tad let out a hiss and hunched farther over the bike. The runner on the left pulled a weapon out and pointed it at me. A gun of sorts. Long like a spear with a funny little dart at the end of it.

"Are you kidding me?" I yelled. The gun went off, and the dart flew between Tad and me.

"Shoot them!" Tad yelled again.

I brought up my hand that held the gun as fast as I could, and it slipped out of my hand. I tipped my head back to see the gun rise and fall as we sped away from it. "Oh dear."

Tad groaned. "If you weren't my sister, I'd strangle you."

"That is not how we talk," I reminded him.

"We're not in Kansas anymore, Dorothy Do-little."

The puff of a second gun went off, and I shifted where I sat so the dart missed me. But it hit Tad in the back of the arm, the feathers on the end of it flapping in the wind like a miniature flag.

"Damn it!"

He wobbled and drooped forward.

"Tad! Don't do that!" I reached around him and grabbed the handles of the bike, somehow keeping us going. Even though I wanted to stop, I ended up gripping the throttle and shooting us forward. We left the bikes behind as I screamed into the wind.

"Mother-humping whales on the beach!" What in heaven's name was I going to do? How did I stop this thing and not wipe out?

Tad slumped to the side as he mumbled, "Dmfffhphh."

I had to let go of the one handle to catch him. The bike unbalanced and we were bucked off at high speed, on asphalt without helmets. I let go of him. The bike spun in a screeching circle below us, the tires burning rubber on the road, the metal crying out as it tore.

I closed my eyes as I went face-first toward the ground. This was going to hurt; there was no way around it.

But I never hit. Something snagged me around the waist and yanked me sideways. My eyes flew open. A rather large and solid-looking man wearing a suit of hard materials stared down at me. Flinty blue eyes. That was all I could see.

"You're under arrest for running from the Supernatural Division of Mounted Police."

"I wasn't running. We were on a bike." The words escaped my mouth before I could filter them. The blue eyes hardened further.

He spun me around, I squeaked, and he clamped a pair of zap straps over my wrists, tightening them until they bit into my skin. "Hey, that's not necessary." I twisted to look at him.

"You are in serious trouble, missy."

I looked around for Tad. He was nowhere to be seen. Had he gotten away and left me behind? No, I didn't think that was the case at all. "I really didn't know what was happening."

"Save it for the captain." He shoved me forward, through the wreckage.

My thoughts were all jumbled and messy, but something didn't seem right. "How did you catch me? I was falling and everything happened so fast."

He grunted. "I'm a shifter."

"Yeah, but how did you catch me?"

He spun me around to face him. "How new are you?"

I frowned. "I don't know what you mean."

His eyes widened and he laughed, but there was no smile to go with it. "Load her up, boys, we got a real fresh one here. Wet behind the ears."

Someone else barked a laugh. "I'd like to see where else she's wet."

I flushed, the heat in my face enough to bake a cupcake. Flinty Eyes stared hard past me, and no one else spoke a word.

Fresh, he didn't mean I was *being* fresh. He meant I was fresh off the delivery truck. Green as a Saint Patrick's Day cake. Raw as my infamous chocolate chip cookie dough.

"You're new to being a supernatural, correct?" He stared at me and I nodded. "Let me be the first to welcome you to our side of the Wall, then. This is your home, get used to it."

That wasn't possible. I'd been on Whidbey Island, and then . . . well, I suppose anything was possible. Not like I knew how Merlin did things.

They lifted me into the back of the semitruck, which had finally caught up to us, and stuffed me into the back. Where Tad already lay, flat on his back. He snored as they turned the big rig around and headed back the way we'd come. The slower pace gave me time to really see where we were. Surrey. The sign to the right of the road was clear as day. We were north of the border then, on the Supes' side of the Wall, exactly as Flinty Eyes had said. "A place for everyone" was the tagline for the town. I highly doubted that.

We drove past Merlin's place, and I was sure I saw a flash of his face at one of the windows. I lifted a hand. "Thanks a whole heck of a lot, Merlin. Some warning would have been nice."

A groan rumbled up from my feet. "I tried to warn you. Why didn't you shoot them?"

"I don't know how to use a gun, you dink," I snapped at Tad. "Since when do I know anything like that? Give me a frying pan and I can do some damage, even a rolling pin and I could have flattened them."

He sat up, rubbing at his arm where the dart had been. "First lesson: SDMP uses a fast-acting tranquilizer that only works on supernaturals. They shoot first and ask questions later."

I went to my knees beside him, tucking my heels under my bum. "But aren't they supposed to be the good guys? Aren't they the police here on this side of the Wall?"

He snorted. "They're paid thugs. The Supernatural Department of Mounted Police, SDMP, works for the human government, so their job is to keep us in line, to keep track of us, and make sure we know our place. And they can be bought, sister dear. Which means we are royally screwed."

"Oh dear, that can't be good." I mean, when had being screwed ever been good? Certainly not with Roger.

"Yeah." He scrubbed a hand over his hair. "We can't get out of this, Lena. They're going to put tracking devices in both of us. They've been on my case since the beginning, but I've been able to dodge them until now."

I reached out and took his hand. "I'm sorry that I messed this up for you. How bad is the tracking device?"

"Keeps you from crossing the Wall. They won't say that, but it does. You remember the shock collar we had on Petey?"

Petey had been our German shepherd. He'd loved to run, and we'd finally gotten him a shock collar that was tied to an underground wiring system. The farther he got from home, the more the collar shocked him. I swallowed hard. "Unfortunately, yes."

"Same theory."

"Oh dear." I put a hand to my neck. "So what do we do?"

He shrugged. "Get ready to be implanted."

"I don't want to get implanted."

"Little late for that."

Our conversation stalled as we pulled up to a large building that was actually quite pretty. The exterior was done in sheet metal polished to a high sheen so that it was a mirrored reflection. It looked like a giant version of the aluminum cookie sheets I had in my bakery. Three stories tall, it towered over every other building in the area. From what I could see, there were at least three wings to it, all of which circled around a central area.

Two sets of double doors were at the top of the stairs, and they opened up to the courtyard. In the center of the courtyard was a large fountain with an abstract painting–type sculpture thing that at first looked like someone had let a child design it. Water spewed everywhere from multiple spouts on the fountain. The SDMP pulled us out of the back of the rig. Tad fought with them, trying to get free.

I didn't; I couldn't stop looking at the fountain. It called to me, and as I was escorted to the doors, which gave me more views of the fountain, I realized why. The fountain was actually a tree bursting out of the ground with such force the earth had exploded around it. But from the back all you saw was the mess of earth in every direction.

"Oh, that's lovely," I breathed.

"You aren't on a field trip." My escort with the blue eyes jerked my arm, making me stumble.

"You don't have to be mean, you know. I'm not fighting you," I said. "Mean-spirited people have holes in their hearts where all the goodness leaks out." I quoted my mother without thinking. "I bet you have lots of holes."

The men around us laughed, and even my escort chuckled. "Enough holes. You want to see them?"

My face flamed hot as I realized what I'd said and inadvertently stepped into. "That's not what I meant."

"I would make an exception for you," he muttered softly, low enough that I was sure only I heard. "What are you?"

"What do you mean you'd make an exception for me?" I looked up at him, knowing that his friends had heard me.

Several guffawed. "Making a move on her? Smithy, you're going to get your ass ticketed if you even think of it."

My escort, Smithy, went stone-faced. He all but dragged me up the stairs so my feet barely touched the granite surface.

"Hey!" I yelped as he shoved me through the doors. I spun and ended up landing on my butt in a heap. "That wasn't nice."

He glared down at me. "This world isn't nice, harpy. Get used to it. Nice people die here."

I fully admit my jaw dropped open. "I am not a harpy! You are a horrid man, and I hope you think about what you said the next time you kiss your mother with that mouth."

He handed me off to someone else, who took me through several more sets of doors before stuffing me into a tiny interrogation room. I was shoved into a chair, my zap straps were cut off, and then I was left alone.

I rubbed at my wrists. The room wasn't much. A table and two chairs. A large plate-glass window. On the other side stood three people. All men. I stood and walked to the window, putting my fingertips on it.

The vibrations of their words rumbled along my skin, and I heard them clearly, as if there were nothing between us.

"She was with the snake. You think he was going to make her like him?"

"No," the man in the middle said. "She's related. Same blood, but different creature, I'm sure of it. Naga smell like snakes. She doesn't. She smells human."

"Not possible. We spotted her coming out of Merlin's place, and she's dumb as a stick when it comes to supernatural goings-on."

Dumb as a stick? I frowned and tapped on the glass, but they ignored me.

The other two shrugged, and the man in the middle turned. "I'll see what I can get out of her. Maybe a date if she really is human." He winked.

I stepped back from the window. I didn't smell like a snake? Had Merlin saved me and kept me human somehow? Hope soared for a split second. Who was I kidding? I'd just listened in on a conversation using my hands as a microphone. That was not normal.

That was not human.

I went back to my chair and sat down. I smoothed the skirt over my legs and then pulled my hair across my shoulder, running my fingers through it over and over. The door behind me opened, and the man who'd stood in the middle of the trio stepped into the room.

He reminded me a bit of Smithy. They had the same pale-blue eyes and hard edge to their jaws. Though Smithy was a bit leaner than this one, their builds were close enough that I wondered if they were related. They were both big, strapping men who could probably bench-press three hundred pounds without breaking a sweat.

"My name is Captain Oberfall," he barked out as he strode around to the other chair. He yanked it out from the table and sat down across from me. Placing his hands on the table, he leaned forward. "We can do this hard or easy."

"My name is Alena," I said. "Why did you chase us?"

"How new are you?"

I frowned, feigning innocence. "I don't know what you mean."

He let out an exasperated sigh. "Merlin turned you. When did he do it?"

From the window came a laugh. "Merlin loves the dumb ones, doesn't he? She's too stupid to even understand a basic question."

I had to force myself not to react to the other man's comment. "Umm. I guess not long. A few days maybe, I'm not sure."

That much was the truth.

"A few days, then. When did you wake up?"

I blinked several times. What harm could it do to tell him the truth? "A few hours ago."

His eyebrows jumped. "Goblin piss, that is new. Okay. Here's the rundown. I am in charge of this town, do you understand? Nobody shits, eats, sleeps, or fucks that I don't know about it. You got that?"

"Why would you want to know if someone poops? That's disgusting." I crinkled my nose up and leaned back.

He glared at me. "You will stay to your own kind. There will be no fraternizing with other species. You will be situated with a tracking device that will be implanted into one of your major organs while you are under anesthetic. You will not cross the Wall."

"Lots of don'ts." I made myself sit still when all I wanted was to jump up and run out of the tiny room that held the overbearing Oberfall. "What am I supposed to do here?"

"What did you do before?"

"I was a baker."

He grinned. "Good. We don't have any bakeries, and I'd kill for a donut. You and I are going to be friends. Understand? You will do what I say, and I will make sure you stay safe. It's a harsh world, Alena. And this is the harshest place for a delicate flower like you. Now." He pulled a folder out from behind him and slapped it on the table. "I want all your information in here."

He flipped the folder open and pushed several sheets across to me along with a pen. I took the pen and filled everything out. Name. Age. Previous residence. Occupation. Blood type.

I paused at the "Married"/"Single" boxes. "I was married."

"Not anymore. Unless he got turned too?" Oberfall asked.

I shook my head, but my pen hovered over the "Single" box. I moved it to the "Married" box and checked it. Oberfall shook his head. "Firstamentalist?"

"I was," I whispered.

From the window came a low groan. "Assholes, all of them. Think they're right, won't conform. Won't change. My family was turned in by a local group of them." A pause. "Usually end up offing themselves in the first six months. They claim it isn't suicide, since they were already dead to the world."

Someone laughed from the other room. "Bet she doesn't last even that long. Shame. I'd like to see what she's got under that frilly skirt."

I swallowed hard. "I'm not going to kill myself." I stared at the next question and was fully stumped, so I left it blank.

Oberfall raised his eyebrows. "Good to know."

I pushed the sheets back at him. "That's everything I know."

He glanced over the papers, shuffling through them. "You didn't fill this out. What is your designation? What species are you?"

I didn't hesitate. "I don't know."

He snorted. "You can't not know. What are you?"

I shrugged and leaned back in my chair. "I really don't know. Merlin said I was a special snowflake."

Oberfall growled, low and deep, and as he leaned forward I got a whiff of pine forest and deep snow.

Gray fur, howling at the moon, pack family.

Wolf.

The image flickered through my mind, and I swallowed hard. "Maybe a psychic?"

"That's not a supernatural designation," he snapped. "And a maybe psychic? No more games. What. Are. You?"

"I'm not playing games. This isn't tiddlywinks, you know. My brother is a naga. That's what he said I was going to be." I pushed back from the table and stood up. He leapt to his feet, his hand going to a gun at his waist.

"I have every right to shoot you where you stand if you don't give me the answers I want. You aren't a naga. You don't smell like one."

Oh dear, this was not going well at all. Not that I'd really expected it to.

I lifted my hands slowly above my head, fear cascading down my spine. A funny tingle started in my toes and crept up my legs. "I really don't know what I am, then. I told Merlin I didn't want to be a vampire, werewolf, or witch. I wanted to be something else. Something different and as human as possible." The words poured out of me, and his trigger finger eased.

"Something special. But you aren't a naga."

I nodded.

A loud thump reverberated through the room, stopping the conversation in its tracks. Oberfall ran for the door. It opened and he leapt out, shouting, "Get the UV guns."

UV guns? Did he mean ultraviolet? I stood and stared at the now-open door. I should stay put. That was the good-girl thing to do, to conform and do what I was told.

And get a tracking device shoved in my liver. Maybe not.

I hurried to the door and peeked out. The Supe Squad dressed themselves in hard black body armor with red slashes on the arms, but they weren't the only ones wearing armor in the hall anymore. They had been joined by an influx of new additions. The new guys, or girls, it was hard to tell, had their own kind of covering. Four of them ran by me, chasing two SDMP members. I jerked back with a gasp. The ones swarming the station wore full-on coverage, from the top of their heads down to their toes, a strange shimmering black material that looked like it would hold out every stitch of light. Even their faces were covered, giving them an eerie ghostlike quality. All of which could only mean one thing.

Vampires.

Two ran by me, barely sparing me a glance. I didn't know what was going on, but I knew I could use it to my advantage. With my back to the wall I slid down the hallway to the next interrogation door. I opened it and peered in. Tad sat in a chair, strapped down to it, his head resting on his chest. Stepping into the room, I shut the door behind me, then groaned. I was an idiot. One quick twist of the doorknob told me all I needed to know.

I'd just locked us in. But at least we were together.

"Tad. Wake up." I hurried to his side and crouched next to him.

He groaned and lifted his face. In the short time we'd been there he'd been roughed up bad. His face was swollen. He had cuts and growing bruises on both cheeks. I gasped and put my hands on his face. "Why would they do this to you?"

"They didn't like my answers. Can you untie me?"

I slid a hand over the zap straps. Pulling on them would only cut up his wrists, or maybe even cut his hands off. The chair was wooden, though.

I put a hand on either side of the chair and pushed with all I had in me.

It exploded out from under Tad, who tumbled to the floor. "Shit, sis. Ease up."

"I'm sorry, I didn't mean to push so hard."

"No, it's all good." He rolled to the side and slid his feet back through the loop his hands made. He brought the zap strap to his mouth and on one fang cut through it. "They really should invest in handcuffs."

"I'm glad they didn't," I said.

He took the lead and I let him. "The door?"

"Locked. Sorry."

"Stop saying that."

"Sorry," I whispered.

The sound of gunfire rippled through the air, and I backed away from the door.

Tad looked at the door and then to the window. "New plan. Break the mirror."

"You mean window," I corrected.

"No, I mean the two-way mirror."

How had I been able to see through a two-way mirror? Only another question that made me wonder just what I was.

Merlin, what did you do to me?

Tad picked up the biggest piece of the chair, which happened to be the seat, and walked to the mirror. With a yell, he slammed it into the big surface, shattering it. The glass exploded, sending shards everywhere in a spray. The ones that landed at my feet blinked up at me as perfect mirrors. Dang, it had been a mirror. But I'd been able to see right through it. I frowned, trying to figure it out.

"Lena, time to go." Tad held a hand out to me. He was on the other side of the mirror, leaning back into the room for me. I took his hand, and he helped me up and over the shattered pieces.

The room we stood in wasn't much bigger than the interrogation room, only this one had more stuff. Weapons of all sorts. Knives, guns, and a few of the type of dart thing that had taken Tad out. He grabbed a bag hanging on the wall and stuffed it until it overflowed with weapons. I just stood there, unable to make myself touch anything.

"Come on." Tad slid the bag over his head and held out a hand to me again. I took it, and he tugged me along, out the door, into a new hallway. We ran, twisting and turning as we searched for a way out. I struggled to keep track of where we were, and then suddenly we were outside the building, in a back alley.

"Take your shoes off, you can't run in them."

With a sigh, I did as he asked, knowing he was right. For my first heels, they were pretty nice, though, and I didn't want to leave them behind. I hooked my fingers through the ankle straps, dangling them from a hand. Maybe I could find somewhere else to wear them.

We ran down the alley as the sun set, sending the world into a dusky twilight of pale purple. It was only then I realized it was January and I wasn't freezing even though I wore next to nothing. Tad was dressed in jeans and a thick hoodie under a leather jacket. Why wasn't I cold?

We were the same kind of creature . . . weren't we?

CHAPTER 6

We stopped at the front edge of the SDMP building, peering out into the street. Tad pointed at the three Hummers in the street. "Vamp wheels. The local mob boss, Remo, and his gang."

"Stay away from vamps, right? That's the deal?" I stood beside him, staring at the array of big trucks.

"You better believe it."

Except I saw someone I knew sitting in the driver's seat. I knew her from the pictures we'd shared. Red hair and a vibrant smile I knew even with teeth. She was stunning. I couldn't help but wave.

"Dahlia!"

Her eyes shot to me and she frowned. Of course. "She doesn't recognize me," I said, hurt more than I'd thought I would be.

Tad yanked my hand down. "Don't be waving at her. We don't need that kind of—shit."

I looked away from him to see Dahlia running at us with a wide grin on her face. "Alena!"

I met her partway, catching her in a hug. "Dahlia, you're okay."

"How did you recognize me?" she asked as she held me at arm's length.

"Your smile." I grinned at her.

"Damn, you look good, girl. I can't believe you did it, but I'm so happy you did!"

I laughed, a light sweet feeling tugging at my heart for the first time in weeks. Happiness seemed a foreign emotion.

"Me too. I think. How did you recognize me?"

She grinned. "You look exactly as I saw you in the hospital. Gorgeous."

And then she kissed me. Heat flushed along my skin, and I pulled away. "Dahlia."

"Oh, get over it. I swing both ways and you are freaking stunning. I had to at least get a kiss in before—"

Tad yanked me away, putting himself between us. "No kissing my sister, fang face."

Dahlia's eyes widened. "Well, well. You must be Tad. I see the genetics run strong with you two." She leaned in and kissed him too. Only he didn't pull back.

I stared as they locked lips, oblivious to the world around them. Men all in black poured out of the building waving guns as they stripped off their masks.

"Ummm, Tad. I think we should go." I grabbed at his arm, but he shook me off and all but picked Dahlia up, his hands tight on her butt.

I grabbed the back of his jacket and jerked him away from her. They unsuctioned with a pop. "I said we have to go."

His bottom lip bled, and he stared up at me with a rather blank look on his face. Dahlia cringed. "Damn, I rolled him."

"You what?"

The men shouted, and one of them called to her. She waved. "Come on, you can come with us. We'll sort this out."

"No, I don't think that's a good idea."

"You want to stay with the Supe Squad?" She ran toward the Hummers, and I knew I didn't really have a choice. Especially when from behind us the clatter of boots on the asphalt told me all I needed to know. We were stuck between a rock and a rock-hard biscuit.

I didn't think, just scooped Tad up over my shoulder and ran for the Hummers. The fact that I was running with my brother over my shoulder only confirmed that I was anything but human, and for the moment I was glad. I wouldn't have been able to get him out without the extra strength.

I pushed him ahead of me into the backseat of Dahlia's Hummer and slid in, sitting on top of him.

Dahlia hit the gas and we peeled out.

"Won't they follow us?" I asked.

From the passenger side a man peered back at me. "You're new, aren't you?"

"Is it stamped on my fricky-dicky forehead?" I snapped.

He grinned, his fangs showing clearly. "Not quite. But close. What are you?"

I didn't want to tell him in case he decided he shouldn't have anything to do with Tad and me, so I kept my mouth shut. One step at a time. "Dahlia, can you drop us off somewhere?"

"Nope, sorry. Remo said to bring you in."

I groaned. Of course the big bad mob boss wanted to talk to us. Or worse. Eat us. What a mess.

I took a breath and tried to sort through the last few hours of my life. In that time I'd been in a motorcycle chase, been interrogated by a werewolf, run from gunfire, and been kissed by a vampire. A girl vampire, no less. As if picking up my thoughts, Dahlia grinned into the rearview mirror. "I didn't swing both ways before. But that's part of being a vamp. It ramps up your hormones like crazy, makes you irresistible. Which is why we're supposed to stay away from the humans."

I thought for a minute. "What did you mean when you said you rolled Tad?"

The other passenger glared at her. "Yeah, what *did* you mean by that?"

She didn't shrink in her seat, only shrugged. "I'm still learning, Max. You know that." Her eyes went to me again. "Basically means

I made him a bit of a pet. It's temporary, but the more you do it the harder it is to undo it. Right?"

"But not with me?"

"No, I tried to roll you. I couldn't." She stared hard at me and I stared back.

"You look like you're bunged up and trying too hard to push to squeeze a poop out." I leaned back in my seat. Tad let out a groan, stirring, but not waking.

Max burst out laughing. "Oh shit, Remo is going to like her."

Dahlia nodded. "Yeah. I'm thinking he might too. I just can't decide if that's a good thing or not."

Max shrugged and smiled over at me. "If Remo likes her, we all have to."

The vampire was handsome; I'd give him that with his dirty-blond hair and dark-brown eyes that seemed to be full of mischief. "How long have you been a vampire, Max?"

"Ten years."

That was before the Aegrus virus had appeared on the scene. He grinned at me. "Yup, I did it just because I wanted to. I loved the idea of never seeing the sun again, my family, or the world I'd grown up in."

Shame flickered over me. "I'm sorry, I shouldn't assume—"

"Everyone does it, kid." His smile softened. "Especially in this world. Are you human? Are you a Supe? Are you a monster or a magician? I didn't become a vamp because I wanted to. My wife was dying and I tried to save her, selling myself to the highest bidder to pay for her chemotherapy." He shrugged again. "So am I still damned to hell, or am I a hero wrapped in monster clothing?"

His words hung in the air between us. "I don't know."

He turned away from me. "I do. I'm a monster. Just ask my wife."

Oh, God. The pain in those four words all but resonated in my chest.

Tad woke up but kept his eyes down as he squirmed underneath me, breaking the silence. "Why did you go with them?"

"Not like we had a choice," I said. "Besides, Dahlia's my friend. I trust her."

She grinned at me and I grinned back, though it was a strain after what Max had revealed. "We almost died together. Now here we are, being chased by the SDMP. Together again, just like old times."

"Exactly."

The SDMP gave up faster than I thought, their lights fading behind us as we drove out through the valley toward the mountains. Dahlia didn't slow the Hummer down, though. We drove for over two hours, out of the city and into the lower floodlands that met with the base of the coastal mountains. Dahlia and I laughed and talked. I told her about how the nurses all thought she'd died, and Max kept looking at me oddly. Like he couldn't decide what to make of me.

I didn't care. We were safe and with a friend.

Only . . . One of those wasn't right. We weren't safe at all, not if we were going to meet a vampire mob boss.

"Why were you guys at the detachment?" Tad asked.

Dahlia shared a look with Max. "Looking for something the boss wanted."

"Did you get it?"

They shrugged in unison and said no more.

Dahlia pulled the Humvee off onto a dirt track that bounced us around, our heads brushing the low ceiling of the vehicle. The road twisted and turned, and around a sharp right-hand turn we came to a stop. "Here we are."

I peered out through the windshield. "Tad, look at this place. It's huge!"

That was an understatement. It looked like a castle had been plucked out of Europe and plopped in the middle of the floodplains. Right down to the moat circling around the place and the drawbridge that lowered as Dahlia crept the Hummer forward. I counted at least seven spires curling up into the sky.

"Shit. We can't go in there, Lena. We'll never get out."

I glanced at him. "Really? Never? Never ever, never, never ever?" Dahlia giggled and high-pitched her words. "Never ever ever?"

"You two are unreal," he muttered, and Max grunted in what I assumed was a form of male agreement.

The four of us slid out of the Humvee as the other two armored trucks pulled up on either side. No one came to greet us, but vamps spilled out of the other vehicles. I wanted to press against the Hummer and lower my eyes. But . . . Tad was vulnerable. I wasn't for some reason, which meant I had to do this for both of us. I thought about the last meeting I'd had with a banker who'd thought he could charge me a higher interest rate on my loan because I was a woman. I didn't let that happen then, and I wouldn't let either of us get taken here any more than I would let that banker take me for a ride.

I stood up straight and met each vampire's gaze with one lifted eyebrow.

Tad stayed behind me. "What the hell did Merlin make you that you can't be rolled?"

"I'm a naga, like you. Maybe the females are just naturally stronger." I didn't want to say I didn't know. But I didn't want to say nothing. Tad shot a look at me and I shrugged. "Well, it is a possibility."

Dahlia motioned for us to follow her. "Come on. We didn't get what we were looking for at the SDMP, so Remo is not going to be happy."

Max put a hand on my arm, tugging me forward. "All the more reason to distract him with your friend here. Right, Alena?"

He pulled me in the opposite direction from Dahlia, and I went along. Not because I wanted to, I just didn't want to fight if I didn't have to. He led Tad and me into the castle, and I realized again everyone else was bundled up, whereas I was completely comfortable in my tiny dress. "Tad, how are you doing?"

"Fine. Embarrassed. You know I hate redheads. They're stupid, and just from kissing her I could catch the dumbs."

I gasped, spun, and slapped him hard, knocking him back several steps. "Don't you talk about Dahlia like she's a horrible person. As far as I'm concerned she's one of my best friends. So you just shut your fat mouth."

He lifted his eyes to mine, shock filtering through. "I came back to you from the dead only a few hours ago, and you'd put your friend you've known for weeks ahead of me?"

I stepped closer to him and lowered my voice. Not because I thought it would actually keep the vamps from hearing. No, that wasn't it at all. "I lost you five years ago. I cried every day for years. Every. Day. You were my best friend, Tad. If it had been reversed, I would have sent a letter or called, or just shown up. Something to tell you I was okay. That I was alive. I wouldn't have let you grieve like that."

His face paled. "I couldn't get out until recently."

"Buffalo balls." I spit and spun on a heel. "You are in my bad book, Mr. Budrene."

"I paid for you to be turned!" he yelled. I whipped around, my hair flying out in a twirl along with my skirt.

"You owe Merlin a favor. You didn't pay him."

Tad stepped closer to me so we were nose to nose. "I did pay him. You turned him down. I had to offer him a favor in order to get you another chance."

Chagrin flowed through me. I put a hand to my forehead. "I'll fix it, then. You won't owe him anything."

"How?"

"Merlin can have the favor from me."

A low, sensual laugh rolled out from behind us, and I slowly turned. The man who walked toward us was not what I'd expected. A vampire mob boss made me think of the old Italian bloodlines, fine-boned men with heavy accents and suits custom made for their slim builds. Maybe an extra-long mustache.

This man who approached us was anything but that. He was taller than me by a good five inches, which put him easily at six five, and was built as though the person in charge of his genetics were making a Viking warrior. Thick muscles in his arms and chest strained against the long-sleeved pale-gray shirt he wore. His hair was shorn close to his head, a perfect buzz cut that gave off only a hint of color. Light brown, I was guessing. In his chin were two piercings that looked like fangs hanging from the middle of his bottom lip. He lifted his top lip in a tight snarl, and the effect was obvious. What was better than two fangs as a vampire? Four, of course. As he drew closer, the tattoos on his neck were visible, a curl of dark ink I couldn't fully make out other than it started from somewhere under his shirt.

I finally locked eyes with him. Dark eyes, like the night in which we stood right down to the hint of purple that flickered in their depths. Damn, he made Roger look like a total pansy. Not that Roger wasn't a pansy, but if I stood them side by side, my husband would have fit in this man's shadow in more ways than one.

He frowned and I frowned back. "Who are you?"

"Alena." I lifted an eyebrow. "And who are you?"

Around us a quiet, collective groan rose in the air. He smiled, though it was a mere hard line of his lips. "Remo. And I am master here, so watch how you speak to me, Alena."

Something in his tone reminded me of the pastor at our church. Like I was not good enough to stand in his presence, let alone disagree with him. Anger snapped through me. No more, I was not going to let another man try to put me in my place.

I pulled myself up to my full height and tipped my chin in his direction. "I will dang well say what I want, to whom I want, regardless of how important they think they are."

The crowd around us shifted back with another low groan. Remo stepped closer and I put out a hand, stopping him, poking him in the chest with a single finger. Even that much contact sent a flare of awareness through me. This man was dangerous.

And a part of me rather liked that fact.

"Personal space. Respect it."

Both his eyebrows shot up. "What are you?"

I shrugged one shoulder. "I'm not telling." I wanted to groan, because the words did not deter him but only seemed to draw him closer. Dang it all. Maybe that wasn't a bad thing. What was I saying?

"I think I could make you tell me." His eyes roved my body once, sliding down and then back up to stare into my own again. "Anything I wanted."

"I doubt it." What in the world was wrong with me? He brought out the worst in me, the parts I'd tried my whole life to tamp down. The mouthy, sassy girl who got in trouble for making inappropriate jokes during Sunday school. I'd almost forgotten about her. She'd been far more like her yaya than Mother had wanted.

We stood there staring into each other's eyes for several minutes. He frowned, opened his mouth, shut it again, and then smiled. A slow curling of his lips, just enough to show the flash of white teeth again.

"Oh, I think I like you. Apparently you are right, I can't make you do what I want. At least not in the conventional sense. You seem immune to being rolled, and there's some fire in there. You weren't always a firebrand, though, were you?" Remo reached out and touched a finger under my chin. I twisted my head away from him and batted his hand away. The feel of his skin on mine was far too personal.

"Did I give you permission to touch me? No, I didn't. Let me be crystal clear. You don't touch me or my brother without permission." I stepped back. "Tad, we're leaving."

"There are no cars that come out this way. No public transit." Remo smirked.

"We'll walk. We have a lot to talk about. And we won't turn into crispy critters when the sun comes up." I herded Tad ahead of me as if I knew where I was going. I waved to Dahlia as we went by. "Thanks." She tossed me something and I caught it. A set of keys.

"Take it. I'll catch up with you later." She winked at me and I winked back.

Remo growled from behind us. "Dahlia, you are going to end up in the box."

I didn't know what the box was, but I doubted it was anything good. I couldn't let her suffer for us. I stiffened and spun. "Dahlia, you want to come with us?"

"Yeah"—she glanced at her boss, then to us—"I do."

Remo smacked the wall next to him, and the room trembled along with the remaining vampires. "I am the law here. I will not be disobeyed."

"Really? That's what Oberfluffel said. He was the law and I had to respect him. You want my respect? You can earn it."

Remo's lips twitched. "Oberfluffel?"

"Whatever his name was. He thought he was in charge, and you showed him he wasn't. Maybe you're about to get the same rude awakening, Remo." I purred his name a little too much, and something in the air shifted. His eyes widened, and he drew in a slow breath.

"What are you that you can draw me?"

"Never you mind, it's not a single bit of your beeswax." I gripped Tad tight, unable to believe the words that flowed out of me.

Dahlia and I pushed Tad ahead of us, leaving behind a vampire mob boss with, at last glance, his chin on the floor.

I handed the keys back to Dahlia, and she ran ahead of us to a tiny purple punch-buggy car. I laughed and piled in, Tad with me.

"Dahlia," Tad said, "you can't leave here. The sun will come up and Alena is right. Crispy critters are not the worst of it."

"Worried about me, lover?" She smiled. "I'll be fine. There's a safe house in the city, we can go there for the night. Remo will calm down. He always does. He's really not as bad as he seems. He's just on edge right now."

"He's a horrible donkey butt," I said as we sped out of the castle and back the way we'd just come.

She snickered. "You mean an ass?"

"Yeah, that."

"Still not cussing?"

"No. I've broken so many rules, at least I can hold to that one. It's simple."

Tad shook his head. "You aren't breaking rules, Lena. You're surviving. There are no rules when it comes to making it in this life."

I shrank into my seat and stared out at the night sky; the cold stars so far above us had in the past been a source of solace, a thought that one day when I was dead and gone I'd be there, in the heavens, with all my loved ones who'd gone on before me.

Dahlia reached over and took my hand. "The loneliness fades. Honest."

I put a hand over my eyes, tears slipping past them. From behind me, Tad reached forward. "Don't cry. She's right, it will get better."

But they didn't know why I was crying. It wasn't the loneliness, though that was there under my skin too. It was the reality of being forced to face that maybe everything I'd believed for my entire life was no longer what I could hold on to, not even with my fingertips.

The rock I'd thought was solid turned out to be nothing but a pile of sand that tried to hold me down, burying me under the weight of beliefs I could no longer turn to for solace because now, I was everything I'd once believed was evil.

How did one reconcile a belief system with a reality like that? There was only one answer.

You didn't.

We reached the safe house, and Dahlia let us in with a flourish of one hand. "Make yourselves at home, I've got a few things to do."

The morning was a few hours off, but she disappeared as soon as she made sure we knew where everything was.

"She's gone to feed," Tad said, and I startled.

"Feed?"

"Drink blood. They probably have someone chained up in the basement. They're animals, sis. Seriously. You can't be friends with—"

I pushed past him, running in my bare feet after Dahlia. She wasn't like that; I couldn't believe it of her that she would be okay with holding someone against their will. Through the house I bolted, skidding to a stop on the white tile floor of the kitchen. The fridge door was open, and Dahlia peeked out around it. "You hungry?"

My stomach rumbled. "Apparently. You don't have anyone chained up in the basement, do you?"

Dahlia grinned. "No. That's a story Remo spread around. He's not the badass he looks like. I mean, I wouldn't seriously cross him, he's stronger than any of the other supernaturals, but he's kind of a softy."

"He's not going to punish you for helping us?" Tad asked.

She shrugged and stepped away from the kitchen, pushing the fridge door shut with a foot. A glass milk jug in one hand and a glass in the other were her only accessories. If it weren't for the bold-red filling of the milk jug, it would have looked normal. "Nah. I might have to do day duty, which sucks because we do need to sleep contrary to what others will tell you. And a few days up on both shifts is no fun."

She pulled a pot out from under the counter and poured the contents of the milk jug into it, then put the pot on the stove. Her eyes met mine. "It's better warmed up on the stove. The microwave does weird things to it."

"Of course," I murmured. A twist of hunger rolled through me. "Is there other food here?"

"Yup, the basics."

Tad and I went on a search. I found crackers and cheese, and a can of some sort of processed meat. He found a half-opened box of pastry tarts and a jar of jam.

We cracked it all open and dug in.

I dipped a pastry tart into the jam, the multilayers of sweetness making my teeth ache at the same time that I couldn't help but want more. I flicked my tongue out to take the jam from my lips.

"Holy hell, now that's a tongue." Dahlia stopped stirring her pot of blood in midmotion.

I put a hand to my mouth. "What?"

"Your tongue is long, my friend. I didn't notice when I kissed you. You're a naga like your brother?"

I swallowed hard and looked at Tad. "I think so. But Oberfluffel said I didn't smell like a naga. Could he be wrong?"

Tad licked crumbs off his fingers. "I told Merlin to make you the same as me. There's a couple of other nagas around, but they're solitary. Here, let me see your teeth."

He scooted over and I obediently opened my mouth. He peered in. "Damn. Where are your fangs?"

I shrugged. "I don't know."

Dahlia tapped her spoon on the counter, then poured from her pot into her glass. A steaming glass of blood. I shuddered, I couldn't help it. "Vampire fangs are always there too. You're sure hers aren't retractable?"

Tad shook his head and opened his mouth. Tiny fangs, almost unnoticeable, were there. Much smaller than a vampire's mouthful.

The idea of retractable fangs, though, that would be okay. No one would ever know I had them unless I bit them. Which I would never do. With my mouth closed I flipped my tongue up and touched the roof of my mouth. Two fangs were indeed there, along the roof of my mouth. Only two, thank God. But they went way back, far further than I thought they should have.

"I think Dahlia's right. I can feel them in my mouth."

Tad grabbed me and tipped me backward. I grunted and opened my mouth again.

"Shit, you're right, those are not naga fangs. That bastard Merlin! I told him what to do."

"He gave me options. I said I wanted to be something unique."

Tad shook his head. "But that's just it. We won't be allowed to be around each other."

"We're doing it right now. So what as long as we're both alive?" I pointed out, and Dahlia nodded.

"Yeah, so what? The SDMP is too stupid to find out, and besides, we're small fish. They won't be looking for little old us."

My brother paced the kitchen. "Yeah, except they're cracking down for some reason. They're shutting the border crossings next week. Not even those with legit day passes will get through."

"Temporary. Remo isn't concerned." Dahlia took a sip of her drink.

"No." He shook his head, his green eyes worried. "For good this time. No more day passes, no more nothing passes. They are shutting down the hospital on Whidbey too. When people get the Aegrus virus they'll be shipped over the Wall from now on."

I felt like a child listening in on the adults' conversation. "Why would they do that?"

"The virus. There's been another outbreak way deep down in Sonoma County in California. Government is putting a stop to all connections. They'll ship in blood and willing bleeders for those who live off the blood." He took a bite of a cracker, swallowed it, and went on. "At least, that's what they're saying."

"They can't let us starve up here, and they can't really keep us in. It's a willing thing for us to stay; we can leave if we really want. You know that," Dahlia said, but there was no fire in her voice. Tad looked at her, and then away.

"What would happen if no food sources came in? You'd start targeting the other supernaturals. You'd wipe us out within fifty or a hundred years. Maybe less."

Whatever hunger I had fled. "You think that's what they're going to do?"

"It's a distinct possibility. Let the monsters kill each other, then the problem of what to do with them is solved."

"Then we have to get over that border before they close it down." I stood up and brushed off my dress. "We need to go see Mom and Dad right now. Tell them we're alive. They have to know."

"You aren't even going to ask to phone them?" Dahlia paused with her glass halfway to her mouth. I shook my head.

"The phone lines are blocked across the Wall. Even I know that."

Tad put a hand on my shoulder. "There are bigger issues than visiting Mom and Dad."

I took a step back. "How do I get a border pass?"

"You have a tracking device put in, and then you can maybe get a border pass," Dahlia said softly. "I could get one."

"You're tracked?" Tad pushed away from the counter; Dahlia hunched her shoulders.

"I didn't have a choice. Vampires more than anyone else are stuck with a device. The only one who doesn't have one is Remo."

I put a hand on her arm. "You don't have to be ashamed, Dahlia. You're alive. That's what matters."

Tad grunted and I swung a hand back at him, smacking him hard enough to knock him off his chair. He landed on the floor with a thump.

"Hey!"

"Don't you 'hey' me. You have seriously forgotten your manners since you died. Don't be rude to someone who saved us and is a *friend*." I half turned to glare at him. "Now, you know another way over the Wall. Right?"

His eyebrows shot up. "Why would you say that?"

I leaned forward. "That jacket-hoodie combo? Same as the old man who ate my bagels. Same old man who gave me the Aegrus virus."

Dahlia sucked in a sharp breath and Tad blanched. "It wasn't like that. I didn't know I was sick. If I thought I would hurt you, I never would have come near you. Merlin suggested I go for a visit, to see you. I missed you, Alena. And I knew I could get close to you, but not Mom and Dad."

The fact that he didn't deny it was him who infected me . . . I wasn't sure if that made what happened worse or not. Not that it mattered now. Better to focus on the task at hand.

No point in prepping batter meant for a cake yesterday.

"How do you get over the Wall?"

Tad cleared his throat before answering. "First thing in the morning they do a shift change. The guards are lazy and sleepy. It's easy to make it past them."

"Then it's settled," I said. "First light we'll get over that wall and go talk to Mom and Dad. Neither of us is sick, so we won't be putting them in any danger."

Dahlia looked at the clock on the stove. "It's late enough that I have to get underground. I wish I could come with you."

I smiled, but it felt strained. "You've done a lot. Thank you. For still being my friend even though we have—"

"Different fangs?"

I laughed. "Yeah, something like that."

She drained the last of her glass and licked her lips. "There are extra clothes in the upstairs bedrooms, if you want to change." Dahlia wiggled her fingers at us and left the room. For several minutes, neither of us said anything. Five years apart, and now dealing with everything that had happened, I wasn't sure what to say to him. Or if I wanted to say anything at all.

"Lena, you have to know I didn't mean for this to happen," Tad said, his tone soft. I closed my eyes and nodded. That much I believed. Tad would never hurt me intentionally, not even when we were children and fought on a regular basis.

"I know. That doesn't make it any easier. Why didn't you just send a letter?"

"No postal system here. Even our landlines and cell phones won't call outside this area. We aren't supposed to exist, so they are slowly wiping us out."

I struggled to believe him, simply because it was a long-standing argument with him. Paranoia ran deep in our family. Of the government, conspiracies, an asteroid sent by aliens to destroy our world, and of course the supernatural. Some of it was the upbringing with the Firstamentalists, but some of it was just the way our family thought.

Everyone, and everything, was out to get us in one form or another if you asked any Budrene.

"Really, Tad? Maybe it's just that Super Dupers are too strong, too fast, and too dangerous to be a part of the rest of the world." I was halfway up the stairs to check out the other clothes.

"Do you know that Roger gets everything? Nothing is yours. In the law, you are dead. So even if you showed up on his doorstep, proved you were still alive, he would have to give you absolutely nothing. Not a single penny, not a single piece of that house you love."

Yeah, I'd not forgotten about that bit. "Yes, I'm well aware."

"Doesn't that bother you in the least?"

"Bothers me more that he's boinking Barbie. That he's selling Vanilla and Honey to fat-nosed Colleen—"

"Excuse me?" Tad jogged up the stairs to catch up to me. I strode forward into the first room. I went straight to the closet and started to rifle through the variety of shirts and pants.

"He's got a new love. Her name is Barbie, and they're opening a dog-grooming business together. And cats, they're grooming cats too in order to make the business legit. And he's selling my bakery. You know, the one you sat in front of for free food?" I'd said it to make him laugh at the absurdity of it, to take away the sting.

"Oh, Lena Bean, I'm so sorry." His soft tone and the old nickname from my childhood undid me, but I didn't stop what I was doing. I rifled through the clothes through blurry eyes, going by feel more than sight.

"Help me find something. Please. You know I have no fashion sense."

He put a hand to my back, just a gentle touch, and then he was in the closet too. After a few minutes we'd found me a pair of yoga pants, a long-sleeved shirt and hoodie, and a pair of runners that fit me reasonably well.

Dressed in my new clothes, I felt more like myself than I had since waking up with this new body.

We headed out of the house and crossed the street. "How far are we from the Wall?" I asked. I'd seen it only once and from a good distance when Roger and I had gone on a lazy Sunday drive. We lived in the Queen Anne area, near Kerry Park, where we'd met; the drive to the border, and the Wall, was easily two hours, so it wasn't something I'd done often. Or ever, to be fair.

"About fifteen minutes to walk." Tad dropped an arm over my shoulder, and I wrapped one around his waist. "You remember stealing cookies from Yaya and getting caught? How she chased us with the wooden spoon screaming like a banshee?"

"And how she used to make us believe she was a consort of Zeus? That she could handle a lightning bolt if she caught one." We laughed, and that was how we walked to the Wall.

"Did you ever wonder how she got mixed up into the Firsts? I mean, I understood Mom doing it, because she was always so afraid, but with Yaya . . ." I glanced over at Tad.

He was thoughtful. "I overheard Dad and Yaya talking once. I thought it was nothing, but now I'm not so sure. I don't think Yaya or Dad really believe what the Firsts do. They said they only went to keep Mom happy."

I frowned. "Yaya has always done her own thing."

Tad nodded. "Since Uncle Owen died, though, Mom is all she's got left. Maybe that's why."

He had a point. Losing Uncle Owen when he was so young had sent Yaya into a downward spiral. It had been only in the last few years that her spunkiness had shown back up, and by then she was firmly ensconced in the religion her daughter had chosen.

As we walked, we told stories about our parents and grandmother, reminiscing about the past and pushing away the fact that we walked toward a Wall that cut us off from those we loved.

Who hopefully still loved us.

CHAPTER 7

"This is a big dang wall," I whispered. The monument—and that was what it really was—stood over forty feet tall. Made of concrete blocks, it had natural handholds and breaks you could clearly see through. It made sense now why the Super Dupers were able to climb over so easily. But then why even make the farce of a Wall?

I frowned and put a hand to the pale-gray concrete. "Now?"

Tad hooked a hand through one of the openings and glanced back at me. "I'm going to climb first and see if there is anyone on the watch. To be safe."

I grimaced at him but let him go without me.

He pulled himself up, hands and feet working in concert easily as he scaled the concrete blocks. I rubbed my arms and looked down the line of the Wall. A hundred feet away, several other people crept out of the bush and moved to their section of the Wall. I lifted a hand to them, and they turned away from me.

"Snobs," I muttered.

"Let's go!" Tad hissed down at me. Startled, I jumped and stumbled forward.

I took his lead and started up the Wall. The rough concrete scraped at my skin, tearing off tiny bits and pieces; nothing serious, but enough to bleed. Halfway up the Wall I stopped and stared at where I'd nicked myself.

"Alena, hurry up!"

I couldn't move, though. My hand, where the skin had been torn away, held my gaze as if I were hypnotized. Scales glittered up at me, shifting with every pulse of my blood flowing under them. Jeweled scales of purple, green, and blue flickered in the early-morning light.

"Alena, move your ass!"

Swallowing the roll of nausea rising in my throat, I forced myself to move again. Hand over hand, the glittering scales caught my eyes every time I reached over my head. I just couldn't look away from them.

Tad grabbed me as I drew close to the top and hauled me up the last foot or so. The Wall was ten feet across, and we were climbing down the other side before I had time to register anything around us except for the fact that Tad was not happy.

We climbed side by side, and I tipped my hand so he could see the scales. "Is this like you?"

"Shit. No. I'm going to kick Merlin's ass for this," he snapped. But really, what could he do? Could he make Merlin change me into something else? Call it a hunch, but I had a feeling that wasn't possible.

We hustled down the Wall and dropped to the ground. Tad grabbed my hand, and we bolted across an open section as shouts erupted behind us. I sucked wind hard and put everything I had into getting away.

Until the screams started: the high-pitched cry of terror of someone who was about to die. I understood that feeling all too well. I slid to a stop and spun around. The three people who'd been waiting down the Wall were on the top, with three Supe Squad members coming in from either side.

"Tad, we have to help them."

"They wouldn't help us. That's not how this works." He reached for my hand, and I knew he would pull me away. Just like Roger had done when I'd told him about the old man who was hungry.

"Let him starve. He put himself in the situation, he can get himself out."

If I'd listened to Roger, things would have been different. But I couldn't regret my choice then, and I wouldn't pander to Tad now.

"No, I'm going to help them." I ran back the way we'd come, angling toward the section of the Wall they stood on.

Tad grunted, and then he was running beside me. "We don't have magic powers, Lena. It's not like that."

"We can help. Maybe we can distract them."

He didn't answer me and I hurried, arms and legs pumping hard. A few feet from the Wall, I leapt and caught handholds. I pulled myself up as fast as I could, not caring about the scrapes and bruises, hardly feeling them. Above us the three cornered Super Dupers pleaded their case, though after dealing with Smithy and Ober-whatever, I knew it would do them no good.

"Please, we're not sick. We have family on that side, and we haven't seen them in years. They don't even know we're alive."

Their words tore at me, spurring me on. What the heck I thought I was going to do once I got up there I didn't know. But I couldn't stand by and do nothing.

I had to try to help.

The SDMP didn't seem to notice me climbing, so focused on those they were trying to capture that they'd blocked out everything else around them. I peered up over the edge of the Wall, right at the foot of one officer. Before I thought better of it, I grabbed his ankle and yanked him backward out into open space.

He let out a yell and the other SDMP members spun. Still they didn't see me. Tad grabbed an officer to the right of the group and shoved him off on the Supe side of the Wall.

The remaining four SDMP members swung around, all holding those dang dart guns. Worse? One of them was Icy-Blue Eyes: Smithy. He saw me, lifted the gun, and pulled the trigger. I flattened myself against the Wall and the dart missed me—barely.

I popped my head up, waved at the runaways. "Hurry up!"

They didn't need any more prompting. They dropped to the edge and shimmied over as the SDMP officers leapt for them. Icy-Blue Eyes caught the tiniest girl, a petite blonde who looked light as a feather. She kicked out at him, her hooves catching him in the knee. He snarled and dropped her. She fell, and rolled over the edge in that split second.

Flinty Eyes glared at me. I gave him a weak smile. "Sorry we keep meeting like this, Smithy." I scooted down the Wall, a part of me wondering why they weren't chasing us. Because they really weren't. Even the guy I'd tossed off the Wall just dusted himself off as he headed back to climb the Wall, ignoring us.

Tad, the three Super Dupers we'd helped, and I dropped to the ground within seconds of each other and bolted away. No chasing, though, no pursuit from the SDMP.

Fear and adrenaline drove me, along with a fair bit of euphoria. Tad and I had saved someone from the SDMP and their crooked ways. I couldn't help feeling like I'd won a prizefight.

Even if it was more of a schoolyard tussle.

We ran for ten minutes until we hit a natural line of trees and bush that provided decent cover. I stopped, clinging to a tree as I panted for breath. "Tad, why didn't they chase us?"

"They're too lazy," the petite blonde gasped out. I looked at her, really looked, and realized she was not going to pass for human in any way, shape, or form. Two tiny horns curled out from the side of her head, ivory colored, so they blended in well with her white-blond hair. Her ears were pointed at the top like they'd been cropped, and they twitched every few seconds as though the wind tickled them. Her eyes were two steps off normal, the pupil running vertical in a slit imitating that of a goat. Maybe all those differences could have been hidden, but there was no way she could cover her legs. Under the jeans, her legs were a strange shape from the knee down, bent like a horse's back leg and ending in two solid black hooves. Not exactly what I'd call easy to blend in, even in a crowd.

I racked my brain for the right Supe denomination. "Dryad?"

"No, satyr," she said. "Natural."

That made me pause. "I don't understand, what do you mean by natural?"

She laughed. "You've obviously been turned. My name is Damara. I'm a natural, which just means my parents were satyrs. I was born like this."

"I'm Alena. I guess . . . not natural?" I wasn't sure how else to denote myself. *Turned* sounded like I'd been turned to the dark side. I didn't like the connotation.

She laughed, her smile wide as her ears twitched, though there wasn't a mean thing about any of it. "Good enough. Nice to meet you, Alena."

I glanced at the other two with her. Two men. Both with the same characteristics as her with the strange legs and eyes, blond hair, and curling horns. "Are they your brothers?"

She grinned, her wide, expressive mouth giving me the impression that there was a joke I didn't understand. "Boyfriends. Tim and Gavin." They grinned at me in unison.

"Oh my," I whispered. She laughed softly and put a hand on my shoulder.

"Thanks for the help. You didn't have to do that. It's been a long time since Supes helped each other out."

"That's what I told her," Tad said.

Damara glanced at him. "She may have saved the world by helping us."

My eyebrows shot up. "Excuse me?"

Damara waved for me to walk with her. Tad tried to pull me away, but I wanted to hear whatever it was she had to say. A gut feeling, perhaps, but there was something about her that called to me.

Like she fit with me somehow, which made no sense. I had no horns, no hooves. Yet the feeling persisted.

"We're going to see if we can't find Zeus. He can fix this mess of a wall and the humans herding us behind it. He's got it in him to rule, to show the humans we can all live side by side." She pushed aside a huckleberry bush and held it for me, and I stepped through the opening. The cries of birds cut off in midtweet as we walked, and I looked up. The birds hadn't left; they'd only gone silent as we passed. Why did I think it was my fault?

Call it a hunch, but I was betting most birds didn't like a snake near their homes.

"I'm sorry, Zeus? Greek god of thunder and lightning?" Tad bit the words out with more than a little edge to them.

Damara nodded as if he hadn't been rude. "We need a leader for the Supes who is not a vampire. Someone impartial who can actually do the job. Someone who can advocate with the human government. Remo is strong, but he isn't strong enough, and the humans will never fully trust him because of what he is. We need someone who's done this job before. Zeus ruled Olympus for a long, long time. He defeated a lot of bad shit out there and kept the supernatural world running smoothly for thousands of years."

I raised an eyebrow. "Did he not also cause his own amount of trouble too? From what I recall of Greek mythology, he was hardly a saint."

Damara sniffed. "Most leaders aren't, Alena. And if someone in charge says they *are* a saint, they're a liar."

Tad grabbed my hand. "Well, good luck with all that. You know, finding a god that no longer exists."

The two satyr boys shared a glance, and Gavin shook his head. "You don't understand. There have been sightings of the old heroes. Someone is bringing them back to life."

A laugh burst out of Tad. "That doesn't mean shit. Someone who dresses up like Hercules and straps a sword to his waist does not make him Hercules. Makes him a nut."

Damara didn't seem bothered by his assessment. "The heroes only arise when there is a need. Think of it as being woken from a deep sleep and called out of retirement."

"Wait." I held up a hand. "I know the stories. The heroes all died at some point no matter how strong they were. Even those who were demigods like Hercules. So how can they be called out of retirement?"

Damara shook her head before I even finished my question. "A true hero never really dies; neither do the old gods, for that matter—but I'm getting sidetracked. The heroes only show up when the monsters—the true monsters—begin to revisit this world. Heroes and monsters, they are tied to one another. Which means we need to be on the lookout for the big bad uglies. Someone is changing the game, and we need to take advantage of it."

A shiver ran through me. "What kind of monsters?"

"Hydra, Drakaina, Cerberus, Gorgon, Medusa. They are the ones the heroes were brought forth to fight in the past. If the heroes are showing up, that means the monsters are going to show up too, if they haven't already. Can you imagine the human government trying to figure out how to deal with Medusa as she turned people to stone around her? The humans would go mental and bomb every Supe in sight simply because they found a really bad apple." Damara lifted both eyebrows.

She had a point. Turning people into stone when you tried to have a discussion with them would be a problem. "And finding Zeus could fix this?"

"He could manage the relations between humans and Supes. That was his job description back in the day," she said.

We came to a small clearing where two paths branched off. Damara, Tim, and Gavin headed to the left. Tad tugged on me to the right. "Let's go."

Damara turned and lifted a hand. "Good luck, you two. And thanks. If you ever have need of me, you can call on me."

I waved back, but before I could say anything else they melted into the foliage as if they'd never been there.

"Do you think they're right?" I asked Tad as we walked along the slowly widening path.

"No. The old gods are gone. They have been for a long time, even assuming they existed in the first place. We're on our own, and they're on a wild goose chase."

"Then how do you explain Damara? She said she's a natural. She isn't like us, turned into whatever we are."

"I know what I am." Tad glanced at me. "It's you we have to figure out. And there are naturals in every species, except vamps, of course. You do know how babies are made, right? You and Roger did have sex at least once?"

"I am not discussing my sex life—"

"Or lack thereof," he interjected.

"—with you." I glared at him.

He went on as if I weren't trying to pin him to the ground with my eyes. "Didn't you wonder why Damara had two guys with her? Those satyrs are known for their sex parties. Not that I've ever been, of course; Mother would disapprove, and I'd never do anything to make her upset with me."

That was a total lie, but it took me a moment to realize what he'd implied.

I blanched, moral outrage making me splutter. "You've . . . been . . . to one of the parties, haven't you? Tad, that's awful!"

"Actually, awful is not exactly the word I'd use."

I breathed a sigh of relief. Good, he wasn't going to do it again.

He grinned at me and shook his head. "It was the best sex I've ever had. Even if I'm not really sure who it was with." He winked, and I stood there with my jaw hanging.

My mouth flapped open and closed, my teeth clicked, and I couldn't get a word out.

Tad went on as if we hadn't just talked about . . . what we'd talked about.

"Just because Damara is a satyr doesn't mean she's right about the heroes and old gods."

I pulled myself together, doing my best to block the last few minutes from my mind. Despite everything else he said, he had a point about Damara. She could be as fanatical about Zeus as Mom was about the Firstamentalists.

We worked our way through the last of the bush and stepped out into a park that was cultivated and well groomed. Even in the dead of winter, it was green. All the rain we had kept things lush and growing despite the fact that we were on the forty-ninth parallel.

At the edge of the park we stepped out onto the sidewalk, and I took a deep breath. The differences on the two sides of the Wall were startling.

Grungy, dark, and untamed on one side with imminent death or confinement waiting on every corner.

Clean, proper, and cultivated on the other with no sign of someone trying to kill us.

I swallowed hard. I would never be a part of this again. Not really.

We flagged a cabbie, and he took us to our parents' house over in the Madison Park part of Seattle. Posh. Comfortable and very, very human. Funny I'd never noticed before, but as we drove across town there were parts of Seattle where I saw glimmers of Super Dupers.

Almost as if reading my mind, Tad cleared his throat. "You know, *Super Duper* is not what most Supes want to be called."

"Dahlia coined it in the . . . hospital." I was careful of what I said, rather aware that the cabbie was listening in.

"You're going to piss off the wrong person using it."

I shrugged. "I don't care." I did care, but I was tired of him telling me how to act. I'd forgotten about that part of our relationship, burying it under my grief. I'd put him on a pedestal when he died. There were parts of Tad that irritated me.

Like his bossy-pants act.

The cabbie slowed. "Here we go, you two. Have a nice visit with your parents. Good luck telling them you're Supes."

My jaw dropped, and the cabbie smiled at me in the rearview mirror, his grin wide and white. A waft of musk flowed back to me. Another wolf. Damn, they were everywhere.

"Um. Thanks."

Tad paid the cabbie and we slid out, silence holding us hostage.

"Mom's going to freak out." Tad broke the quiet first.

"Yeah." There was no denying it. I hooked an arm through his. "She won't recognize us at first."

"Dahlia recognized you, and you her. And you knew who I was."

"Maybe when you care for someone, the changes aren't as big, like Merlin said." I took a step, all but dragging Tad with me up the steps. The unspoken words were that maybe Mom wouldn't recognize us at all.

The house was the one we'd grown up in, and yet it looked foreign to me.

"You think Mom doesn't care about us?"

"I think she may make herself not care so she doesn't get dragged down to hell with her two wayward, soul-damning children." The bitterness in my words was evident even to me, though I tried not to think about how much truth I spoke.

The exterior of our parents' house was painted a pale yellow with white trim. A two-story home, it had a great view of a soccer field from the back balcony where I'd spent more time than I liked to admit watching the boys' soccer teams scrimmage.

I knew the interior would be clean, spotless to be fair. Mom cleaned every day, the perfect housewife as the Firstamentalists taught her. She'd made no effort to hide the fact that she felt the church had been her place of sanctuary. That it had been the place she'd learned to be an adult.

She always had gourmet meals on the table, hand-stitched the tears in our clothes, and folded fitted sheets like Martha Stewart. There was nothing she couldn't do when it came to the home.

"Jesus, just knock," Tad whispered.

"That is not my name." I raised my hand and rapped my knuckles against the wood. Why we weren't just walking in was beyond me. We never knocked. Surely that would be a tip-off that we were shysters there to try to pull the wool over their eyes.

The door opened and Yaya peeked out. Her eyebrows shot to her curly gray hairline. She called over her shoulder. "Sweet baby Cupid. Beatrice. Clark. You'd better get your hungover asses out of bed."

She opened the door and we stepped in. Formal. "Yaya. Do you recognize us?" I asked.

"'Course I do. I know my grandbabies. Even when they do stupid things like get turned into supernaturals. Hera be damned, you're going to get us all killed." She swatted the back of Tad's head first, then aimed for mine. I ducked out of the way while Tad rubbed his head.

"Yaya, we didn't do anything stupid."

She pointed a finger at me. "I told you to be careful of magic. And what did you do? Jump in with both feet like it was a contest to see who could make life the most dangerous. Pah. Stupid kids." She pointed at the couch. "Sit."

Tad and I sat, our hands clasped in our laps. Yaya paced in front of us. "Maybe we can still fix this."

"Fix it? We're both alive, Yaya. Unless you're planning on killing us both and burying the bodies in the backyard," Tad said.

She pointed a bony finger at him. "Don't sass me, boy, or I'll go get my shovel and start digging."

"Yaya." I held a hand out to her, and she took it. "You told me to make the right choice; what did you mean by that?"

She bowed her head. "It's a long story. And I wasn't at liberty to tell you. Though now there is no choice."

Her words were cryptic and strange, and they made me nervous.

From the hallway a soft groan rolled through the air along with the sound of bare feet slapping the tile floor.

"Mom, stop letting the Mormon missionaries in. They're very nice, but we aren't changing religions no matter how many times you pinch their bottoms."

I stood up, unable to stop myself. My mom, Beatrice to her friends, stepped into the room, yawning. Her pink fluffy robe she'd had for years was tied around her waist. She had the same dark-brown hair and brown eyes that I'd had before I'd been turned, and though she'd always been shorter than me, the difference was marked now.

"Hi, Mom," I said.

Her eyes popped wide, and she clutched at the throat of her robe. "Alena?"

Tad stood up. "Hi, Mom."

She wobbled where she stood, tears welling up in her eyes. "My babies."

I didn't care what the Firsts thought about me. I was me, and she was my mom, and she recognized me and that was all that mattered. I ran to her, wanting nothing more than to grab her in a hug. Tad was right behind me and snagged my arm before I could reach her, snapping me to a stop.

"Don't. Look at her eyes, Lena. She's afraid of us. The church will punish her for being near us, for even touching us and acknowledging we're still alive. You know that as well as anyone."

We were maybe three feet away from her, close enough that I could see the horror in her eyes, the tears on her cheeks. I froze where I was. "Mom. We aren't sick."

Tad tugged me back. "It's not that, Lena." I knew he was right. It wasn't the possibility of the virus that scared her.

It was what we were.

Super Dupers. Supernaturals.

Monsters.

Yaya came up beside me and slipped an arm around my waist. The warmth of her arm centered me, and I felt a tiny pulse of strength flow from her to me. Knowing she stood by us was enough to keep me there, facing my mother even when I knew what was coming.

"Beatrice. You hug your daughter right now." Yaya shook a finger at her daughter. "I raised you better than this."

That was just it. Mom had turned to the church for guidance even over her own mother's teaching. The church had become the place where her every question was answered.

Mom didn't move; she stood as still as if she'd been turned into a statue. "I can't. She isn't . . . Tad isn't . . . They aren't themselves. They're monsters, not my beautiful babies. My children are dead. They brought it on themselves, sinning. This is their punishment." Her mouth moved with two words I didn't think we were supposed to hear. "And mine."

How was this her punishment? That made no sense.

I stepped back, a final cold wash of understanding flowing over me like ice water poured on top of my head. This was what she believed: that we were some sort of demons now. I'd known it; it was what I'd believed most of my life. What I'd believed when I'd looked Merlin in the eye and told him to turn me in order to live.

"You would choose the church over us. I get it. We're lost to you. I just thought you should know we aren't dead. That we're still here." I turned, surprised I wasn't sobbing my heart out.

Because I think maybe I'd known all along this was a futile trip. That Mom would turn from us, and even with that, I'd needed to be sure we were outcast. I'd needed to see it for myself in order to put the past, and what was left of my family, behind me. "Come on, Tad. Let's go."

"What about Dad?"

A bitter, harsh laugh I didn't recognize escaped me. "You think he'll be any different? You think she'll let him?"

As if speaking about him had summoned him, our father, Clark, strolled down the hall in nothing but his pajama bottoms. Lean like Tad, he had green eyes and darker hair. Tad and I resembled him more than our mother now.

He lurched to a stop behind Mom, his jaw dropping open. "Alena. Tad." He made a move to step around Mom and she put an arm out, stopping him despite the size difference between them. He looked at her, then us.

"Bea. You can't be serious."

"The church doesn't allow interaction with supernaturals. You know that. They could kick us out."

His green eyes met mine and he smiled. "Unless you've put cameras in the house, they won't know." He pushed her arm down gently and walked toward us.

He caught Tad in a hug first, thumping him on his back while I stood there in shock. "Good job. I didn't think you'd be able to convince her."

"Almost didn't." Tad grinned at him, and then Dad came to me. He pulled me into his arms and held me without the back thumping. "I'm glad you came home, Lena Bean. We . . . I hoped you would take the cure."

I jerked back. "The money was from you?"

Mom gasped.

Dad half shrugged. "Life is life. Even if I couldn't see you, I wanted to know you'd had a choice. That I'd done what I could to make things better and given you the freedom to live a life outside of what—"

"Clark, when the priests find out they're going to kick not only you, but me out too! We'll go to hell!" Mom grabbed his arm, seeming to forget that it brought her closer to both Tad and me.

I held still, not sure how I felt about what she was saying. A part of me understood she wanted to be obedient to what she believed, but another part of me would never grasp turning away from her family. Not even for my soul.

Dad grabbed her arms and gave her a shake. "Bea. This is not the world they tell us it is. Our children are alive. They're here. We are a family. You think you'll go to hell because you love your babies? Babies we fought to have? You'd let them go so easily?" His words seemed to hit her like slaps, and she flinched with each thing he said.

Babies they'd fought to have. I looked at Tad, and he shook his head. There had been no stories of difficulties getting pregnant. What else didn't we know about our family's past?

A knock on the front door stopped all the words, and the five of us slowly turned. "Do you have company coming today, Yaya?" Dad asked.

"Nope. You two kids go hide." She shoved at Tad and me, and I stumbled down the hallway to our parents' bedroom, Tad right behind me.

Voices rose in the other room as we closed the door. I looked at Tad and he shook his head, finger to his lips. Yaya could be heard over everyone else.

"You are not welcome here, you, don't make me hurt you. Bunch of pointy hat–wearing monkey balls."

I looked at Tad. His eyes were wide. "I don't know. SDMP doesn't come this far off the Wall. Ever."

"We can't leave them out there."

"What if it's Firsts?"

"They don't wear hats, it's forbidden. You know that. God might not see them if they cover their heads from him."

His lips twitched. "I'd forgotten about that one."

That it wasn't Firsts made the decision easy for me. I shoved the door open and strode down the hall, focusing on the anger that kindled in my belly. Foreign and invigorating, the emotion was so unexpected I rode it all the way to the main room.

I skidded to a stop at the scene in front of me. Six men stood positioned around the room. Each held a gladiator sword in one hand and a shield in the other. They wore helmets with bright-red crests running down the center, along with a band of metal running down the middle of their noses. Armor wrapped around their chest, and leather kilt things hung to their knees.

The man who stood next to Yaya pointed his sword at Tad and me. "Serpents."

I pointed a finger back at him. "Donkey butthole."

He pulled his helmet off and threw it on the floor. Dirty-blond hair that looked like it had been crammed in the helmet for more than a few hours stuck out everywhere on his head. His eyes were dark, like the color of unsweetened chocolate. "You would insult me, monster?"

"You started it. And do I look like a monster to you?" I cocked a hip and put a hand on it, feeling for the first time the power that came with a body and face that could stop traffic.

His eyes traveled down my body, then back up to my face. "You hide behind beauty. It's the way of your kind, to seduce and destroy. But I will not fall for your evil."

Yaya moved to the center of the room. "This home is under my protection; would you forfeit your right to Zeus's guidance?"

The men shifted, leather skirts creaking and sandaled feet shuffling on the floor.

"This is not a shrine of Zeus. Besides, we do not answer to him." Blond Boy turned his back to Tad and me in order to face Yaya.

She drew herself up to her full five-foot-nothing height. "I am a priestess of the god of thunder and one of his favored women. So what are you going to do about that . . . Achilles?"

CHAPTER 8

"Achilles?" I spit the name out, my tongue flicking along the *s* a little too long. He spun, his sword raised to my face.

"Do not speak my name, serpent."

I mock-frowned at him while a distant part of me freaked out. A man was pointing a sword at me, and I wasn't afraid. Shouldn't I be terrified? Quivering with fear? Achilles was the one who took down Troy, the one who defeated Hector. Achilles was the greatest hero of Homer's *Iliad*. And he was standing in front of me, threatening to kill me. He was a hero of heroes. Yet I felt nothing but a slight irritation.

Maybe my mom was right, maybe there was something wrong with me. Maybe I had no soul and therefore could no longer feel true fear—

He pulled his arm back and whipped it forward, the sword catching the light. I leapt sideways into the coffee table, stumbled, tripped, and fell to my hands and knees while my heart did triple time. So much for not being afraid.

The soldiers laughed and Achilles grinned down at me. "I will be merciful, for your beauty softens my hand. Be still, and I will take your head, ending your suffering."

"What? Why?"

"You are the serpent I am to face. You are the first of the five monsters reborn to the earth. The first of five who must be destroyed so our queen can rise again."

"Oh, well, that clears up nothing." I pushed to my feet. "Sorry, it's been a long day, and I don't know why you want to hurt me, because I don't even know what I am. My mother won't hug me, and you're standing here with your sword sticking at my face."

Yaya snickered. "His other sword would be better, I think. He's quite good in bed from what I hear."

"Yaya!" Tad choked on her name, and I struggled to keep a straight face. Achilles, on the other hand, didn't seem to have a sense of humor.

"It matters not to me which sword I stick you with"—he moved around the side table—"or what you think you are, only that you are the first to die."

He raised his sword again and I stood there, staring at him. Because surely this wasn't happening.

My dad shoved Achilles from behind, throwing him toward me but also forcing him to deal with the coffee table between us, which he fell flat on, cracking the glass top, falling with the shards to the floor.

"Lena Bean, run!"

The other soldiers had a different idea. I took a step to the right and one grabbed my arm, yanking me toward him. I dug my heels into the carpet and jerked backward, fear making me pull with all I had.

He flew through the air, over my head, his eyes as wide as Mom's fine china dinner plates.

Tad pushed one of the other soldiers down, creating a tiny pocket for me to slip through. He grabbed my hand and we ran through the house, through the kitchen, and out the sliding glass door. The yard was soggy with rainwater and we were in bare feet. The mud and grass squished through my toes, but it wasn't cold. Not like it should have been.

All thoughts of cold feet flew from my head as the glass doors behind us shattered, and Achilles and his men poured out into the backyard. I backed up, already knowing we were screwed.

The fence completely circled the yard, was eight feet high, and had no gate, which was a long-standing argument between my parents. Dad wanted a gate; Mom said it would only encourage thieves to sneak in through the back.

Right at the moment, I was wishing we'd given the thieves an in.

"Boost me!" Tad ran to the fence and I followed. I cupped my hands and he put his foot in. I boosted him up. A little too hard. He flew fifteen feet into the air, his body twisting as he fell on the other side of the fence.

"You have no one to save you now, monster." Achilles approached, swinging his sword in a lazy circle.

"That's what you think," Yaya said from behind him. He spun as the arc of the frying pan flew straight and true. The cast iron smashed into Achilles's head. He dropped to the ground in a crumpled heap.

"Ooh-eee. Did you see his eyes roll back?" Yaya waved the pan at the soldier closest to her. The soldier seemed less than impressed as he pulled his sword arm back and held up his shield. As if going to do battle with a true foe.

Yaya was going to get us both killed.

But I was a Super Duper now. There had to be perks to being one of the monsters. Most were stronger and faster than humans, and if flinty-eyed Smithy was any indication, I should be able to outmaneuver these soldiers. Time to see if there was any truth in that. I ran toward Yaya, scooped her up with one arm, and bolted for the house before I questioned if what I was doing was even possible. All in the matter of barely two heartbeats.

"The glass, Lena!" Yaya shouted, and I leapt. We soared over the broken glass of the table, and I landed in a crouch well inside the kitchen, Yaya still tucked tight under one arm like an oversized, mouthy football.

"Mom, Dad. I gotta go. Don't tell Roger I'm alive," I yelled as I ran through the house, still clutching my yaya. "I want to surprise him."

Yaya cackled with laughter as we raced through the front door and out onto the steps. Yaya's baby-blue 1981 Granada waited for us, Tad at the wheel.

"Thanks, Yaya." I kissed her on the cheek and put her down.

"I'm coming with you, Lena Bean." She swatted me on the bum, and I scooted down the steps ahead of her. She made her way down the steps, all but dancing. I slipped into the backseat, leaving her the front. She got in and tapped on the dash. "Go, boy. Before that meathead wakes up."

We drove away at a good clip, all three of us quiet for a moment before the silence was broken.

All three of us tried to talk at once, a mash-up of questions and explanations. "Stop, both of you." Yaya held up her hands.

I closed my mouth. Yaya looked over the bench seat at me. "We need to figure out what Merlin did to you. Your brother is a naga. It's the only form that was allowed. Merlin is dabbling in things he shouldn't again."

I frowned. "You're talking about him like he's *the* Merlin and not just some wannabe who decided it was good name."

Yaya stared hard at me. "How do you know he isn't? The world is a much bigger place than you and your brother were ever shown. You were kept blind to the supernatural, more so because of our family history than anything else. That is the only reason I allowed your mother to go crazy with the Firstamentalists. It was a way to keep you all safe from . . . things I thought you'd never need to know."

Tad turned onto the main highway, sped up, and merged into traffic while the Granada's engine protested. "Yaya. You aren't really a priestess of Zeus . . . are you?"

"Of course I am. Why do you think I don't give two horny figs if I went to church with your parents or not? I went to keep your mother happy, and I only took her at all because I needed to look like I'd renounced my vows. That's all. I don't actually think that crap they dole out about supernaturals being the devil is right. Or even reasonable. You know, some of my best friends back in the day were supernaturals."

I reached up and gripped the back of the bench seat, the pleather creaking under my fingers. "Yaya. Why did you make us go to church, then? Is it because of Uncle Owen?"

"Because I was trying to keep you safe." Her eyes filled with tears. "When I lost Owen, all I could think about was keeping the rest of you away from danger. I couldn't bear the thought of losing any of you. One thing about the Firsts, they are safe." She shook her head, her gray curls bouncing. "I tried, but your bloodlines are too strong. I told your mother your father would be trouble if she married him, but she didn't listen to me. And now look. You two are both supernaturals just like—" Her teeth clicked shut and I shot a look at Tad. I had a feeling my eyes were probably as wide as his.

"Just like who, Yaya?" Tad asked.

"Never you mind. Don't matter. I have to pick some things up from the Blue Box Store. The one on Forty-Ninth Avenue and Homer." She leaned back in her seat, pulled her headphones from her pocket, and slipped them on. "Now let me sleep. I've had too much excitement and need to calm my heart before we get to Blue Box. The new one, not the crappy ones outside town."

The steady thump of techno music pulsed out of the earbuds, loud enough that I could easily hear it. Worse, the music crawled over my skin, the vibration as intense to my body as to my ears. I shivered and rubbed at my arms.

"Cold?"

"No, don't you feel that?" I pointed at Yaya.

Tad shook his head, frowning at me in the rearview mirror. "Feel what?"

"The vibration of the bass, the music. It's the same as when the Supe Squad came up behind us in the big rig. I could feel the pulse of the engine on my skin."

"Weird. You definitely aren't a naga. I couldn't have thrown you over the fence like you did to me. And I don't feel vibrations on my skin—ever."

"What kind of Super Duper does?" I asked, my voice quiet even though I didn't need to be. It wasn't like Yaya was going to hear me.

"I don't know, sis. But whatever you are, there's no doubt about it. You've stirred up a hornets' nest just by existing."

"That's a comforting thought," I muttered.

"I know, right?" He laughed softly, but the sound faded. "I am sorry, Lena. I didn't want this to happen to you. None of it."

I put a hand on his shoulder. "Don't be sorry. Things happen for a reason, right? Maybe you and I are meant to be like this." The words were the kind of platitudes I'd heard my whole life, but they'd always applied to other people. People who had bad things happen to them.

But not me.

The words didn't feel as deep or comforting coming out of my mouth this time.

"You really believe that?"

I opened my mouth to say yes. Shut it, and tried again. "Maybe."

He laughed again. "Who do you think Yaya was comparing us to? She was going to say we were supernaturals just like . . . and then nothing."

I put my chin on the back of the bench seat and stared out the windshield. "We don't know anyone who was a supernatural. At least no one Mom and Dad talked about."

"Grandma and Grandpa on Dad's side. They were strange," Tad said. I let out an exasperated sigh.

"Grandpa was an illiterate mill worker, and Grandma never lived anywhere farther than three miles from where she was born. Weird, yes. Supes? No way."

"What about Aunt Betty, on Mom's side?"

I snorted. "The lady with the affliction of terrible hats? Bad taste is just bad taste, Tad. You're stretching here."

"I want to know who she was going to compare us to. How else are we going to figure it out?"

"How about asking her?" I leaned away from the front and stared at the material ceiling of the car. I reached up and touched a hole that was almost the same size as the hole in my sheet back at the hospital. From one death trap to another. The thoughts rolled around in my head and I couldn't stop them. Two days ago, I'd been in the hospital dying just for existing.

Now I was facing some sort of death sentence just for existing. My lot wasn't improving as much as I'd hoped when I'd told Merlin to turn me.

"We're here, Yaya." Tad reached over and touched her on the shoulder. "We're here. Do you want to wait in the car and I can get whatever you want, or do you want to come in?"

"I want you to stop saying *want*," she grumbled, *then* slipped off her earbuds. Had she heard everything we'd been talking about? Call me a cynic but I was betting yes. "I'm not telling you who you're like now either. Not my place. Not my story."

Bingo.

How in h-e-double-hockey-sticks had she heard us over that heavy bass, though?

The three of us got out of the car and headed across the parking lot, weaving between cars to make the straightest route possible. The doors slid open. We stepped into the box store, the artificial lights buzzing high above us. My skin itched with the sound, and I wanted to scratch at every inch of me.

I settled for clamping my hands under my arms and then strode forward with Yaya.

"Yaya, what are we doing here exactly?"

"I need to talk to someone. Well, you need to talk to him too." She grabbed a stock boy and twisted him around to her. "Where's the manager?"

"Ah, I don't know." He tried to pry her off, his eyes flicking to Tad and me as if we would be on his side.

"I'd tell her, she bites when she's angry," Tad said. I laughed, falling into old patterns. No matter how ridiculous, we backed each other up. Even if it was an outright lie.

"You remember that time she bit the postman, barking at him like a dog and grabbing his ankle?" I smiled and shook my head as if remembering.

Tad grinned. "He had something like thirty stitches on top of a tetanus shot."

Yaya gave a sharp nod. "And I'll do it again if I need to. Go all the way up the leg to where the meat is soft and easy to bite off."

The stock boy paled. "Manager is in receiving, I think."

Yaya let go of him and patted his blue vest. "Good boy." With that, she spun and strode farther into the store. Tad looked at me, shrugged, and fell into step behind her.

People hustled through the store, pushing carts, pushing children, pushing items on the shelves. A woman shouldered between Tad and me and shoved me backward. She was maybe in her fifties with thick glasses and teeth that looked like she'd deliberately painted them black. That was the only explanation I could come up with for the dark shade several of them were.

"Move," she snapped, and I did, mostly because I didn't want to send her flying through the air like I'd done to my brother earlier.

The top of her head barely came to my chin and smelled heavily of body odor, with a faint undercurrent of moldy bread. I shuddered, wrinkled up my nose, and hurried to catch up to Tad and Yaya.

She was filling him in on something. "So you see, your father knew you were okay all along. He was the one who paid for you to be turned, but you knew that, Alena didn't. We were trying to keep her safe from persecution from the Firstamentalists. If they knew her brother was a Supe, she'd have an even harder time. Your mother never knew either, and that was the plan. But when Alena got sick, we didn't want you two to be separated again. So we made sure Merlin would turn Alena into a naga too."

"Why a naga?" I asked as we cut through the plastic tub aisle.

"The naga is a creature of Eastern mythology. We thought that was perhaps the best chance for you both." Her words softened and she shook her head. "But it looks like Merlin has decided on other things. Things that are going to cause no end of trouble."

"Do you know what I am?" I asked, hoping she had the answer.

"I think so. But I know someone who can tell for sure, just by looking at you. He can see through glamours and guises. Part of his old job."

We passed through the sporting goods and were working our way toward the car section, if the rotating tires above the aisle were any indication. A strong odor of rubber and oil crossed my nose, confirming our current location. In front of us was a tall man with big arms, a blue vest, and a perfect square-cut jaw I could see in profile as he followed at a distance behind a man who had obviously not ever had a mirror in his life. That was the only explanation for what I saw in front of me.

The man in the lead wore bright-pink leopard short-shorts, cowboy boots, and a tank top that was cut off at the midriff. Over all that he wore a see-through lacy trench coat. And he clutched a giant lollipop between his teeth.

The guy in the blue vest stalked him like a hunter after prey, with his camera phone as his weapon of choice. The scene was strange, but not surreal, as so many of my waking hours had been lately.

"That is not for real," Tad breathed.

The man in the blue vest with the great profile spun and laughed. He held up a cell phone. "The Real People of Blue Box is an actual thing, my friend. I document whenever I can. I have millions of hits and thousands of followers. Makes me feel alive again!" He grinned and a lightbulb burst over our heads, shattering into a million sparkling little pieces.

I hunched, Tad yelped, and Yaya stepped sideways to avoid the falling bits.

The man in blue grinned and flexed his arms. "Sorry about that. Happens more often than I like even after all these years."

I stared at his blue vest, reading the tags on it. *Best in customer service. Store Manager. Zeus.* "Sweet baby Jesus," I whispered.

Zeus looked at me, his gaze flicking up and down my body several times as if seeing me for the first time. "Well, well. What have we here?"

Yaya stepped between us. "That's why we're here, Zeus. We need to know what's going on. You have information and we need it. After all these years and all the times I stood up for you, we deserve your help."

She hardly blocked his view of me, yet he craned his head to look around her. "Flora, why did you bring me a siren?"

I slapped both hands to my chest. "I am *not* a whore."

He shook his head and one long finger. "No, not whore. Siren. Very different. And I think a rather special kind of siren."

Yaya fluffed up her hair, then tapped her forehead with one finger. "Zeus. Is this really something you want to discuss in the middle of the store?"

He spread his hands wide. "This is my kingdom now. I rule here, I am the overseer of this world."

"Are you serious?" Tad spluttered. "This isn't a world. It's not a kingdom. It's a box store." He looked at me, and I lifted my hands in surrender. What did I know about dealing with someone who thought he was Zeus?

"Don't look at me. The last twenty-four hours feel like some sort of dream to me as it is. Why can't Zeus be ruling a kingdom within the confines of a Blue Box Store? Just another weird twist to an already bizarro situation."

Zeus clapped his hands together, and a distinct rumble of thunder rolled through the store. "Flora, I have everything I need here. Food, drink, clothing, entertainment, and women. Lots of women." He winked at Yaya and reached as if to caress her face.

She swatted his hand down. "You like anything that will take you into their bed. Men. Women. Sheep."

He grunted. "Low blow, my love. I seem to recall you didn't mind my indiscriminating gaze."

Tad and I turned in unison to Yaya, who blushed a furious red under our curious eyes. "I'd like to forget that chapter of my life, thank you very much. I've moved on to much greener pastures."

Zeus chuckled. "Well, at your age, forgetting the past . . . that's entirely possible, isn't it?"

Yaya gasped, and I felt the dig as if it had been aimed at me. I shoved between them and put my finger into his sternum. "Listen here, hamster balls. You don't talk to her like that. Nobody talks to *my* yaya like that. Not even some trumped-up douche who thinks he's a long-dead god."

He grabbed my hand and rubbed my finger up and down in a far-too-suggestive manner. "Or what, darling? I think you and I could have a fine time together. Feisty, just like Flora with a longer set of legs. Yes, we could have some real fun."

Just like Roger, he thought he could pull the wool over my eyes with his deception. As if he could seduce me, making me blind to how he treated my family and me.

Just like Merlin, who'd lied to me, he thought he could seduce me with words and a future that didn't really exist.

Anger snapped through me, firing my blood like an open flame. I opened my mouth and my fangs dropped down. They hung out under my top lip and brushed along the lower edge of my bottom lip, beads of moisture dripping from them. A long low hiss slid out from deep in my throat as my eyes narrowed. Zeus stumbled back, slipped on a thin patch of oil, and fell onto his butt. He was up fast enough that I couldn't be sure he even fell if not for the fact that he brushed the back of his pants off and his hands came away slick.

"Drakaina," he said. "That's what she is, Flora. Whoever turned her did it with the intention that she would die."

My mouth dropped open wider, and with the dissipating anger, my fangs retracted, folding back as nicely as you please. "What?"

I seemed to be saying that a lot. *What. Why. Where.* I didn't like not knowing.

Zeus snorted and the lights above us flickered. "Drakaina. Serpent. Siren. Shape-shifter. Monster. That is what you are, granddaughter of Flora, long-ago priestess of mine."

"I don't want to be a monster," I whispered, forgetting I'd been angry with him only moments before.

He shrugged. "Not my issue, snake. You're a true monster, that's how it is. Not just any old supernatural, but a monster through and through. As bad as they come. Eating people, destroying cities, ruining lives: that is your calling card now."

His words were too much, the final straw piled onto my shoulders. I spun and bolted back the way we'd come, running for the front entrance. Tad shouted, begging me to stop. I couldn't, though. All I could think was that I wasn't going to be able to fit in at all. That people would know me for what I was as easily as Zeus did.

I choked on a laugh, the edge of it more than a little hysterical.

I was a monster. A snake woman who could seduce people and apparently scared even Zeus.

The lady who'd blocked us as we came in glared at me. "Out of my way, girl. I'm a-shopping, you know."

I didn't slow down but shoulder-checked her as I went by. She flipped right over backward and landed with an explosion of air as she belly flopped on the hard floor.

Mouth flapping wide like a fish out of water, she finally sucked in a breath only to let out a wail. "Assault! She assaulted me and I peed myself!"

A sharp tang of urine flooded the air, giving credence to her claim along with the puddle that slowly spread around her ponderous body.

Zeus, mighty god of thunder, was the Blue Box Store manager. His voice boomed over the PA system.

"Cleanup in aisle seven."

I slapped a hand over my mouth, but the shriek of laughter escaped me anyway as I spun and ran out of the store. There was only one place I wanted to be, and I couldn't stop myself. Couldn't keep my feet from taking me to the home I'd shared with Roger. The place I'd felt the safest since my earliest memories.

We didn't live that far from the Blue Box, a scarce fifteen-minute drive, down to Galer Street in the Queen Anne neighborhood. But that was driving and I was on foot. I didn't slow, though, as if running would take me away from the craziness my life had become.

The first hill was no problem as adrenaline pushed me up it in record time. The second hill was tougher and the third I walked up, panting and sweating despite the chilly weather.

I reached the top of the third hill and stood there, staring at my house. My grandparents' home. The place I'd thought I'd live until I died. Which in a way, I had. Only I wasn't truly dead. Even if I had a large stamp of *Deceased* on my birth certificate.

"Don't get melodramatic," I scolded myself. "You don't know what's on your birth certificate now. Could say *Monster* for all you know." My pep talk didn't help any.

Parked in the driveway of our house was a black sports car with glittering silver paw prints all over it. I made myself walk up to the car and peer in. The interior was filled with fast-food bags, wrappers, and empty pop cans.

"Disgusting," I said, as though my being a monster were any less disgusting than the car filled with garbage.

Why had I come here? Not just because it was my safe place, not if I was being honest with myself. A small part of me wanted to be held, to have someone tell me it would be okay. Roger had always been good at telling me what I wanted to hear.

I stepped away from the car and headed for the front door. The house was old, a hundred years and counting. Three stories, it towered over the other homes in the neighborhood, and yet I'd never felt like it was ostentatious. It needed some love; the shingle roof needed to be replaced, and the windows needed to be swapped out for double pane. Lots of love, sure, but I'd been willing to give it what it needed. To take the time . . .

The window that looked out over the front yard was our bedroom, and the light was on, and it was only then that my heartbeat slowed enough that I could hear Barry Manilow playing. Loud enough that the words were audible.

That was Roger's lovemaking album. The music he'd told me put him in the mood only for my kisses, and never for anyone else.

Something in me snapped. Roger was never going to hold me again. And I didn't want him to. He was a dirty donkey's butthole.

I opened the front door and headed straight for the stairs. Taking them two at a time, I passed the second level and kept moving on to the third. The bedroom was actually the entire third floor, and while it was smaller than the second floor, it was still a thousand square feet.

One feature I'd never minded before, though, was now a real problem. The top level was an open floor plan, and there was no door on the bedroom. I stood on the steps a few feet below the landing, the music a low, mindless tune I'd always hated. Always. Why hadn't I told Roger I'd hated it?

Because he'd told me how much he'd loved it and I'd wanted him to be happy. I'd always been trying to make him happy. To prove I was worth his love, to prove I was worth being his wife.

I squared my shoulders and took a step. A female giggle rippled through the air, and I made myself keep moving. Kept walking up the final few steps. The view didn't make sense at first, as there was just a humping, bumping black blanket on the bed.

"Roger, you are frisky tonight. Naughty Chihuahua," she—I assumed Barbie—*yipped* out at him. As if she were the Chihuahua.

He growled and snapped his teeth. I rolled my eyes, put my hands on my hips, and broke up their party. "I hardly would call him naughty. More like dumb. Or useless. Maybe lazy, that's another good word for Roger."

They spun, the two of them sitting up in bed like pop-up dolls.

"Roger, who is that?" Barbie said. I had to give her credit. Her hair was perfect, and from the shape of her chest under the sheet, her boobs weren't half bad either. Power, though, Zeus said I had power.

A siren, was I? Well, let's just see what that got me.

I flipped my hair back over my shoulders and took a step closer. "Roger. Who. Am. I?"

He stared at me, looked me up and down, and in slow increments his mouth dropped. "Alena?"

I smiled, feeling a strange sense of confidence roll through me. Roger swallowed hard and slid to the edge of the bed as if he would come to me. I held a hand up. "You stay there."

"That's your *wife*? Her pictures don't look like that. And isn't she supposed to be dead? How are we going to have the money if she isn't dead?"

"Excellent question, Barbie." I paced in front of the bed. "I mean, really, he's not all that good in bed, so the money is very important, isn't it? How much did he promise you for your business venture exactly?"

"I am an excellent lover," Roger spluttered. "Caring, considerate—"

"You couldn't find the G-spot in an alphabet." I snapped my fingers, waving a hand in the air. "Seriously, how often do you fake it, Babs? Ten out of ten? I know I did."

Her lips tightened, and I wasn't sure if it was laughter or anger holding them shut. Roger spluttered and spit but couldn't manage a single word.

"Here's the thing." I paused and pointed at Roger, feeling the strength of my words grow with each syllable. "He's not going to have any money when I'm done with him. This is my house. The inheritance is mine. The bakery is mine, and that fat-nosed Colleen isn't going to have a single sugar cube from it. Got that? He's going to have his stinking little brown Fiesta hatchback, a bag of clothes, *and if he's lucky*"—I approached them—"his little girlfriend." I snapped my fingers at her and she flinched. Roger, though, hadn't taken his eyes from me.

"Alena, I've never seen you like this. If I'd known you'd be like this, I never would have looked for someone else. I didn't know you were going to survive." He crawled across the bed to me and I stepped back.

"Are you for real?" I said at the same time Barbie slapped his butt hard enough to make him jump and his drooping man bits wobble and deflate.

"Ouch!"

"I'll do more than 'ouch' you, you asshole. You said you loved me, that you never loved her but married her because she was a good girl and would do what she was told. That you always wanted me more." She pouted at him while not so subtly pushing her chest out.

But his eyes swept back to me, a bright, hot lust raging in them. "Alena, we can work this out. I know we can. Every couple has a bump in the road, and this is ours. Give me a second chance. Please, baby."

My heart leapt, and for just a second I thought about it. A second. No more than that, because what happened next hit me like a blow to the belly.

My eyes locked with hers, and the smug curl of her lips told me the truth of her and Roger, even though I still had to ask.

"You were with him before I was sick, weren't you?"

She smirked and ran a hand over her chest. "You don't actually think you were satisfying him, do you? Miss Missionary."

I drew in a slow breath, anger kindling along my synapses as I swung my gaze to my husband.

"Roger, not for anything in the world would I go back to you. Not for money, fame, fortune. Nothing. I will never come back to you." I turned, paused, and looked over my shoulder. "You'll be hearing from my lawyer. And Barbie?"

I locked eyes with the blond bombshell one last time. "Good luck on teaching him how to pleasure a woman. You know what they say about teaching stupid dogs new tricks. Impossible."

His mouth dropped open and she glared at me. "Maybe all he needed was someone worth pleasuring. Maybe a little brown church mouse wasn't all that fun to play with."

Oh, she did not go there. I spun on a heel and faced her. "Do I look like a little brown church mouse to you?"

She stood up on the bed, buck naked, and put her hands on her hips. "I think you wouldn't know what fun was if it snuck up and bit you on the ass. Roger is better off with me. As is the money, because I'll at least do something interesting with it."

Gobsmacked was the only word I had to identify the emotions running through me. A small part of me wanted to strangle her.

Okay, a large part.

The rest was just confused, and that part won out this time. "Our whole life together was a lie, wasn't it?"

Roger shook his head, but I saw it in his eyes a split second before he lowered them. The truth. I was just a stepping-stone for him.

I snorted softly. "You two have fun. I'm taking you for everything you've got and then some. *Rog.*"

I turned again and headed down the stairs, making myself not hurry. Forcing my feet to go at a sedate pace. I refused to run from the two of them.

But maybe if I'd hurried, I would have made it out before the bad guys found me.

Okay, I was assuming they were bad guys. But really, good guys don't burst into a house wielding large weapons.

Nor do they normally look like bulls from the waist down.

I swallowed hard. *Here we go again.*

CHAPTER 9

"I think you have the wrong house!" Roger yelled from the top of the stairs. "We gave at the office."

I twisted around to glare at him, wondering what I'd ever seen in him. Spineless twit. No wonder he couldn't even manage a cash register.

"You the Drakaina?" a deep voice asked.

The question turned me back to face the things in the lower foyer. Men from the waist up, bulls from the waist down, which included hairy legs, cloven hooves, and oversized bull bits. Each of them had a strap across his chest with an emblem engraved in gold. One that looked suspiciously like Achilles's chiseled jaw.

"What's a Drakaina?" Barbie whispered, and the Bull Boy at the front pointed his sword at her.

"Back away, puny human. The Drakaina is a dangerous beast full of poison."

"Actually, *poison* is not quite right. *Venom* would be correct if you're referring to my fangs." I took a breath and backed up a step.

Bull Boy raised an eyebrow at me. "You the Drakaina?"

I shrugged as a niggling fear began to gnaw at the base of my neck. Achilles had sent his goons after me. I went with coy. "Maybe."

"What do you mean, maybe?" He pointed his sword at me.

"She's a human, not some draco thing," Roger said, though his words wavered at the end. "Right, Alena?"

Bull Boy grinned up at me. "That's her. Alena. Boss said it was her name."

He took a step, his large hooves tromping onto the bottom stair. The wood groaned and I lifted an eyebrow. "I don't think that was a good idea."

"Drakaina, we're taking you to Achilles."

I glared at him. "What is it with all the men in my life trying to make me do what they want?"

Barbie snickered. "Because you haven't learned yet to make them do what you want them to. Idiot."

I didn't want to think she had a point. But maybe she did.

Bull Boy let out a snort, leaned forward to step up . . . and went straight through the stairs, the old wood busting out underneath him with a monstrous screech of breaking lumber and rusted nails letting loose all at once. His hands flung up as he went down, and he bellowed as the house seemingly swallowed him whole. The remaining six Bull Boys stared at the hole, their hooves shuffling on the wooden floor. Their furry legs twitched as they backed away from the pitch-black hole.

"You'd better leave. I can't guarantee the rest of you will make it out alive." I took a step forward. They backed up farther, their eyes trained on my every move.

They were afraid of me.

A wild urge gripped me, a power like I'd never known. Not magic, but the realization that just by existing, I frightened them. Gathering myself, I leapt the rest of the way down the stairs and over the hole the lead bull had opened up in the floor. I landed in a crouch on the main floor. Achilles's goons scattered to one side, the clatter of the hooves filling the air.

"Holy shit, she *is* a supernatural," Roger breathed.

The bulls snorted, shaking their heads and holding their weapons out in front of them, though they were far less certain without their leader. Like a real herd of bovines, they weren't about to step away from the group and face me on their own. I grabbed the front door, opened it, and moved to step through. Hanging beside me on the wall key ring was a set of keys with the name *Barbie* in bright-pink crystals. I scooped them up along with my set of keys from Vanilla and Honey. No way was Colleen getting her hands on these.

"Alena, you can't leave us here with these things!" Roger yelled. I glanced up at him, the dark sheet he held to his waist highlighting how pale his skin was.

Barbie glared at me. "Don't you dare touch my baby!"

I didn't think she meant Roger. My husband took a step and I pointed a finger at him, freezing him as if that were a new power of mine.

"Go to . . . *hell*, Roger." The word quivered on my lips, but I said it. His jaw dropped and I slammed the door behind me.

I strode out to the shiny black sports car, opened the door, pushed the junk off the seat and out onto the ground, and slid in. Key in ignition, I revved the engine, shifted into reverse, and hit the gas pedal. The tires peeled in the loose gravel, spitting rocks everywhere. The sound of pebbles hitting the sides of the car gave me a wicked sense of satisfaction. Spinning out onto the road, I shifted into gear and hit the gas again. From the side mirror, a rampant group of bull men chased down the road behind me. They gave up when I hit the on ramp to the highway and opened the sports car up.

The car was light to the touch and responded quickly. It didn't take long for me to recognize the direction I took. Vanilla and Honey was on the outskirts of downtown, close enough to get good traffic, but not so close that the rent was impossible.

Tears trickled down my cheeks as I thought about the last twenty-four hours, my life, the last few weeks, and the realization that nothing prior to my being sick had been what I'd thought. Nothing in my life had prepared me for what I'd gone through and what I'd learned about those people I thought were on my side. I sniffed several times. "What the heck happened to me?" Not that I expected an answer. So when I got one, to say I was surprised was an understatement.

"Well, this is what happens when you get mixed up with gods and goddesses. Or in your case, when your family gets mixed up."

I jerked the car to the side of the road and threw it into park. Beside me in the passenger seat floated a mostly naked cherub who sported a pair of cream-colored wings and a barely-there loincloth made of pale-pink satin.

"Umm, excuse me?" I had to be seeing things. Naked cherubs didn't just appear in the air. They were in frescoes and paintings, not real life. He tugged at his loincloth, scratching at his crotch.

"I said this is what your family gets. For meddling."

I rubbed at my eyes. "Wait, are you . . . Cupid?"

"I am not!" He floated up to the ceiling of the car, his face pinking up to match his loincloth. "That miserable interloper has nothing on me." The color in his face bled down his neck to his chest.

"Sorry, I'm not up on my mythological . . . deities." I sniffed back the last of my tears. "Who are you, then, and why are you in my car?"

"Not really your car now, is it?" He grinned, and the red faded from his skin. "Name is Eros. But you can call me Ernie. I like it better. More new-age sounding."

"Ernie. Okay, so . . ." Wrapping my brain around this newest addition to my life was a struggle. "What are you doing here, Ernie?"

"Well, the boss felt like a shit, being as he used to knock boots with your granny and all, and since it's kind of his fault you ended up like you are, he wanted me to bring you a message and tell you to meet him at the club tonight and he'd tell you everything he could." He drew in a deep breath, his chest swelling. That was a lot of words in a single sentence for such a little guy.

I narrowed my eyes. "So what you're saying is my yaya gave Zeus what for and he's trying to make nice now."

Ernie grinned and gave me a big wink with one baby blue. "You betcha. I always liked Flora. She didn't put up with the boss's nonsense like the other priestesses. I don't put up with it either." He let out a sigh and floated to the seat. "Where are you going?"

"To my bakery," I said without thinking. He lit up like a Christmas tree with ten times too many lights.

"I love sweets."

I put a hand on the stick shift and then glanced at him, my mind working. I couldn't afford to let the opportunity slide by, which meant I had to embrace the weirdness 100 percent.

"I'll give you all the sweets you want . . . if you answer some questions for me."

"Sure thing, toots." Ernie settled into the seat and grinned up at me. "What do you want to know?"

I pulled back into traffic and picked through all the questions I had. "Tell me about what I am."

"Ahh. A Drakaina. Interesting choice of monster for Merlin to make you. I heard what you said to the Bull Boys; you're right about the venom-versus-poison thing. Venom in the fangs, but you are not poisonous. Your venom will kill anyone, including heroes. Including gods and goddesses." He shifted in his seat. "It's why Zeus fell over trying to get back from you when you showed off your fangs."

"You saw that?"

"I was sitting in the rafters eating my lunch. Got a good view of the whole encounter."

I took the next off-ramp, clutched the steering wheel, and made myself ask the next question. "That's not all being a Drakaina is, is it?"

"Nope. You're a shifter. Should be able to turn into a giant snake. Big as a house. And you're sensitive to vibrations and smells. You can see in the dark, and of course being something of a siren, you can seduce men and women right out of their clothes if you put your mind to it."

Wonderful.

"Okay, what else have you got, beautiful?"

"Don't call me that. I'm a monster."

"A beautiful monster." He grinned. "That's got to count for something." I hunched my shoulders. "Okay. Who in my family is a Super Duper?"

He laughed, falling onto his back and flashing me in the process. "A Super Duper? Are you kidding me? That's not what you call supernaturals, is it?"

"Stop laughing. That's what we called them in the hospital."

"Say that to the wrong Supe and you're going to have a fight on your hands." He grinned and I glared at him. "Okay, okay. I don't know who in your family is a Super Duper"—he half choked on the words—"but you're right. Someone is supernatural, or you never would have caught the Aegrus virus."

"What do you mean?"

Ernie cleared his throat. "The virus only attaches to those who carry some amount of supernatural blood. It can't attach to pure humans. So Flora, being a pureblood, and your mom, being a pureblood, would never be able to pick up the virus. A pure-blooded Super Duper"—he snickered—"can pick it up but just gets sick. It's you halfers that get sick and die. The virus is too much for the little bit of each."

The epiphany hurt my brain, and I ran it through my brain twice before I realized what he was saying.

"If my mom is pure human, and I caught the virus, it means—"

"That your papa is most likely some form of supernatural. You got it." He shimmied deeper into his seat.

Fricky dicky, that was a revelation I'd not been ready for. Dad was a Super Duper? How could we not have known?

"Don't beat yourself up for not knowing," Ernie said. "Most Supes hide from their families too. It's better that way with the current atmosphere."

I counted my breaths in and out as I did my best to calm myself. Nothing I could do about Dad right now. Though a little honesty would have been nice. I frowned. "Why wouldn't he have said something when we went home?"

"No idea."

Me neither.

"Okay, back to the other stuff. The halfers who get sick, they're the only ones, right?"

"Yup." He fluttered his wing tips over his head as if egging me on. "Keep going."

I scrunched up my face, the thoughts coming together in bits and pieces. "That's why the government hides away those who are sick in places like Whidbey. They don't want everyone to know how many halfers there are out there? Because if they knew how many halfers there were, people would realize how many supernaturals there were?"

"You got it now. You're a smart one. In the whole wide world, at least half of the population has some amount of Super Duper blood. They don't have to be halfers like you and your brother. Just a speck of the supernatural, down to I think something like a sixteenth the last time I asked, was enough to make you vulnerable. That's about half the population in the world. And that's a big kill zone. Imagine what would happen if half the population keeled over. Or became . . . Super Duper like you and your brother." He grinned again.

"Wow," I whispered as I pulled into my parking spot at the back of the bakery. "Ernie, thank you."

"Anytime you want info in trade for food, you've got it."

I stepped out of the car and he followed, flying near my shoulder. I glanced at him. "Do you mean that?" He'd been more honest with me than anyone else so far.

"Sure. I like you. You remind me of Flora when she was young. Feisty and full of life. Nice rack too."

I rolled my eyes as I walked to the back door. I pulled my bakery keys out and held them in front of the knob. No need to use them, though; the door was cracked open.

The bakery hadn't been open since I'd gotten sick; I'd closed it down thinking I'd be back soon enough. Before I'd known it was the Aegrus virus. My main helper, Diana, was supposed to be checking on things every day, making sure all the fridges and such were running so nothing spoiled. But that was an early-morning task.

There was no way Vanilla and Honey should have been unlocked this late at night. I held a hand up to Ernie, motioning him to be quiet.

The back of my bakery was the kitchen, pantry, and cold storage as well as my office. Even though my office wasn't sealed off, I didn't mind. When I was doing the numbers I liked to feel I wasn't separated from the rest of the bakery and goings-on.

Behind my office desk, three men dressed in black pried at my wall safe, their backs facing me.

"John, get that pry bar. We'll take the whole thing."

One of the men turned around, saw me, and froze. "Boss. We got a problem."

"I doubt it, Johnny. Get the damn pry bar."

"We got company."

The other two men spun around so all three were facing Ernie and me. The cherub floated up to the ceiling. "You got this. Kick their asses so we can bake some cake!"

"I don't know how to fight." Who was I kidding? This was my bakery, my baby, and they were ransacking it. I wasn't going to just stand there and let them take what they wanted.

"You don't have to, your instincts should ramp up and help you out." His blue eyes twinkled down at me. "Here they come."

What did he mean, I didn't have to know how to fight? I tore my gaze from him as the first thug approached me, grinning from ear to ear.

"Here I thought we were taking cash, and we're going to end up with a beauty prize as well." In his hands he held a length of rope he slowly spooled out in a loop, like a lasso. I took a step back, my butt bumping up against one of the countertops.

I reached behind me, my hand gripping something familiar and solid. I swung the rolling pin, catching the goon on the side of his head. He dropped like a sack of potatoes.

"Atta girl! Now the other two!" Ernie cheered me on and a rush of adrenaline zipped through me. I'd never felt so . . . alive.

I strode toward the next would-be thief and brandished the rolling pin. "Get your friends and get out."

He pulled a gun from his lower back and pointed it at me. "This is *our* heist. Get out or I'll shoot you right in your pretty face."

I didn't even think. I dropped to my knees and lashed out with the rolling pin, catching him in the knee. A rather satisfying crunch of bone filled the air. He let out a scream as he fell and the gun went off, firing into the ceiling. Goon number three—a.k.a. Johnny—let out a yell and ran for the back door.

"Throw the pin!" Ernie yelled.

I spun and threw the rolling pin, surprised I could do what he said so easily. The heavy wooden pin flew end over end several times before crashing into the back of the fleeing Johnny's skull. He fell forward, facedown on the pavement.

I stepped toward the still-conscious thief and pushed the gun out of his reach with my toes like I'd seen on every cop show I'd ever watched. I leaned over him and grabbed the phone off my office desk, dialing 911.

"I'd like to report an attempted robbery by three complete idiots."

Ernie snickered and I gave him a thumbs-up.

Minutes later, the police pulled into the back parking lot. It didn't take them long to cuff the three thieves. The police took a statement from me but ignored Ernie.

"He saw what happened too, he can back me up. That will make a stronger case, won't it?" I lifted my eyebrows at the young officer.

"I'm sorry, ma'am," Officer Jensen said. "We don't take statements from supernaturals. They don't exist in the human court system." His dark eyes darted away from mine and then back again. "I'm sorry. For what it's worth, I would take his statement. But it would get the entire case thrown out when the judge realized he was a Supe."

"That's discrimination." I frowned up at Ernie, who shrugged. What would they say, then, if I told them I was a Super Duper too? Would they have even come to help? I had a feeling that they wouldn't. Or worse, they would have sided with the robbers because they were human . . . and I wasn't.

"Yes, it is discrimination." The officer nodded, lifted his hat, and scratched the top of his head before putting his hat back in place. "Nothing to be done about it. If you need anything or remember anything else, please don't hesitate to call." He handed me a card that had his name and a cell phone number on the back of it.

I tucked it in the palm of my hand. "Thank you."

He smiled and backed out as his walkie-talkie squawked to life. He pressed the button and spoke softly into it. Maybe he thought I couldn't hear.

"Yeah, boss, she's here."

My blood ran cold and I swallowed hard. I could only guess who he spoke to. I wasn't fool enough to believe it was his chief of police. Achilles most likely, even though the image of the Greek hero on a cell phone was a hard one to believe possible.

I forced myself to walk forward and shut the door behind Officer Jensen. "Ernie, I think your time at my bakery is going to be cut short."

"What? Why? I haven't had a good piece of home-baked goodies in years. I've been living off that cellophane-wrapped crap in the store." He whined at me and I smiled, though my lips trembled.

"Officer Jensen just said, 'Yeah, boss, she's here.' So I think we can't stay. Or at least, I can't stay." I gathered up my keys for the bakery along with Barbie's keys and walked to the door. "Maybe you should go your own way."

"Nah, you're interesting. I've been bored out of my head for the last thousand years. A monster shows up, and things finally start to happen again."

I paused at the door. The officers had taken my wooden rolling pin for evidence, but I had another one. A metal one I used for making fondant. I reached for it, the cool stainless steel in my hand a nice weight. I glanced at Ernie floating at my left shoulder.

"Just in case."

He grinned at me. "Not going to be a matter of if you need it, Alena, but a matter of when, I think."

I pushed the back door open a crack. The moon was only partially up, giving the back parking lot a gloomy look of dodgy shadows among the dark purple of the night. Officer Jensen sat in his police cruiser, his head bent over something. Maybe more paperwork. "Do you think he's watching the bakery?"

Ernie floated up to peer out over my head. "Pretty good bet. If he's ratting you out to someone, then they'll want him to keep an eye on you for sure."

I closed the door and backed away. Hurrying, I wove through the bakery, around the counter, and to the front door. I peered out into the growing darkness. Across the street from the bakery sat a police cruiser identical to Officer Jensen's.

A loop of claustrophobia tightened around my neck. Trapped.

"How am I going to get out of here?"

Ernie floated around so he was directly in front of me. "Walk out, see if they follow or try to stop you. They might be here to make sure no more break-ins happen."

A frown settled on my face. "Really? Do you believe that?"

"No. But I don't want you flipping out and shifting in here. You might bend my wings. Worse, you could wreck your bakery, and that would mean no pastries for me. Which would totally suck rotten eggs."

I put both hands on the door and stared hard at the officer. "Ernie, why would I shift? I don't want to be a giant snake. I'm never going to shift into one."

The very thought made my skin crawl, and that only made me shudder more. Who in their right mind would want to be a snake so big it could swallow a horse whole? No. That wasn't—

"You won't have a choice. If you're threatened or scared bad enough, you'll shift."

"I don't want to!"

"Sorry, but you will. It's not a matter of if, but when." He fluttered his wings and did a slow circle.

"You like saying that, don't you?"

He shrugged. "It's a good saying. Not if. When. That's life. Not if you die. When. Not if you fall in love. When. Not if you get your heart broken. When."

"Not if you turn into a giant venomous snake the size of a two-story house," I whispered.

He nodded. "You got it now. So what's it going to be, beautiful? Door number one? Or door number two?"

Paralyzed by indecision, I stood there in my bakery and bowed my head. "Achilles is going to keep coming after me, isn't he?"

Ernie didn't answer right away. He floated over to the cash register and lowered himself to it. "He's only been woken up to kill you. I think."

I put a hand to my eyes to cover the prickle of tears. The stainless steel rolling pin in my hand seemed a silly thing now, useless against a hero who had a sword and knew how to use it. I dropped it to the floor with a clatter. "Maybe I can sneak by the officer in the front."

I flicked the lock and stepped out of my bakery, leaving behind the comforting smells of dough, yeast, and flour. Moving quickly, I strode down the street, putting the bakery and the officer behind me. "Ernie, can you see if he's following us?"

"Yup, he's doing a U-turn."

"Donkey balls," I bit out, and hurried my stride.

"I don't think speed-walking is going to get you out of this. Go. I'll catch up with you later if I can," Ernie said as he flew above my head and off to the side.

I broke into a run. The buildings whipped by in a steady blur, and behind me the police car's siren rent the air, shattering the false silence.

I took a hard right down an alley and kept moving as fast as I could. I leapt dumpsters and sleeping homeless people, climbed two fences, and took three more turns before I let myself slow down. The siren had been turned off, or I had outrun it. I wasn't sure which, and really it didn't matter except that I'd bought myself some time.

My hand brushed against the old brick building and I leaned into it. Just what was I going to do now? I had a hero who wanted to kill me. How was I going to stop that from happening?

I didn't realize I'd spoken out loud until someone answered me.

"I can help you, Alena."

I spun around with a gasp. Behind me stood Remo, the vampire mob boss. He leaned against the building, a lit cigarette dangling from his lips. The tip burned bright as he drew a breath, the color flickering over the metal fangs in his chin. Violet eyes stared hard at me, as though trying to see through me. I glared at him, hating the way I felt around him. Equal parts intrigued and scared, irritated and amused. Even I knew that was a dangerous combination for a recipe.

"I don't want your help. And you shouldn't sneak up on people, it might be bad for your health."

He smiled around the edge of his cigarette. "Threatening me right off the bat? That's amusing."

I didn't like that he used the word I'd been thinking about him. "Go away. I'm not on your turf."

"It's all my turf, Alena. Now, are you sure you don't want my help? I think you're going to need it. Rumor is you pissed off some mighty powerful people. I would think you would like an equally powerful . . . friend." He pushed off the building and walked toward me. Each step he took reminded me of something, the same as when I'd first met him. Like a tiger sliding through the jungle, seen and then not as its stripes blended into the foliage. That same slinking, muscled walk in a man his size was, to say the least, unnerving.

"You move like a cat," I said, the words escaping my filter before I could stop them.

His eyebrows shot up along with one side of his mouth. "Pardon?"

I couldn't help the blush that heated up my face, unable to take my eyes from his lips. "Never mind. I don't want to be your friend. Besides, we aren't allowed to interact. You being a vampire and me being . . . not a vampire."

He smiled and flicked the cigarette behind him. "I want to be your friend, Alena. You're a powerful Supe. Beautiful. Deadly. Confident. Everything I want in a *friend*."

I blinked and he was standing right in front of me, our eyes locked as though our gazes had tangled. My earlier assumption was right; he *was* a good five inches taller than me, which left me craning my head to look up at him. I took in a deep breath, and his scent coursed over my tongue.

Cinnamon and a hint of honey, as if he'd dipped his tongue in a jar of it. My fangs slowly dropped, and I slapped my hands over my mouth. "Sorry."

He grinned, a slow lifting of his lips. "Did your fangs lower on their own?"

I nodded.

"I must smell good to you, then." He stepped closer and in a blink had me pressed against the wall with his body. Every hard line of him ran against me: chest, hips, and thighs lining up perfectly with mine. I placed my palms flat against the wall behind me.

"Get off me." The words I meant to come out in a shout slipped by my lips in a whisper.

"I think you like me on you. In fact, I'd lay money on it."

"All the same," I breathed out. My fangs retracted and I moved to shove him away from me. All I could think about was how much my mother would have hated him. How she would have demanded I break off whatever I had with him and find myself a good boy. One who went to church. A doctor. Someone with an education and no tattoos or piercings.

I blinked up at Remo, grabbed the sides of his head, and kissed him. He let out a surprised grunt, then leaned into the kiss, his tongue flicking in and out of my mouth in a way I'd never felt. He slid an arm around behind me and grabbed my bum, tugging me tighter against his very obvious attraction to me. A groan slipped from me, the sound full of want and need I'd never known. Desire pulsed between us so thick and heavy I would drown in it if I didn't do something.

I couldn't help but compare him to Roger, to the sense of duty I'd felt with Roger. The feeling that I had to have sex with him, not because I wanted to, but because he wanted to.

And in that moment all I could think about was how badly I wanted to see where the rest of Remo's tattoo went, where it began or where it ended. Maybe trace it with my fingers.

I sucked in a gasp and pulled my mouth from his. "Enough."

"I think we're just getting started." His dark-violet eyes sparkled, little lights dancing in them that sought to draw me down into their depths.

Batting my eyelashes, I pushed his chest and he stumbled back a good ten feet. "I said, enough." Power coursed through me, and I pulled myself up to my full height. "I'm sorry, I shouldn't have done that. You should go. Achilles will be here soon, and the last thing I want is more people getting hurt because of me."

"That idiot couldn't find his sword when it's in its sheath." He snorted. "I sent him on a wild goose chase out to the edge of the Rockies. He'll be there for at least a few days searching for you."

"No, I heard Officer Jensen. He said . . . oh. You're the boss he was talking to?"

Remo grinned, and my knees wobbled at the impish grin on the big vampire's face. "Yes, I'm his boss. I asked him to watch out for you."

"Why?"

"You intrigue me in a way no woman has in a thousand years, Alena. All the power, all that strength. And yet"—he drew closer again and ran a hand through my hair, catching the ends and drawing them to his nose—"there is an innocence about you. As if you have been kept from the realities of the world and believe you cannot be corrupted. I find it intensely attractive."

I tugged my hair away. "Let me guess, you want to be the one to corrupt me?"

"On the contrary. I like you just the way you are. This mix of beauty and power. Of innocence and strength. I want you to be my First, Alena. Come with me, I will keep Achilles at bay." His hands pressed against the wall on either side of me, trapping me once more with his body.

His First?

"I don't know what that is, your First, but I—"

"As in the First one in my bed. You would be my favored woman, the one I hold closest to me in the deep of the night, our skin flushed with the heat of passion and blood, or slick with our lovemaking."

A flush of desire roared through me, his words painting a rather vivid image. But the desire was followed close by a cold flurry of horror. One of many women he would parade through his life.

"You want me to be your whore? You think I would share a man with other women?"

"Call it what you will. Many would beg to be offered to be my First."

I shook my head as my fangs lifted away from the roof of my mouth. I pushed them back up with my tongue. "You can take your help and shove it where the sun shines brightly, Remo. I will never be your whore, and for the record, you would only need one woman if you had me."

His lips twitched and he dropped the tip of his tongue to touch one of his piercings, and I couldn't help but track the move with my eyes. "So tough. Fine. You know where I am, Alena. When you realize you aren't strong enough on your own, you can come to me. I will take you. But the price will be steeper then. Interest, you know. Everything goes up in value if you don't have a buy-it-now policy." He winked, turned, and walked away from me down the alley. There it was again, that image of a tiger in the jungle, his body visible and then fading into the world as if he weren't there from one step to the next.

"Yeah, well, you suck." It was the worst thing I could come up with, and all it did was make Remo laugh. His shoulders shook and his laughter floated back to me.

"Alena, you are something else entirely, I can't wait till you come to me on your knees. Begging."

Again his words gave an image I could all too easily see in my head. I was a wanton woman if my mind went to the gutter so easily. I shook my head.

Dang, I was no good at the insults. Maybe I needed lessons.

Remo disappeared around the corner and I stood there, thinking. Where to now? Vanilla and Honey was as good a place as any. I'd slept there more than once when I had big orders coming in. A tiny cot I had tucked in the closet would do nicely. I started back to the bakery, my thoughts swirling.

Mostly they centered on the handsome vampire whose mouth I couldn't stop feeling on my own. Or the way his body pressed against mine and made me think things I was pretty sure would send me straight to hell. That being if I wasn't already going there. Who was I kidding? I was a monster. I was going to hell according to my mother.

"If I'm going to h-e-double-hockey-sticks, maybe I should do whatever I want," I whispered to myself. The thought was both electrifying and terrifying. To live without a myriad of rules, answerable only to my own sense of right and wrong. What if I turned into a bad person? Other than being a monster, I really wasn't any different. I hadn't done anything wrong. Had I?

But did it matter? By virtue of what I'd become, I was damned.

My thoughts consumed me, keeping me from noticing anything around me, including Ernie as he flew in from around the next alley. His wings fluttered frantically and he was breathing hard. "This is why

I let Hermes be the damn messenger." He all but collapsed above me. I caught him in my arms, cradling him so I wouldn't bend his wings.

"Are you all right?"

"Just winded. You're damn hard to keep up with when you're running. And I got news you're going to want."

"What news?"

"Those thugs you embarrassed at your place?"

"You mean the Bull Boys?"

He grunted. "Sure, the Bull Boys, I've got dibs on them you're going to want."

I nodded. Why did I think this was not going to be good? Instincts. I was beginning to hate them. "What are they doing now?"

"Well, they've gone after Zeus and are currently demolishing the Blue Box Store."

I shrugged. "Why would that matter to me?"

"Because unlike your vampire friend who just left"—Ernie twisted around and launched back into the air—"if you help Zeus, he'll owe you a favor. And let me tell you something, in your situation, you could use a favor from the god of thunder and lightning, previous ruler of Olympus."

He had a rather good point there. But if Remo was telling the truth, I had a reprieve from Achilles. If I went to help Zeus, the Bull Boys would tell Achilles where I was and that small window of time would be lost to me.

"No, it's too risky. Besides, I can't fight. I don't know how."

"I thought you might say that." He fluttered up and out of my arms, his baby-blue eyes deadly serious. "The thing is, your yaya and brother are still there. And they're right in the center of things."

CHAPTER 10

I clutched the steering wheel of the sports car so hard the plastic creaked under my hands. The vibration of the engine transmitted through the wheel and up my arms, which made me want to scratch like crazy. That or get out and run beside the car and burn off the excess sensations rolling over my skin. The feeling was so insistent, demanding of my attention, I had to grit my teeth and force myself to keep my hands clamped tight. The last thing I needed was a wreck at these speeds, seeing as I had my foot jammed to the floor, the pedal as far down as I could push it without driving it through the floorboards.

"Slow down, I think I'm going to shit myself," Ernie gasped out as we sped off the highway, the off-ramp curving hard enough that we were pushed into the side of the car by the g-force. Rubber squealed on the pavement and the car tipped precariously, balancing on only two wheels. Ernie yelled and I made myself ease off the accelerator a fraction of an inch. As soon as the road leveled out and the car dropped to all four tires, I punched it again.

"Where did you learn to drive like this?" Ernie yelped as I wove around cars, into oncoming traffic, and then back into my own lane.

Cars and trucks laid on their horns, and a big rig jackknifed as I took a hard left in front of him.

"Gran Turismo."

"We're going to die," he whispered.

I spun the wheel and did a full drift through the next corner, the sports car responding as though it were a part of me. "Nope. But those Bull Boys are about to get a surprise."

"You realize it's probably a trap?"

"Yes." I couldn't look at him and still keep us on the road. "Stop talking, Ernie. We're almost there."

Behind us came the flashing lights and sirens I'd expected right off the bat. Not that I cared. Nobody was going to get between my family and me. Not when they were in danger, not when I'd only just gotten Tad back.

With a second spin of the wheel we drifted into the Blue Box parking lot. People mobbed outside, peering in through the main doors. Above the store, a storm cloud gathered, dark and violent as it rumbled and flickered lightning as if it couldn't contain the energy.

At least the humans were out of harm's way.

I slammed the car into park, was out the door and running across the asphalt before the engine quit humming. Behind me, the police shouted at me to stop.

I didn't pause, didn't even consider it. A few short weeks ago, the old me would have put her hands up and tried to explain. Tried to get them to help.

A few days . . . who'd have thought a few days would be enough to turn my world upside down? That a few hours could suddenly make me flout rules I'd followed my whole life? Certainly not me, I would never have thought I was capable of such blatant rebellion.

My mom would be horrified. Who was I kidding? I'd already disappointed her; what was another reason to make her think me a heathen?

"Get out of my way!" I yelled as I drew close to the front doors. The mob jerked as a unit, and a small opening appeared. I ran through it and slammed a shoulder into the doors. I'd meant only to push them open, but instead I shattered the glass. People screamed and I kept moving, limbs flailing as images of Yaya and Tad being hurt filled my mind. Maybe I couldn't fight, but I could distract the Bull Boys and give my family time to get away. That had to be worth something.

Through the candy aisle, pop and chips, and cooking department I raced. I paused in the cooking aisle and grabbed my weapons of choice, then was off again, running toward the sounds of battle and the show of thunder and lightning in the corner of the giant box store.

I skidded to a stop as lightning danced at my feet. "I'm on your side!"

"Sorry, I'm out of practice!"

"Yaya?"

It wasn't Zeus throwing lightning bolts, but my yaya. She held a thin rod out in front of her, and wherever she pointed, lightning flung out in wild arcs. Blue and red, green and yellow, the colors were anything but natural. But they kept the bad guys at bay, and that was enough for me.

Between her and me, though, was a bigger problem than the lightning. The Bull Boys had increased in numbers. At least three times as many as had met me at my house now ranged out through the different aisles.

Not one of them looked at me; their focus was all on Yaya. One of Achilles's minions held a net out in front of him. "Let's tag and bag the old lady, boys, and the snake will come to us."

A trap indeed, Ernie was right about that much at least.

"Hey, you ding-dongs. Why don't you try me on for size?" I yelled, brandishing my weapons at them.

The big bull, the one who'd fallen through my stairs, turned slowly and glared at me. His face was scratched up, and a few wooden splinters were clearly visible under his skin. I cringed. That had to hurt.

"You."

"Yes." I waved him toward me. "Me. Why don't you pick on someone your own size?" I grinned as I said it. That was one line I'd always wanted to use but had never been big enough to say.

He bellowed and rushed me with his head down, anger making him stupid. Even with my lack of fighting skills I could see it was a brash, foolish move. I sidestepped him easily and brought the thick cast iron frying pan down on the back of his head with everything I had.

The boom of metal on skull and the crack of bone echoed through the suddenly silent store. My arm shuddered from the impact, and it rippled all the way up to my shoulder.

He went down, the ground crumpling under his body. Waves of cheap linoleum rolled out around him like a mini-earthquake.

"Oh, now that was a good hit. You should use a frying pan more often, I think." Ernie situated himself on the top of the rafters. "Damn, girlfriend, I think you killed him."

I stumbled back from the body at my feet. "No. I didn't kill him. I didn't hit him that hard . . ." I lifted my eyes to see all the Bull Boys staring at me with open mouths. At my feet their leader lay lifeless, without a single twitch or heave of his chest.

"I didn't mean to," I said. Not that my protesting did me any good.

"She killed him, get her!"

As a herd, they rushed me.

I had a choice. Fight them off, likely killing more of them, or stand there and let them take me to Achilles, who would surely kill me and maybe my yaya and Tad too.

While the choice might have seemed obvious, I didn't react to the raging herd until the last second, my past and present warring within me for dominance.

The first two Bull Boys in the lead swung their overlong swords straight at my head.

A strangled squawk burst out of me and I fell to the floor, the whoosh of the weapons whistling through the air where I'd stood only a second before. Right under my nose was their leader I'd killed. Blood trickled from the cracks in his skull, drawing my eyes, holding me in place as I stared at the damage I'd done.

"Move!" Ernie yelled, and I rolled to the left, right into the base of one of the stacks of goods, hitting it hard. The stack wobbled and tipped backward with a groan. Plastic jugs of bright-blue windshield washer fluid hit the floor, creating a near-instant lake that smelled vaguely of soap. I leapt to my feet and whipped around, frying pan in one hand and rolling pin in the other. My arms shook and my mouth was dry as a brownie made without enough buttermilk.

"To your right!" Yaya said, and I spun, but not fast enough. A head wrapped in horns slammed into my ribs and sent me flying through the air. I arced over the electronics section high enough that I could see the cashier crouched down behind the register as I passed. The cashier with the white-blond locks, chiseled jaw, and store manager's name tag.

I hit the ground hard, rolling across the slick floor and stopping only when my skin finally stuck to the linoleum. I sat up, my legs too wobbly to actually stand. "Zeus, why aren't you fighting?"

"Can't. It's against the rules. No fighting of the gods and goddesses. There's too much damage when we duel."

I glared up at the rafters and the flutter of white and pink. "Ernie, we are not friends anymore, you bat-winged liar!"

"I wasn't lying!" He swung down right in my face, his eyes pleading. "I was only telling you what I got from the hotline."

He moved sideways when I waved at him, forcing him out of my way. The Bull Boys had split up, most of them coming my way. But three had stayed with Yaya. There was a flicker of movement as the bull in front of Yaya swung a fist, catching her in the jaw. She fell backward, boneless.

The moment stretched, I felt it pull at me like taffy being strung out, holding together far longer than it should: Yaya falling, her eyes rolled back, her body hitting the floor with a distant thud.

A strange sensation rolled through me, a feeling of not being able to control myself. An anger so hot and wild I knew it would burn me up if I didn't let it out gripped me. I flung my head back, opened my mouth, and screamed. The sound echoed through the store, a cry that slid from the upper octaves down lower until it was nothing but a low rumbling hiss that echoed from my chest.

"Oh, they've done it now," Ernie said, his voice from somewhere to my left. "Alena. You're going to shift."

"Don't fight it. It will only take longer and hurt if you don't let it happen," Zeus chimed in.

Don't fight what? I fell to my knees, my eyes locked on the Bull Boys as they dropped into identical crouches, inching their way to me, their weapons weaving from side to side. A roll of smoke swirled up around me, blocking them from view. I tried to stand, to move forward. I had to stop them. I had to save Yaya.

What if she was already dead? A blow to the jaw and a fall . . . they were enough to kill someone her age. The thoughts pounded through me as I struggled to move, and again Ernie yelled out to me.

"Stop fighting it!"

Only, I wasn't fighting whatever was happening. Or at least, I didn't think I was. I tried to take another step and stopped as my body rippled forward. I blinked and the scene around me shifted. The smoke cleared and nothing was as it had been. My head was in the rafters, and the Bull Boys far below backed away from me. My body was a beautiful mixture of multi-colored scales: purples and pale greens with a flicker of silver here and there.

Beautiful was not a trait I would have ever attributed to a snake, certainly not a snake that filled up the interior of a box store. But even I had to admit the scales were something else, a rainbow that caught my eye, mesmerizing me for a split second.

"Cut her tail off, boys, we'll have roast snake for dinner!" One of the Bull Boys laughed. "She don't even know what she can do. Too damn new! Achilles won't even have to deal with her."

They laughed with him and ran forward, weapons raised. Two of them swung down at a section of my coils. I braced myself for the impact. They were right; I didn't know what to do.

The weapons bounced off, as if they used plastic toy swords and I was made of steel.

I opened my mouth to yell at them, but all that came out was another rumbling hiss, and in it I felt my strength for the first time. Saw the fear in their eyes and knew it was because of me. Because of what they knew I could do to them, even if I was still learning the depth of my own ability.

Think of it like learning a new technique in the kitchen, girl. You can do this.

Maybe being a monster wasn't so bad after all; at least not when it came to protecting my family.

I flicked my tail forward, slamming it into the stacks on one side of my enemies. Sweeping the merchandise at them, I cleared the section of everything but the floor and a few bolts. I bunched my muscles and slid across the floor, scales catching the light, flickering it around like a living prism.

The three remaining Bull Boys ran from my yaya. I snaked my head toward them, mouth open and fangs bared. So fast . . . I had no idea how fast I really was until two of them filled my mouth. I bit down, driving a fang through each of them.

Ernie flew by my head. "You don't have to kill them. You can make them your minions with your siren abilities. It's your choice."

I rolled my eyes to him and he flew back a few feet. That would have been nice to know about ten seconds previous. "Damn, girl, you've got the beauty and the beast all rolled into one package. Don't get pissy with me, girlfriend. I'm trying to help."

The boys in my mouth writhed and I shook my head, flinging them across the store. One hit the plus-sized women's clothing, and the other hit the stacks of toilet paper. I didn't want them to be my minions.

I dropped my head and sniffed at Yaya. Her heartbeat echoed across my skin along with the buzz of the lights. I swept my head back up to the roof and did a swift arc with it, taking out the lights closest to us. The buzzing eased a little and I dropped my head again. Yaya didn't move and I looked up at Ernie. I wanted to ask him questions, but couldn't.

Apparently being a giant snake had its disadvantages. As the adrenaline faded, the smoke rose up around me again, and my body sloughed off the snake form like a dead skin that faded away until I stood there, buck naked, in front of my yaya.

"Beauty indeed," Ernie murmured, and I glared at him.

"I heard that."

"Sorry, but you've got an ass that won't quit and legs—"

"Shut up, Ernie."

I ran forward and crouched beside my grandmother, taking her hands in mine, pressing them to my chest. "Yaya, talk to me, please."

"I'm alive, though I'm going to have a headache the size of Zeus's ego." Her eyes flickered open and I smiled.

"Can you stand?"

Her eyes flicked over me. "You shifted?"

I nodded and gave her a somewhat wobbly smile. "Yeah, it wasn't so bad. I killed someone. That was worse."

"Ah, my girl. I'm sorry." She sat up slowly and cupped my chin with one hand. I burst into tears and bowed my head, pressing my face against her shoulder.

"I am a bad person. That's why I'm a monster, that's why Merlin made me this creature. It's a reflection of who I really am." At least that was what I tried to say; it was hard to actually tell through the sobbing hiccups what the words were.

A blanket settled over my shoulders, and Yaya wrapped her arms around me. "Pull yourself together, Lena. The night is not over yet."

I lifted my head and wiped my nose. "It's not?"

"They took Tad."

My heart sank. "I was hoping he'd made it out. Or left before this mess started."

"No. We tried to talk Zeus into spilling the beans, and then I decided to get some groceries. You know how it is, once you start shopping you keep adding things, and before I knew it, hours had passed."

Zeus cleared his throat and we both looked up at him. To be fair I looked, and Yaya glared.

"You fool. You think you can escape your responsibilities by hiding here?"

"I'm not hiding. And your granddaughter is not my responsibility, Flora," he said, but there was hesitation in his words. As if even he didn't really believe them.

Yaya snorted. "Please. That's the least of my concerns. Hera is up to something, and you know it!" She pointed a bony finger at him.

Zeus shook his head. "We've been separated for years. If she'd give me the damn divorce, I'd do it in the heartbeat of a hummingbird. But you know her; she's a jealous bitch. You didn't get that family curse for nothing."

Shock zipped through me. "What family curse?"

Yaya's mouth pinched to a thin line, and she wouldn't meet my eyes.

"What curse?" I repeated.

Zeus looked over our heads as if searching for an answer from the heavens. "Tonight, at Charlie's Club. I'll tell you what I can there. If you still want to hear it. Seeing as you did save my kingdom from complete destruction."

I rolled my eyes, forgetting I sat there naked as the day I was born. Until the police came rushing down the aisle, Officer Jensen in the lead. His dark-brown eyes widened when he saw me sitting there, and I wiggled my fingers at him.

"Hello again, Officer."

"How am I not surprised?" he said under his breath.

The cops called in the EMTs for Yaya, but she waved them off. "I'm fine, stop touching me, you grabby perverts." This to the ambulance attendant trying to get a stethoscope on her.

I put a hand on her arm while still clutching the blanket tight. "Maybe you should go with them, Yaya. Call Mom and Dad and tell them . . ." I didn't know what she'd tell them. Or what good it would do. Not like Mom was going to let Dad help us again. Another burst of anger at my parents and fear for Tad snapped through me. A hand locked onto my shoulder, pressing me into the ground. I stared up at Zeus. His blue eyes held mine. "Not here. Not now."

What was he talking about? He gestured with his head and I looked to my feet, where the scales I'd seen in my full snake form wrapped up my leg. Nothing else, just scales. I stared at them, unable to look away.

There was no more denying that I wasn't going to be able to live as a human, no more believing things could go back to the way they were. I was a Super Duper. And not just any Super Duper, but one of literal and most epic proportions.

Officer Jensen was the one who questioned me about the incident. I listened in to Zeus's account from thirty feet away. Obviously the police had no idea he was a supernatural, or they wouldn't be taking his statement at all. Nor did they consider me a supernatural, or they wouldn't be taking mine.

Zeus was explaining that the Bull Boys were disgruntled employees, and they'd trashed the place and beaten each other up, and then the remainder of them had left. I echoed his words to Jensen.

"And the accounts of a giant snake? People from the doors swore they saw a giant snake head touch the ceiling at one point. You didn't see that? How could you miss it?" Officer Jensen held his pen over his notepad as his brown eyes narrowed. As if he knew I was the one to blame for that particular section of testimony.

Oh dear, this was going to be hard to explain. "Did anyone get a picture of this supposed giant snake?" I did my best to put some sarcasm into my words, but I wasn't very well practiced.

"No, there were no pictures, unfortunately. Apparently it all happened too fast."

Relief swept through me.

I shrugged and let a bit of the blanket slip down my shoulder, baring the pale skin. His eyes slid away from me, and the expression in them softened. "Ma'am. The giant snake."

Here I was, about to break another rule that had been drummed into me since I was a child. Thou shalt not lie. "I would think if there was anything like that, Officer Jensen, we would see it. Wouldn't we? It's not like a giant snake can just disappear into thin air."

I took a breath; the blanket slipped a little farther so the tops of my breasts peeked out. Just skin, no nipple, but it seemed to do the trick.

"Of course not," he said, agreeing with me far too easily. Even though I was grateful for it, I wondered if it had to do with who his boss was. If again, Remo was somehow trying to make it so I owed him something.

He jotted something on his paper and turned away. Pausing, he looked back. "The boss. You've got him riled up, and he's not a guy to rile up easy. Try not to get on his bad side, will you?"

I frowned. "Not my fault he's got sex on the brain and I don't."

Officer Jensen's mouth dropped open. "Sex? Why would you say that? He wants you on his side, not in his bed."

Oh dear, what had I stepped into this time? "Nothing. Never mind. I'm not interested in his offer. That's what I meant."

He didn't look away, and I couldn't hold his gaze. Yaya ranted at the ambulance attendants as they wheeled her away on a gurney. I waved at her, glad she would be looked after and kept out of harm's way. Whether she wanted to be or not.

Zeus and I stood to one side, away from the officers as they tagged and bagged the remaining Bull Boys. That is, the ones that had been killed. By me.

Nausea swam up through my guts, threatening to spill out of my mouth.

"Go get yourself some clothes. No charge." Zeus shoved me toward the other end of the store. Which in effect turned me away from the body bags.

"I want to know where my brother is. Who has him?" I whispered my questions, knowing the police would want the info if they knew Tad was missing. And knowing they couldn't help even if they did know.

"Tonight. At Charlie's Club," he whispered back, giving me another gentle shove.

I took a step, stopped, and turned back. Yaya had a rod that made lightning. I looked over the area where she'd been lying. No rod of lightning. Ernie flashed his wings, getting my attention. "It's with her. Kinda like you, it's compact in its less deadly form."

I frowned up at him. "Don't talk to me, you little jerk. You lied about what was going on. Zeus didn't need my help. He doesn't owe me anything now."

"But he's going to help you anyway. Besides, when you get information that there's a lightning-and-thunder show going on inside a Blue Box Store where Zeus works, it logically stands that it's Zeus. Not one of his priestesses. And really, would you have left your yaya here to fight on her own?"

I shook my head. "No, of course not. I'm sorry, I just . . . everything has happened so fast."

My feet slapped on the cheap tile as I hurried across the store. Thinking at all about what had happened only made me want to either throw up or burst into tears. Time for not thinking. *Don't think about Tad missing; don't think about the dead Bull Boys. Don't think about turning into a giant snake again.*

I focused on trying to find clothes, underwear, and shoes that fit.

"Here, try these." Ernie tossed something at me. A pair of leggings that glittered with snake scales in black and green, edged in gold.

I glared at him. "Funny."

"Well, you're going to a club later. It's not like they've got clubbing clothes here, and you want to fit in as much as possible."

Dang it, he had a point. I grabbed some underwear and the leggings he'd tossed at me.

"No, no. You need a thong for those leggings. Otherwise your panty line shows, and that would be a crime against *your* nature. Friends don't let friends be frumpy." Ernie threw a piece of string at me. String. I held it up on one finger. Make that three pieces of string. "This. Is not underwear."

"It is when you wear tight pants, honey butt."

I pulled the thong on under the blanket, grimacing as the thin strap slid up between my cheeks. "Who the heck thought this was a good idea?"

"A man. Same as the pants. Only a man would want a woman to be fully dressed and yet still be as close to naked as possible." Ernie fluttered around the racks of clothes.

"You're probably right." I pulled on the leggings and had to admit that both the thong and the tight pants were pretty comfy, if rather revealing. Ernie tossed me a tank top in plain white.

"Kinda cold for this time of year, don't you think?" I held it out from me.

"You been cold at all since you've been turned?"

"No."

"You run hot, like the rest of the shifters in our world. Which is weird because you're a snake and not a hot-blooded animal in nature. But something about the way Drakainas are put together makes them burn. Maybe the venom in their system?" He tipped his head and slowly nodded. "Yeah, that's probably it."

"So cold won't bother me?"

"Nope. Neither will extreme heat."

I dug through a bin of bras and found one in my size. Making sure my back was to Ernie, I dropped the blanket and put the bra on, slipping the tank top over my head quickly.

"Shoes next," Ernie called, and I followed his voice. A small part of me knew what he was up to. And I was grateful. Maybe he wasn't a jerk.

A distraction was what I needed to get me through the next little bit, so I could break down elsewhere, after this mess was dealt with. Like after we found Tad. After I convinced Achilles I was harmless. I snorted to myself. That was going to be like selling ice to an Eskimo. Harmless? After I killed three of his Bull Boys?

Ernie fluttered by a rack of high heels. "What do you think? More height?"

I ran a hand over the black glittering heels that had to be at least four inches high. My mother would have had a complete breakdown. While they weren't as nice as the ones from Merlin's, they were certainly nicer than anything I had in my closet at home.

An image of Barbie going through my clothes and throwing them out while shouting "Brown church mouse!" made me grit my teeth.

"Easy, Lena, your skin is showing again. It'll get easier each time now that you've shifted once. So watch your emotions," Ernie said.

I pulled the shoes down and jammed my feet into them. I didn't even wobble as I strode out of the store. No, I didn't stumble or wobble until I got back to the car and slid into the seat.

I leaned forward and burst into tears. I'd killed at least one Bull Boy, probably more than that with the venom from my fangs, depending on if they survived. I wanted to believe they were alive. I'd lied. Kissed a man when I was technically still married. Worse than all of that, because of me and what I was, Tad had been taken.

Because I'd chosen this path, with my eyes wide open, knowing I would become a monster.

"I deserve it all," I whispered. "Everything that's happened."

CHAPTER 11

"That's enough of that bag of Cerberus shit," Ernie barked at me. "I mean it. Whatever you're thinking you deserve, you're wrong."

I wiped my eyes and turned to him, wondering how he'd gotten in the car when I'd not even heard the door open. "You don't know anything, Ernie."

"I do. Let me guess. You think that the way you were raised defines everything you are. It doesn't. You have to figure out who you are. Who is Alena? Once you figure that out, everything else will fall into place."

"Figuring out who I am won't bring Tad home! It won't bring those I killed back to life, or make me human again!" I yelled at him, and then slapped my hands over my mouth. "Look at me. I've never yelled in my life. Never wore clothes this tight. I'm doing everything I was always taught was wrong. Terrible. Things that would make me a bad person. Things that would damn my soul."

"Defending yourself and your family isn't wrong," he said softly. "Come on, let's go to the bakery. You owe me, and we've got time to kill before Zeus will be at the club." He settled back into the seat and closed his eyes. Not unlike how Yaya rode in the car.

I turned the key and shifted the car into gear, the engine purring nicely like some large jungle cat, which made me think of Remo again.

I pushed him out of my mind. The last thing I needed was to add the feel of him kissing me to the tumult of emotions and fears tumbling in my head.

The smell of his cinnamon-and-honey, hot-and-sweet kiss. I groaned and shook my head, did my best to push that away.

I gripped the steering wheel. Barbie might not have the greatest taste in men, but her taste in cars wasn't half bad.

Damn it, and now I was back to comparing Roger to Remo. And really, there was no comparison. I had a feeling Roger would fall short in every category. My mind went straight into the gutter as I contemplated Roger's small endowment. And how he'd said it wasn't the size that counted, but how you used things. And my mind rolled over to the size of Remo's hands as he'd cupped my bum. If there was any relation between size of hands and size of—

I turned the radio up, as if that would drown out my wildly inappropriate thoughts.

"Hey, why is your face all red?"

"I wasn't thinking about him," I blurted out.

Ernie laughed. "I didn't ask who you were thinking about. But I think maybe I should. Who you thinking about, girlfriend?"

I glanced at him, considered telling him. "I . . . that mob boss."

"Oooh, yeah, he is a dish, isn't he?" Ernie flew to the dash and sat so he faced me. "Seriously, he's got the whole bad-boy vibe going on."

"He kissed me," I blurted out.

"Oh. My. Gods. Tell me, was he any good?" He clapped his hands together like an excited little girl.

I wasn't sure if he was mocking me or not. I went with mocking. "Stop it. Don't tease me. I'm a married woman and I kissed—"

"No, you aren't married." He pointed a finger at me. "You cut ties with the human world. Now give me the deets."

"Deets?" What was he talking about now?

"The details. Was he any good? I mean, I think he would be good. I'd kiss him."

My eyes widened. "You would kiss him?"

He grinned, "Alena, something you should know about most of the Greek pantheon . . . we aren't picky. Beauty is to be honored in all forms, appreciated however it is shown to us. That vampire is the boss with a capital *B*, and there is more than one Greek god or goddess whose eye he'll catch. You'd best watch over him or he might get stolen from you."

"He's not mine." The words came out far more sullen than they should have. Because Remo was not mine in any way, shape, or form. Not mine.

Bad Alena.

I cleared my throat and changed the direction of the conversation. "Ernie, why are you really helping me?"

He slid off the dash, his face thoughtful. "I thought you were going to be another throwaway monster, Alena. Someone for Achilles to use as a stepping-stone."

I flinched at his choice of words, the echo of my own thoughts about Roger coming home to roost. "And now?"

"Now, I think you've got it in you to show the world not all the monsters are . . . well, monsters."

A flush of warmth spread through me, some of the cold fear hounding me chased away by his belief. "Thanks, Ernie."

"Anytime. That's what friends are for, right?"

I smiled. "Yeah, it is."

The rest of the drive back to the bakery was quiet. Uneventful. Which was good and bad. Good because I wasn't sure how much more upheaval I could handle without completely losing my mind. Bad because my thoughts were all my own and I couldn't escape them.

Could my whole life have been . . . wrong? Could Ernie be right and everything my mother presented have been skewed?

I tapped my fingers on the steering wheel as I tried to come to grips with the tiny epiphanies as they rolled through me in rapid-fire succession.

I would always defend my family, and Ernie was right about that. Protecting my family would never be wrong. If I were put in the same position again, I would fight with all I had even knowing the outcome. I felt bad for the deaths I'd caused. But I wouldn't let it eat away at me. I straightened up in my seat like a weight had slid off my shoulders.

Being turned into a Super Duper . . . maybe I was going to hell for that. But was it worse to not be human or to turn away from a chance at life? Really, if I hadn't fought to live, was that not like a form of passive suicide? Which was also wrong according to my mother and the Church of the Firsts.

That worry slid off me until there was only one left. My mother. Her condemnation, and her belief that I no longer existed. That I was no longer her daughter, all because I didn't look right. I frowned and stared out into the dark night. I tried to put myself in her position and realized if Tad had come to me, if he'd told me he was a Super Duper, I never would have turned from him. Even though I feared the supernatural, I never would have turned from someone I loved.

The fact that she'd turned away from Tad and me when we'd needed her most . . . Perhaps I needed to reevaluate my belief system if that was the kind of people it produced.

I thought about what Dad had said. That Tad and I were the babies they'd fought for. Was there something in Mom's past that drove her to the Firsts? Something she thought she could protect herself with by being better than anyone else?

I pulled into the bakery, feeling hopeful for the first time since I'd agreed to Merlin turning me. "Come on, Ernie. Time to bake."

He grinned up at me. "Now you're talking, honey butt."

"That is a horrible nickname." I let us back into the bakery. I flicked lights on and got the oven heating up.

"Well, until something better comes along, I'll just keep trying them on for size. Baby."

I snorted. "That's off-limits. Roger used to call me baby."

"Hmm. That the ex?"

"Yes. The ex who couldn't even wait for me to kick the bucket before finding a new girlfriend. And telling me what he was going to do with my life insurance."

"He didn't."

"Yeah, he did."

Ernie sat himself on the top of the counter near the sink. "He sounds like a total dick of epic proportions."

I grinned. "I'd hardly call it epic. More like forgettable."

Ernie's jaw dropped and he fell backward. "Oh, goddess. Tell me. I love gossip."

That was something I was beginning to see. So while I got things going, I told him all about Roger, the story punctuated by the opening and closing of the fridge and Ernie's guffaws of laughter.

Within a few short minutes I had the food processor going full tilt, the loud purr of the powerful, compact engine doing that same weird vibration to my skin. This time, though, I kept my hands on the sides of the bowl. In the past, I'd always done things by feel in my bakery. With the extrasensory issues going on, that intuition was heightened even further. I dumped walnuts and cinnamon in and pulsed them until they were partially chopped. I actually *felt* it when the consistency was spot on and flicked the processor off. The scent that rose up as I lifted the lid made me close my eyes. Cinnamon, that had Remo all over it.

"You're thinking about the mob boss again."

My eyes flew open. "How do you know?"

Ernie winked. "Heart rate, flushed skin, parting of the lips. You're so hot for him you can't hide it."

I cleared my throat. "I need the phyllo dough." I pulled it out of the fridge and rolled it out, covering it with a damp towel.

"What are you making?"

"You can't guess? I thought the phyllo would be a hint." I grinned at him and his eyes widened.

"Tell me you're making baklava!" he screamed, his voice pitching far higher than I thought possible, as his fists shot in the air as if he'd just won the Super Bowl.

"I'm making baklava!" I yelled back at him, laughing. He spun around a few times in the air, and I went back to my baking.

Once I had the pastry in the oven, I let myself stop the distractions. "Achilles has Tad. Another trap for me and one I won't walk away from."

Ernie flew away from the oven door, where he'd been staring at the pastries. "Yes and yes. No one else would take him."

"Remo might," I said softly, scraping the remaining dough off the counter and tossing it into the sink.

"The mob boss? Why would he do that? Doesn't he want to get in your panties?"

I flushed, and dusted off my hands before I glanced up at him. "He wants me to . . . side with him. Thinks he can keep me safe from Achilles."

Ernie lowered himself to a clean section of counter and plopped himself down. "Doubt that he can keep you safe at all. Thing with heroes, the originals at least, is that they aren't really human either. Achilles's mom was a nymph, and his dad one of the original bad boys. Just like the other heroes, he has a background that all but screams what he's going to do with his life. They're made or born to kill monsters and perform ridiculous tasks. That being said, you need to get Tad away from Achilles sooner rather than later."

"But aren't the heroes supposed to be good guys? Shouldn't Tad be safe with him?" Even as I said it, I knew that was why I hadn't been terribly worried. In my head, even though Achilles hated me, I didn't think he would hurt an innocent. That wasn't how heroes did things. Right?

Ernie shook his head. "Tad is a bad guy to Achilles. To all the heroes, what you look like dictates which camp you are in. Which is why they particularly hate sirens. You confuse them at the best of times with your beauty, which to them should make you good. But then you can turn around and kill people, which makes you bad. They are black and white. You are serious shades of gray."

"I am nothing like *Shades of Grey*," I said quickly. "I didn't even read the book."

"That denial came way too fast." He laughed and picked up the previous thread. "Pretty much the fact that Tad is a snake shifter makes it perfectly okay to hurt, torture, or kill him in Achilles's eyes. All in the name of good versus evil. It's not wrong to make the evil ones suffer, you know."

"Tad is the furthest thing from evil." I paced the room while the air filled with the scent of baklava. I grabbed a pot and threw it on the stove, filling it with vanilla, honey, sugar, and water, my movements on autopilot.

This was not happening. It couldn't be. "Ernie, how long do you think we have?"

"Hard to say. Hours. Days. Maybe a week? It will depend on whether Achilles has already killed him."

I froze where I was, unable to move past what Ernie had said. "Killed?"

Ernie flew close to me and put his chubby fingers on my cheeks. "You need to be prepared for the worst. That's life when dealing with the Greek geeks."

I put both my hands on the counter, and the oven dinged. Moving swiftly, I grabbed the oven mitts and pulled the pan of baklava out. I drizzled the honey mixture over the pastries.

Ernie made a "gimme" motion, flickering his fingers at me repeatedly. "Those smell amazing."

"Thanks." The word was automatic. I dropped the pan on top of the stove and pulled the gloves off. Ernie shoved a pastry in his mouth and grabbed two more.

Who would know better where Tad might have been taken? Zeus was the obvious answer. But I still had another two hours before I was to see him. That only left one person I trusted, other than Ernie, who knew the Greek pantheon. Someone who'd been a part of it in her own way.

Yaya.

"Let's go." I turned the oven off and threw the pans into the empty sink with a clatter.

Hurrying to the car, we were on our way in seconds. Ernie licked his fingers the whole way, which kept him busy. Not that I wouldn't have wanted to talk, but I couldn't. My voice kept getting stuck on a single word.

Killed. Tad could have been killed already. I might be too late.

The hospital was only ten minutes away in good traffic, and I made it in less than five. I hurried to the front doors. The receptionist looked up as I entered, his heavy jowls and sallow skin speaking to too many night shifts.

"Visiting hours are from nine to four during the day."

I slumped. "Please, I need to see my grandmother. Just tell me what room she's in and I'll not say anything about you—"

He tapped the sign beside him. "Not my rules."

Ernie was nowhere to be seen. So I was on my own. Time to embrace what I was, and not just the monster side either.

I needed to see Yaya, and I wasn't leaving without talking to her. I slowly turned back to the receptionist, and leaned in as if to read his name tag. "Steven, is it?" I batted my eyes and drew in a slow breath, which lifted my chest up. His eyes dropped and he swallowed hard.

"Yeah."

"I . . . want . . . to know where Flora Dininny is. What room. I'd be awfully grateful." I smiled and tried to think about how to convince him I was serious. What did women do when flirting? Something with the tongue. I ran mine along my top lip and Steven's eyes went wide.

"What are you?"

I caught a glimpse of my reflection in the glass above his head. The very tip of my tongue was forked.

Oh dear. That was not the reaction I wanted. "You *will* help me. *Now.* What room is Flora Dininny in?" I put everything I had, all the need and desire I had in me into the words. There was no going back.

Steven's face went slack and his hands fumbled over the keyboard; his eyes flicked and he pointed. I leaned into his cubicle and read the screen. Fourth floor, room 415.

"Thank you. Pretend I was never here."

He nodded, his head bobbling like it wasn't attached quite right. "Yes. You were never here."

I hurried away toward the elevators. I pressed the button and nothing happened. Of course, they were locked after visiting hours. I paused and looked around for the stairwell. There to my left the door beckoned. I jogged to it and raced up the three flights in a matter of seconds. I wasn't even winded.

At the fourth floor I pushed on the door. Locked. I hung my head, defeated by a hospital door.

Again.

"You're strong enough to break it."

I turned to see Ernie flying up the last few stairs. "I'm not going to shift in the stairwell."

"Even in this form, you're strong enough. Just shove it hard, you'll break the lock." He floated above my head as he pointed at the door. As if I'd forgotten it was there.

I wrapped my hands around the cool metal handle. "Okay. Here we go." Putting my feet against the wall, I pulled. Slowly, I added to the force until the metal began to grind, like a mortar and pestle working overtime. Except all that happened was the handle let go first, snapping off.

"Fricky dicky!" I threw it down the stairwell, the clang of it bouncing all the way down, echoing far louder than I'd thought it would. I flinched. "I hope no one heard that."

"The nurses are probably all sleeping. You wrecked the handle, see if you can pull it apart now." Ernie peered at the door.

He was right; there was a small section of metal that was bent outward where the handle had been. I put my hand into it and fished around for the lock mechanism.

"You'd make a pretty good thief." Ernie smiled. "If you weren't a giant snake, that is."

"Shut up, Ernie." I grasped what I could and yanked it out of the hole. The door leaned open. I grinned up at the cherub. "Got it."

I slipped through the door, Ernie right behind me. The nurses' station was ahead and to my right, and Yaya's room was to the left. Two nurses were sitting, watching a small TV, both with headphones on. That had to be against the rules. But it had worked in my favor. I dropped to my belly and army-crawled forward. "You be the lookout for me."

I turned to see Ernie already floating above the nurses' heads. "They're watching a porno."

"They are not!"

"You want to see?"

I hurried, not answering him, slithering on my belly down the hall until I reached room 415. Moving into a crouch, I reached up and opened the door, let myself in, and finally took a deep breath. I looked around the room, seeing easily despite having very little light. Another perk of being a monster. I went straight for the bed on the right, where Yaya's earbuds lay on the side table.

"Yaya?"

A shuffling of sheets and she sat up, looking around for me. Of course, she couldn't see me like I saw her. She fumbled for her light and flicked it on. "Alena?"

Someone across the room muttered, "Shut the damn light off, you old kook."

I grabbed the curtains around Yaya's bed and pulled them, closing us off as best as I could from the other person in the room.

"How did you get in here?" Yaya's eyes were wide.

"The nurses are . . . distracted right now. Yaya, Achilles took Tad, I have to go see Zeus in about an hour, and I don't know if he'll help me. I don't know what to do. What if Tad is already—"

"Hush, he isn't. I'd know."

"You would?" I sat on the edge of her bed and took her hand. "How?"

"I'm his grandmother. I would know if he died. Just like I knew when Owen slipped away from us."

"Yaya, I have no idea where to start looking for Tad. And I know it's going to be a trap, but—"

"Listen to me. You're going to go to Zeus. He will fill you in on what he can. While he can be difficult, he won't lie to you. I think."

I grimaced. "Well, that's comforting."

She shrugged. "The pantheon can't be trusted, most especially when they say, 'Trust me.' Achilles has the weaponry to kill you, Alena, just as you have the weaponry to kill him."

I bit back the desire to say I didn't want to kill him. He had Tad.

And I would do anything to save my brother, even if it meant I would damn what was left of my soul to hell.

"Where would he go, Yaya? You know Achilles, don't you?"

She sighed. "I know *of* him. I'm old, but not that old, you cheeky girl. Achilles is prideful, like all the heroes. He will want to make an example and a spectacle of you. The bigger the better."

I clutched her hand. "That doesn't really give me an idea of where he might be."

"Somewhere with a TV feed," Yaya said. "He'll want as many people as possible to see how wonderful he is."

My mind raced with the possibilities. Or lack thereof. "How do I . . . kill him?" The words were hard to say, and she tightened her hand on mine.

"Your fangs will be the best bet. Unless he's got a satyr right with him, there is no one who could heal him." She patted my hand. "You can do this, Alena. You are stronger than you realize. In every way. Only someone with the heart of a lion could be turned into a Drakaina; the change is not something easily done."

"How do you know that?"

"Merlin came to visit me earlier. He said there was no one in the world who could have been turned into the Drakaina besides you." She frowned. "Then he spouted off some nonsense that the only way our world was going to survive was if the monsters came back. Then again, he is a magician and they are always full of riddles."

From the other side of the room came a shuffling footstep. "You two better shut up or I'll page the nurses!"

I glared at the silhouette against the curtain and snapped, "They won't like you bothering them right now. They're watching porn."

Yaya's roommate gasped, and I heard a distant buzzer go off. "I'd better go." I bent and kissed her forehead.

She clutched at my hand. "One last thing. Forgive your mother. She has a reason for being the way she is, even if she isn't ready to tell you yet."

I gave her a quick nod. "I'm trying."

Without another word I slipped between the curtains and out into the hall. The nurses were headed my way. The only hope I had was to distract them. "The old man, he's trying to jump out the window!"

One ran toward the room; the other moved to the desk and pointed at me. "Don't you go anywhere, I'm calling security."

I held my hands up. "Of course not."

As soon as she looked down, I ran for the hall, hit the door I'd broken, and was in the stairwell. In seconds I was on the main floor, running across the open entranceway and out the doors. Steven the receptionist waved frantically at me.

"Call me!" I yelled over my shoulder.

"Okay, but wait, I don't have your number!"

I paused, unable to help myself. I gave him Roger's. "Don't take no for an answer from him when he tells you I'm not there."

"Okay!"

Laughing to myself, I hurried to my car as the first flickering light of the police car came into view. I slid into my seat and slumped down. From the backseat Ernie peered forward. "You think they won't notice the car with the silver paw prints they've seen at two crime scenes already?"

I groaned and slumped farther into my chair, the fake leather squeaking like cellophane being rubbed together. A tap on the window brought my head up. Officer Jensen peered down at me.

I rolled down the window. "Hi, Officer."

"Alena Budrene. How am I not surprised?"

I batted my eyes up at him. Because that was about all I knew when it came to flirting to get my way. "What do you mean?"

"Don't try to act innocent."

Carefully, I reached toward the keys in the ignition. "Officer, I'd love to stay and chat, really. You're cute and nice, and wearing a uniform, which every girl loves, but I have things to do."

His eyes narrowed. "Remo is looking for you."

"Good for him." I turned the key and the car revved. "So unless I'm under arrest, which I've done nothing to warrant, I'm leaving."

Ernie snickered from the backseat. "I knew you had a spine under that good-girl exterior."

Officer Jensen stepped back. "I'm going to keep watching you."

I pulled away, waving out the window. "Enjoy the view."

With nowhere to go, I headed once more for my bakery.

"You going to make me something else?"

I put a hand to my forehead. "No. I'm going to see if I can figure out where the heck Achilles has taken my brother."

Easier said than done.

The bakery had a huge whiteboard, for jotting down notes and new recipe ideas. I wiped it clean and grabbed a marker. Making a quick list, I noted all the TV stations I could. And there were a lot.

"But a TV station, that doesn't make sense. There's no room to fight," Ernie pointed out. I ground my teeth in frustration, feeling Tad's life slip further away from me.

"What do you suggest, then?"

A sudden rap of knuckles on the door behind us spun me around. I grabbed for the closest thing to me, which ended up being a wooden spoon.

"That won't work all that well," Ernie said.

I didn't look at him. "I think it might work on a vampire."

"Ooohh, killed with a wooden spoon? A vampire would never live that down." He snickered at his own joke.

"Who is it?" I raised the spoon above my head.

A high-pitched voice that warbled like a bird came through the door. "Hermes. I have a message for the Drakaina."

I looked at Ernie. He nodded. "He's safe enough. Hermes is a neutral party, he has to be in order to deliver messages."

I walked to the door and flung it open. Hermes floated in the air, just like Ernie on the same kind of fluffy cream-colored wings. But that was where the resemblance ended. Hermes had bright-white hair that stuck out behind his head in a perfect swoosh, the windblown look resembling a certain brand of shoes rather well. His eyes were blue, and he was at least twice Ernie's height. But where Ernie was a bit on the chubby side,

Hermes was whip thin, and he had more clothes on. A white T-shirt and shorts along with a pair of Nike Air runners. Maybe the resemblance to the hair was on purpose. My lips twitched despite the situation.

"I'm the Drakaina." The words echoed in the room, and a curl of pleasure coiled in my middle. Almost as if the Drakaina part of me were sentient and knew that what I'd said had more meaning than just the words. That slowly I had begun accepting what I'd become.

Hermes pulled a folded piece of paper from his back pocket and handed it to me. "From Achilles. You want something sent back, I can wait."

I opened the paper and shook my head. "Ernie, I can't read this. It's all Greek to me."

"Ha-ha."

"No, really." I held the paper up so he could see the Greek words. Ernie flew over to me and read the paper, his eyes skimming it quickly.

"Not surprising, and it solves the problem of trying to find him. He's challenging you to a fight. And he's even given you his location."

"Where?"

"CenturyLink Field."

The football stadium? "Wait, the original one or the new one in Bellingham?"

Hermes bobbed his head. "Bellingham."

After the original field in the south of Seattle had burned down in the Supe Riots, they'd built a new one closer to the border, just north of Bellingham. The size of the field, the number of cameras they had there—it would be perfect for what he wanted. It looked as if Yaya was right again.

I swallowed hard. "Does he say anything about Tad?"

"Nope. And that's not good. I hope . . ." His eyes darted to Hermes, who gave a quick shake of his head.

"Sorry, I don't know. I just grabbed the message and have been checking all the places the Drakaina has been spotted the last two days." Hermes scratched the back of his neck and wove from side to side in the air as if he couldn't remain still. "You sure you don't have a message I can take back?"

Ernie took the paper from me and grabbed a pen from my desk. He scratched something in Greek across the backside of the paper. "Here, take this."

Hermes snatched the message and was gone in a literal flash of light. The air sucked around us, drawing me toward the door. I shut it. "What did you say to Achilles?"

"That you would meet him. But only if your brother remained unharmed."

I let out a soft breath. "Will he do that?"

The look on Ernie's face did not ease my worry. Something between a frown and a twist of his lips. "Achilles is a warrior. They can be unpredictable because they don't always think but instead just rush in with their weapons out and their shields up."

I looked at the clock. We were supposed to meet Zeus in fifteen minutes. It would take us at least that long to get to the club. I itched to go by the stadium and see if I could at least see Tad and make sure he was okay. But even I knew that was silly. No doubt they'd be inside the stadium, not standing outside like a bunch of scalpers at a Backstreet Boys concert. And it was too far to get to Bellingham and back to Charlie's Club in the fifteen minutes.

"Don't worry, you'll figure this out. Everything will be okay in the end. That's how these things work, you know." Ernie flew to my left, so we were eye to eye.

I snorted softly. "Have you read any Greek mythology lately? A happily-ever-after is about the furthest thing from a guarantee. The good guys don't always win. The world isn't always saved. People die, Ernie. I can't lose Tad again. I lost him once; I can't go through that again. Besides, if you'll recall, I'm the monster. Not the good guy. I'm supposed to lose."

He flew around to the passenger side of the car. With his free hand he touched his left earlobe and *poofed*, for lack of a better word. I blinked at where he'd been only a second before.

Movement inside the car caught my eyes. Ernie waved at me from the passenger seat. Well, that explained that. I slid into the driver's side and buckled up.

We headed into the city, and it wasn't long before I noticed the same vehicle behind us. "I think I have a tail."

"Well you have a tail, that's for sure. I don't." Ernie shuffled his butt deeper into the leather seat.

"No." I hurried us through a yellow stoplight. "I mean we have someone following us."

Ernie spun around and leaned over the back of his seat. "You mean the cop car?"

"Yeah."

"Could just be going our way."

I frowned. "I'm starting to believe there is no such thing as coincidence. What do you want to bet it's Officer Jensen?"

"He is kinda cute. Has that exotic mocha skin and dark eyes." Ernie grinned over at me. "I could shoot him with one of my arrows. Make him fall for you."

"I think not." Though I did agree Officer Jensen was a handsome man, he worked for the mob boss who was also a vampire, who'd recently kissed me in a way that made every other man look dull and boring.

Not a mark in Officer Jensen's favor. "I keep telling you. I'm married. I can't even think like that until the divorce is final."

"Which of course is never going to happen since the courts will treat you as if you are dead," Ernie said.

I glanced at him. "I may not have the paperwork started yet, but it is going to happen. You can bet your chubby butt on that."

"Except that the human world, where your marriage was performed, considers you a nonentity. If they gave you a divorce, that would be admitting you have rights. That would set off a ripple effect that would go through the entire world. There is no way anyone is going to let that happen. Certainly not a human judge."

My jaw dropped, and I inadvertently took my foot off the gas pedal. The car coasted to a stop in the middle of the road, and it wasn't until the police cruiser pulled up behind me and flicked its lights on that I shook myself out of the paralysis that grabbed me.

I steered the car over to the side of the road. Behind me, the officer got out of the car. Mocha skin, dark eyes indeed. Officer Jensen approached my window. I rolled it down and forced a smile up at him.

"Officer, we have to stop meeting like this."

"I have a report that this car was stolen from a Barbie Bollinger." He looked down at his notepad and then up at me. "I want to see the license and registration. Now."

"Hey, I thought we were developing a friendship. You know: your boss likes me so you have to be nice." Oh dear, did I really just say that out loud?

Officer Jensen's face went a careful, neutral blank. "License and registration."

I didn't have my license with me. I leaned forward and dug around in the glove compartment. I locked eyes with Ernie and whispered, "I don't have all the paperwork."

He shrugged. "You don't need it. Make him forget. You're a damn siren. Use what you've got, girlfriend."

Use it. Like I'd come with an instruction manual as to being a Super Duper. Well, maybe I had, but I'd left it with Merlin. Dang it all. Then again, it had worked on Steven the receptionist. Kinda.

I drew in a breath and sat back up. I smiled up at Officer Jensen. "I don't need a license."

He frowned at me. "Yes. You do."

"You're going to let me go and stop following me," I whispered. He leaned forward.

"If you don't produce a license and registration in the next ten seconds, I'm going to haul you down to the station."

"Ernie, it's not working!" I yelped as Officer Jensen opened the door and pointed at me.

"Who is Ernie?"

I looked back in the passenger seat. Ernie was gone. Of course he was. I slid out of my seat and stood up. In my heels I was taller than Officer Jensen. I stumbled forward, one of my heels catching in a bump in the road. Jensen caught me with a grunt. I looked up at him, our faces only inches apart.

I breathed him in, and a strange sensation uncoiled inside me. A feeling as if I could see into Officer Jensen and everything he ever wanted in a woman. The need to be the one person a woman turned to. Different than what I'd done with Steven, but still . . .

Officer Jensen wanted someone he could rescue and play the hero to her damsel in distress. Someone he could save. I went loose in his arms and let him hold me up.

His eyes softened and he seemed to be drinking me in. "Alena."

"Officer. I have things to do. I *need you* to let me go." The words purred out of me. "I *need* your help."

The words vibrated in the air, an undercurrent of tension that wrapped around Officer Jensen slowly, tightening until the hold I had on him was complete. His eyes never left mine.

"I can help you."

"Thank you." The words breathed out from my lips and into his mouth. He tipped his head as if he would kiss me. I turned my face to the side and the kiss landed on my jaw. "I have to go. You . . ." I was going to tell him to stop following me. But really, maybe having him on my side and with me wasn't such a bad idea. "You tail me. Make sure no one sneaks up on us."

He smiled and gently let me go. "I can do that. I can protect you better than—never mind."

"Better than who?" I whispered, weighting my words with that same sensation of wrapping him up. He grimaced.

"Better than Remo."

Well, that was interesting. "I thought he was your boss?"

"That doesn't make him good at looking after his people. Especially not the women he chases. You deserve better than him. He doesn't know how special you are." He touched my face gently. I stepped away, not liking the direction the conversation was headed.

"I've got to go."

"I'll follow. You can count on me."

I backed away, turned, and slid into the car. I slumped into my seat and Ernie puffed back into existence beside me. I glared at him. "Thanks for the help."

"Well, there was nothing I could do to help you figure him out without shooting him with an arrow. Which you said you didn't want me to do, right?" He lifted an eyebrow and I shook my head. I did not want him shooting anyone with his arrows. "I jumped ahead. Zeus is waiting for you at the club."

I pulled back into traffic and drove the rest of the way to the club with a police escort. A few minutes later I stopped in front of Charlie's Club. The majority of the people lined up were men. But not your regular, average-Joe men; no, these males stood out. Men dressed in leather and chains, some with masks on. Others holding long whips and leashes attached to others in the line.

I turned to Ernie, a slow-growing horror rising through me. A den of iniquity was what I was looking at, and I knew it. "What kind of club is this exactly?"

"One you're going to stand out in like a sore thumb."

Sore thumb? Oh, if only that were the worst of my problems.

CHAPTER 12

After parking the car and making sure Officer Jensen didn't follow me into the club, I squared my shoulders and put myself into the line. The men around me swiveled to look at me, more than one giving me raised eyebrows and a frown.

The man immediately in front of me wore nothing but studded leather that included pants, shirt, and a face mask that covered him from his nose down over his chin. "You're at the wrong club, sweetheart." His words were remarkably clear considering his lips were covered.

I stood a little straighter. This was business, and I could do that. "I'm meeting someone, thank you very much."

He tipped his head to the side. "You thinking of coming to the dark side?"

I frowned. "I don't know what you mean."

He flexed his arms. "I swing for both teams, I'd take you on if you're looking for company. Show you the . . . ropes." With a wink he held up a thin line of braided rope, quickly tying it into a complicated knot. "A tall beauty like you is hard to find." I frowned and he laughed. "Oh, she's cute when she's angry."

Cute when I was angry? I shot a hand out and caught him around the throat without a thought. I lifted him up off the ground as easily as I'd lift my purse to check for change. "I don't think *cute* and *angry* go together in the same sentence with me."

Ernie hooted with laughter while the man I held up kicked his legs and what I could see of his face purpled. The line around us pulled back, creating a perfect circle. But not one of them made a move to help their fellow leather-clad friend.

"Now you're getting the hang of this, Alena," Ernie said.

I dropped the man, more than a little horrified at what I'd done. "I'm sorry."

He choked at my feet, and rubbing his neck he slid the lower part of his mask off and took a deep breath. A white grin flashed up at me. "You'll fit in just fine here." He waved a hand behind him as he stood. "Jimmy, let this one in. She's going to be fun."

I passed him and he pinched my bum as I scooted by. I whipped around and glared. He winked. "I'm just hoping you're as feisty in the sack and that if I piss you off enough, you'll give me a shot at that sweet ass."

I closed the distance between us, my anger making me bold. I poked him hard in the chest with two fingers, sending him stumbling back into the arms of the others in the lineup. "Not in a thousand years would you have a shot at me, donkey butt."

The crowd burst into laughter. "Did she just try to call you an asshole?"

My fury evaporated under embarrassment.

Hurrying, I made my way to the front of the line, the men parting down the middle to let me by. The bouncer at the front was shorter than me but about three times as wide. He wore only leather pants and had straps over his chest that strained when he folded his arms. Or tried to fold his arms. They kinda stuck out from his body because of all the bulk.

"We don't let women in here. There's another club down the road—"

"Let her in, Jimmy! She lifted me up with one hand, and I almost blacked out," my "friend" from the line yelled. The rest of the men waiting rumbled with appreciation.

"I'm meeting someone. Business only," I said, fighting to keep my face blank and not flushed with embarrassment. This was for Tad, I could do this.

Jimmy looked me up and down. "Doubt that."

Irritation flashed through me and I stepped up to him, looking down at his face. "I suggest you let me in, Jimmy. Or you're going to find out just how honest your friend back there is being. Do not try my patience."

A low rolling hiss started up in my chest, and Jimmy backed up a step, his eyes wide. "What the fuck?"

I didn't wait for him to offer to let me in. Just strode up the final two steps and into the club before he could pull himself together. As soon as the doors opened, the sound of wild music poured out into the night, the heavy thumping bass accompanied by a tempo that made my blood jump in time. I wrapped my arms around my torso as the music crawled up and down my skin, blocking me from sensing anything other than its rhythm.

Shivering, I forced myself to move forward. Every table was full of men, dressed like the ones outside with only slight variations in where the leather was placed. And where it wasn't, as I saw more than once. Good grief.

Their eyes tracked me as I moved through the club, and I fought not to notice how many of them were next to naked. Or completely naked. A man wearing nothing but a leash sat at the feet of another man who petted his head, as if he were a dog.

Every step I took showed me far more than I'd ever thought I'd see in my life, never mind what I might have imagined was out there.

I'd walked the entire length of the building before I saw the god of thunder and lightning. Zeus was at the back of the club, leaning against the wall with an arm over each of the shoulders of two younger-looking men. He kissed one, then the other, but his eyes never left mine. I flushed and looked away.

As he lifted his head he grinned as though just noticing me. "Ah, you made it, Alena. How did you get in?"

Was he serious?

He held his hands out. "They wouldn't have let you in without some sort of show. What was it?"

Embarrassed, I all but spit out the words. "I choked one of the patrons."

He slapped his hands on his leather-clad legs, laughing uproariously. "Oh, I wish I had seen it. Who did you choke? Jimmy? He can be a pill, and I would like to choke him myself a time or two, for the sheer joy of it."

I had to remind myself I needed his help. That was the only thing that kept my feet planted firmly where they were. "I don't know. Some guy in line wearing a face mask. I only threatened Jimmy."

Zeus's grin widened. "Too fun. Okay, boys"—he slapped them on their leather-clad behinds—"I have business. Come find me later." He patted the two men on the head as they slunk away, alternately pouting at Zeus and glaring at me.

I rubbed at my arms. "Is there somewhere the music isn't so strong?"

"Nope."

I realized that was why he wanted to meet me here. I was at a disadvantage by not being able to pick up on any vibrations other than the music. Not that I knew what to do with the vibrations on my skin, not really. But obviously Zeus knew it was something I could use in my favor, or he wouldn't try to block it. Not that I really knew myself well enough to even use all the tricks in my bag.

He gestured for me to slide into the booth behind him. I did and he slid in the other side. Ernie floated in and dropped onto the middle of the table.

Zeus waved at him. "Go get us drinks."

"You got it." He zipped off and Zeus slung an arm across my shoulders.

"I don't trust him. I think Hera has him in her secret pocket." His eyes scanned the crowd, and before I could formulate a question in regard to what he meant by a secret pocket, because I wasn't sure I wanted to know, he plowed on. "We don't have much time. A few minutes before he's back with the drinks. Here's the deal." He leaned in close so his mouth was against my ear, his coarse short beard tickling the edges of it. "Hera is up to something, and for whatever reason you're at the center of it. If Achilles kills you, he proves he is a hero. People will flock to him like they did in the old days."

"What does that matter?"

Zeus pulled back so he could look me in the eyes. "Belief is a powerful thing, young Drakaina. The more people who believe in you, the more power you have. The more power Achilles has, the more powerful the goddess he worships will become. He's working for Hera. She could climb the ranks in a way she's never done before."

Ernie flitted back to the table, drinks in each hand. He handed Zeus the beer and handed me a fluted glass that sparkled with something bubbly. "Beer for the boss, champagne for the lady."

I took the drink but didn't sip from it. Thinking about what Zeus could tell me in front of Ernie, I weighed my options. Not that I believed him that Ernie wasn't on my side . . . but I was quickly learning that not everything was as it seemed. Just as Yaya had said.

"Tell me about my grandmother. What is the curse on her?"

Zeus nodded, his eyes sparkling with approval. "Well, after she and I had our tryst, Hera was as usual peeved."

Ernie snorted. "*Peeved* is a bit light of a term, don't you think?"

"Well, the details don't matter now. Hera is always peeved about something." He rolled his eyes, and I thought about Roger cheating on me. How it had sent me into a flurry of self-doubt, anger, and shock.

I put the drink down and glared up at Zeus, thinking that perhaps all men—and male gods—were alike. Obviously Zeus thought nothing of stepping out on his wife. Neither did Roger. Were they all just primed and ready to hump anything that smiled at them?

"I've been cheated on, and if all she got was peeved, I think you got off light. In fact, I think perhaps you deserve whatever you get."

"A lifetime of penance, eh?" He shook his head. "Please, you have no idea what it is to be tied to someone you haven't loved in years. Someone who doesn't even love you but is such a territorial bitch she won't give you up." His words so closely echoed Roger's, I felt like I was talking to my husband for a split second.

I slapped my hands on the table. "I *do* know what it is to be tied to someone I can't get away from, so don't you talk down to me. You might think of yourself as a god, but you aren't any different than any other stupid man who thinks he can cheat and has all the reasons and excuses to do so."

"You're a child who doesn't understand life," he shot back. "People who are happy don't cheat. If you got cheated on, maybe your husband wasn't happy. Ever think about that?"

"Or maybe he's just a damn asshole!" I shouted, shaking all over. I was so angry that I didn't even care that I had just sworn for maybe the first time in my whole life. Mostly because I worried a part of what he said might be right. What if I'd put more time into my marriage and less into my business? Would Roger have strayed then?

There was a moment of stunned silence, and slowly the tension fell.

Zeus grimaced and waved a hand at me as if to wipe all the words away. "The point is, Hera was not happy. Since she can't really do any-thing to me, she always punishes those I've dallied with. In an effort to scare them off from this goodness." He slapped at the small beer belly that edged out over the top of his pants.

I rolled my eyes. "Whatever. My yaya. What was the curse?"

"That she and her family would never find real love. And if they ever stepped back into the supernatural world, they would be destroyed. Which is why Flora let herself get sucked into the Firsts."

"Oh, is that it?" I drawled even as my heart skipped a beat. "Destroyed? That's it?"

Zeus's jaw dropped, but he covered it by taking a sip of his beer. "You're taking this rather well."

"Listen, I've faced more in the last few days than any good girl should ever have to deal with in her entire life. What's a curse of a loveless life and ultimate destruction added to it?" I leaned back in my seat. "Will you help me with Achilles?"

Ernie's head whipped from side to side, looking from me to Zeus and back again, but he said nothing.

Zeus shook his head. "No. Not my area anymore. 'No dabbling' is my motto now."

"Not even a suggestion?" I leaned toward him, wondering if I could work my siren magic on him the way I'd done on Officer Jensen. That slow unfurling of power within my belly curled up through me.

Zeus laughed softly. "Won't work on me. But nice to see you're falling into your role as a monster."

I jerked back from him as if he'd slapped me. Ernie shook his head. "That wasn't nice. She *is* a good girl."

"Good girls get fucked over, Ernie. You know that." Zeus stared at the cherub. "Either she embraces what she is now, or she's going to die. Achilles will kill her. End of her story."

I pushed out of the booth. "Thanks for all your help."

"You aren't leaving, are you?" He seemed genuinely surprised. He slid out of the booth, following me.

"My brother is being held by Achilles. I can't leave him there."

Zeus's face went a careful, neutral blank. "Your brother?"

"Yes." I frowned. "Does that mean something to you?"

Zeus cleared his throat and leaned over the table. "Don't try to save him. That's Achilles's style. Hold a hostage, use them against his enemy, and kill the hostage right as you step onto the stage. To send you into a rage that will make you sloppy."

The music faded into a buzz. "No, that can't be, he won't kill Tad just to make me angry."

"It is. That has always been his style."

Ernie shook his head. "His methods could have changed. He hasn't faced a monster like Alena for years. Maybe he's got a new trick up his sleeve."

Zeus stared at me. "Heroes are, if nothing else, dependable in how they do things. They have their tried-and-true methods; I'd be surprised if he varied from his."

I pushed to my feet, said, "Thanks for the drink," and strode away from the table, through the club, and out the front door. There had to be a way to stop Achilles and save Tad. I refused to believe otherwise. Jimmy tried to grab me as I went by, and I spun around and hissed in his face, spit flicking from the tip of my tongue. "Don't. Touch. Me."

My skin prickled down around my neck, and Jimmy backed away, his mouth flapping. "You're a Supe."

"You bet I am. And not just any Super Duper. I am a bona fide monster that could snap you like a twig if you don't do as I say."

The crowd sucked in a gasp as a unit and Ernie groaned. "Maybe not the best moment to claim your title."

"Shut up, Ernie," I snapped, then strode through the line, pushing men out of my way where I had to, glaring at those who dared to meet my gaze, to where I'd parked my car. I didn't know if Zeus was telling the truth, but I couldn't take the risk that Ernie would turn on me. Or that he'd been leading me astray deliberately.

He popped into existence in the passenger seat. "Where we going?"

I revved the engine and backed out. "*We* aren't going anywhere. Thank you for your help, Ernie. But I'll do the rest on my own."

"What? Why? What did Zeus say to you?"

"Nothing that concerns you. This is my deal, not yours." I pulled onto the main road and headed north. To the Wall. There was only one person left I could tap into. And seeing as he'd put me into this mess, he owed me. Besides, he had my welcome package.

"Where are you going?"

"Get out, Ernie. I don't want you to be part of this, I don't know whose side you are on." I clenched the steering wheel and pressed my foot into the gas. We shot down the highway, Officer Jensen right behind us. I'd almost forgotten about him. A thought clambered to the front of my brain: I needed to pull the troops I could trust together. Which meant only Jensen at the moment. I pulled over to the side of the road, popped the car into park, and got out. Officer Jensen was out of his car in a flash.

"Is everything all right?"

I stepped in front of him, reached up, and touched his face. My plan that had been slowly forming kicked into high speed. "Do you have a walkie-talkie?"

"Yes, why?"

"Get one for me."

He hurried back to his cruiser and dug around in the front seat for a moment before bringing me back a black heavy-duty walkie-talkie. "What's the range?"

"Close to forty miles."

And the stadium where Tad was being held was about twenty from the Wall. "I want you to go to the stadium, the new CenturyLink Field. Wait for me there and report to me on the activity. People in, people out. Anything you see."

Ernie fluttered closer. "What are you doing?"

I spun and faced him, clutching the walkie-talkie behind me. "I need you to leave, Ernie. I can't risk anyone finding out what I'm planning. Please."

"Without me, how are you going to know things?" His eyes darted from me to Officer Jensen. "He's just a human, there's nothing he can do."

"Ernie. You've been great. But I have to do this on my own. I have to. I would feel awful if you got hurt."

"But not if Officer Jenny there gets hurt?"

Good grief, was Ernie pouting? Looked like it. I smiled at him, trying to think of a way to soften things. "He's doing surveillance for me."

"I could do that for you." Ernie brightened. "I can get Hermes to run messages between us."

I thought for a minute. Zeus said not to trust Ernie, but maybe I could work that to my advantage. "Go watch Zeus. I think he's up to something, I don't think he told me the truth at all."

Ernie's eyes widened. "What did he tell you?"

I leaned close, beckoning him to me, the lie forming with an ease that frightened me. "Hera. She wants me to work for her, so she's testing me."

Ernie nodded. "That makes sense, she likes the powerhouses to be on her side. Okay, I'll go watch Zeus. Hera would be good to you, Alena. She's tough, but"—his eyes darted to the side—"I've worked with her. She's been a good boss in the past."

My heart fell, but I smiled at him. "Keep an eye on Zeus. Send me a message only if he moves toward the stadium." Which I was almost positive he wouldn't do. "I can't have him trying to help me."

Ernie saluted and was gone with a small puff of feathers.

I turned back to Officer Jensen. "Stadium. Go."

He saluted and ran back to his car. I flicked on the walkie-talkie and slid the clip over my waistband. This was just like running the bakery. Plan. Rally the troops. Implement. Deliver the goods. I could do this.

I had to or Tad was going to die for real this time.

A huge sigh slid out of me as I drove away from Jensen and Ernie.

Two hours later, after about as much planning as I could manage as I drove, I came to the Wall, and the only official entry point on the southwestern side. The border crossing was only two lanes. One in and one out. In theory. There was no traffic to speak of other than the two large Supe Squad vehicles that sat to either side of the gate. I slowed the car and rolled my window down.

Looked like my luck was not going to hold. Smithy, my old friend, strolled up to the car and peered in, his icy-blue eyes nailing me to my seat. He braced his hands on the edge of the window, his fingers digging into the metal with a low grinding screech. The smell of donuts rolled off him. "You."

"Missed me?" I blinked up at him, batting my lashes with more than a little exaggeration.

"I'm taking you down to the station. Get out."

I took a deep breath and pouted up at him, pursing my lips. That uncoiling sensation rolled through me and I put a hand on his. "Wouldn't you rather help me?"

He shook his head and blinked several times. Confusion washed over his hard features. "What?"

"Wouldn't you rather help me? There are worse people out there than me. I'm harmless." The words flowed out of my mouth and seemed to tighten around him in a slow constriction.

His body stiffened and he began to tremble. Those blue eyes darted from me, away to the Wall and back again. "You're going to stay on your side of the Wall from now on?"

I widened my eyes. "Of course. I don't fit over in the human side anymore. They don't want me. Maybe you know someone who does?"

His eyes softened and he leaned in toward me. "Maybe I do. But I have to . . . you'll go down to the station on your own?" His words were tense but verged on slurred. I increased my hold on his hand.

"Of course. I'm free to go now?"

He pulled away from me, his hand red where I'd clung to him. He glanced back at his comrades. "This isn't the Supe we're looking for."

He waved me through the gate while his buddies stared with open mouths, obviously recognizing me. But not one of them argued with him. I checked my rearview mirror. He stood in the middle of the road, staring after me while he shook his head as if trying to clear cobwebs.

I waited until I was out of sight of the Wall and the guard tower before I hit the gas hard. Screeching the tires, I hurried, knowing time slipped away faster with every second that ticked by. How long would Achilles hold off before he decided he didn't want to wait on me? Before he would torture or even kill Tad? My throat tightened and I tried not to think about what might be happening to my brother. How hurt he might be. I had to do this right and plan his rescue right, or we'd both end up dead.

Merlin's house was lit up like a beacon as I approached, and even from down the street the sound of music spilled toward me. I tightened my lips to keep from snarling. Here I was fighting for my life and for my brother's, and Merlin was having another poker-night party.

I pulled into the driveway, stepped out of the car, and slammed the door shut behind me. I didn't bother to knock on the house door. Just grabbed the knob and twisted. Locked.

I raised my knuckles, paused, and reconsidered. Really, if I was such a powerful Super Duper, I didn't have to play nice. I took a step back, lifted one heeled foot, and snapped it forward, aiming for the knob. My heel caught in the keyhole, and the door burst inward, taking my shoe with it. I slipped the other shoe off so I didn't walk in lopsided. No need to be undignified.

Two steps and I stood in the main part of the house, with every pair of eyes locked on me. A couple of vampires, including Remo's man Max; the same werewolf as before; and two new girls were the full count. Max gave me a wink I didn't understand. Maybe he was here on Remo's request? Not that it mattered to me.

I didn't recognize the two girls, but by the shell-shocked looks on their faces they were newly turned. One was dark-haired like me, her eyes pale enough they were spooky in their incandescent nature. The other girl was the reverse. Blond hair cropped short to her head and dark eyes the deep black of midnight. I turned my attention to the warlock who'd started all this.

"Merlin. You've been a bad boy," I purred, the anger and frustration curling up through me. "You made me into a Drakaina. Do you know what that is? Do you understand what you've created?"

Merlin stood and made a soothing, flapping motion with his hands. "Now, Alena, my dear. Don't get worked up. You could end up shifting into a monster, and you wouldn't want that, would you? Remember, you asked to be special. I gave you what you wanted and then some. Don't go and be a bitch about it now. Don't make me think you're not the nice girl everyone said you were."

For just a split second shame ran over me, embarrassment that I would make a scene.

No. No, I would not be ashamed of standing up for myself.

"This was not what I asked for!" Sudden understanding tightened in my gut like a coiled knot of writhing snakes. "You turned me into this . . . because I was a good girl. Didn't you? You thought I would be . . . what, easy to control?"

A flash in his eyes was the only clue that I was right before he shook his head. "Of course not—"

I took a step forward, my anger growing. "Because you thought I was weak."

Zeus's words came back to me. "That I'd be an easy kill . . . for Achilles."

Merlin stepped back, the smile on his face not slipping for a second, but I saw the fear in his eyes. "Where in the world would you get the idea that I would want you dead?"

"Not you. Someone else. Someone you work for." I closed the distance between us, or tried to. He scooted around the large table dominating the room. I put the pieces together. "For Hera, perhaps?"

His throat bobbed. "I turn all my clients as per their requests. You asked for something special. I gave you that. What you do with your new abilities, and who you make enemies or friends with, is up to you." We circled around the table, the rest of his guests not moving an inch, as if they were statues. Some of them barely breathed, if the rapid beats of their hearts were any indication.

"And what did these two ask to be made into?" I flicked a hand at the two new girls. They glanced at each other and answered in unison.

"Vampires. That's what we paid for."

I raised an eyebrow, a slow burning recognition flowing through me along with their scent. "Really?"

I slid over next to them and drew in a breath, tasting the air along the back of my tongue, and locked it into my mind. "You aren't vampires."

They stiffened at the same time. "No, that can't be," the dark-haired girl said. "He promised and we paid."

One way or another I had to push the warlock to tell the truth. But what buttons to push on him? Let's try button number one: call him out.

"He's a liar." The scent of their skin flickered something in my brain, something a part of me recognized. An image floated in front of me, superimposing over the two girls. Black and gold feathers layered over them, metallic in nature, with long bronze beaks that jutted from the middle of their faces.

Merlin tapped the table with his knuckles, drawing all eyes to him. "Ladies, please. I made you into what you asked for. Deadly man-eaters with beauty so bright as to be painful to the eye. That is what you asked for. Isn't it?"

The two girls blinked up at me, and I saw in them what I'd been only a few days before. Scared, alone, misled.

Weak.

"What are we?"

"Birds. Beautiful deadly birds." Just as I was a Drakaina, I had no doubt there would be some funky name for what they were. I didn't know it, though. The snake in me recognized them as creatures from the same time period.

They clung to each other, hands interlocking. The dark-haired girl shuddered. "I hate birds."

"It's okay, Sandy. We'll figure this out," the blonde said.

Merlin smiled at the three of us. "Our business is done. Get out of my house, Alena."

I moved forward, putting myself between the girls and Merlin. Button number two: take his latest creations from him. "For tonight, we're done, you're right about that. Girls, I think you should come with me."

Merlin startled. "You can't take them."

I lifted an eyebrow, certainty growing fast within me. Button number three: point out how ineffective he was. "You can't stop me. And I want my welcome package while you're at it."

His jaw dropped open, and the other Super Dupers in the room shifted uncomfortably.

"Welcome packages are by the door," Max said. "Not that there is much info in them. A map of this side of the Wall, things to know about the Supe Squad. That sort of thing."

I gave him a nod. "Thanks."

The petite girls clung to each other as they walked to the door. I waited until they stepped through and were clear before following. I took a package from the high-backed bar near the door. "I'll be back, Merlin. You can count on it." I pointed a finger at him.

He snorted, his composure back in place. "Bite me."

"Be careful what you ask for. You might not like my bite." I snapped my teeth at him, my fangs dropping down. Droplets of venom flicked off the tips and sizzled on the floor. Chairs and boots scraped on the floor as Merlin and his posse scrambled backward.

Merlin's smile finally fell. "Go die, Alena. That's all you're good for."

And there it was, the words I wanted him to admit to. Of course I thought they were because I was headed to Achilles.

That was where I was wrong.

CHAPTER 13

SDMP members surrounded my car, and the two bird girls were in their clutches. Literally.

Two sets of scared, confused eyes looked to me. "Boys, you need to let those two go. They're harmless. Like me." I smiled, even though my adrenaline pumped like crazy. Smithy glared at me.

"No more games. All of you are going to the station. Now."

Anxiety kissed at my heels; the need to not cause a scene, to do what was lawful made me step forward before I thought better of it. No. That was not who I was anymore, not if I wanted to survive. Not if I wanted to save Tad.

I stopped, and looked to my bare feet. The top of my right foot had been skinned, and the multicolored scales that blinked up at me seemed to be all I needed to steel my resolve. I slowly lifted my face. "None of us are going with you."

Blue Eyes lifted a dart gun and pointed it at my chest. "Get in the back of the truck now or I'll shoot."

Putting my hands in the air, I took a step forward. The new instinct in me suggested closer was better. He didn't lower the gun, but he didn't pull the trigger either. Which meant he wasn't afraid of me.

"Officer, you said I didn't have to go to the station today." I smiled as I spoke, all while continuing a slow pace toward him. His coworkers whispered to him.

"Shoot her."

"She hasn't done anything," Smithy said.

"That's right. I'm a good girl. Just ask anyone." I was close enough that the muzzle of the gun was pressed between my breasts, the dart pressing hard against my skin. Not that I thought it would actually pierce my scales. If a sword bounced off me, what was a tiny dart going to do?

The part of me I was slowly leaving behind would have passed out, fallen down, and begged for mercy. But the new Alena . . . I dropped to my knees and whipped my hands up to grab the muzzle of the gun, jerking it out of his hands.

The gun went off, and I realized it wasn't just a dart gun, but a live rifle as well. The bullets ripped through the air, and the vibrations of them cutting through the sound barrier were like slaps against my bare skin.

I stood and bent the gun in half, snapping it like a twig. "Go home. I'm not a Super Duper. And neither are these two girls."

Smithy snarled at me, his face twisting as the wolf in him pushed forward. "Bullshit." Apparently he wasn't going to fall for my machinations this time.

I pulled myself up. "You can smell a lie, can't you?" Honestly, I was guessing on that one.

He nodded.

"I am not a Super Duper. Not like you at all." I enunciated each word clearly.

His eyes slowly widened as he drew in a breath. "Then what the hell are you?"

"Dangerous. But I don't fall within your jurisdiction. And neither do they." I pointed at the two girls. They pulled away from the SDMP members who held them. "The three of us will come to the station tomorrow morning. In a show of good faith. I'll explain everything." At least as much as I was able. "There will be no tracking devices. Understand?"

His eyes flicked over me, then to the girls. "Merlin's work. Correct?"

I nodded. "Maybe you should talk to him about what he's been doing."

Behind us, Merlin's door slammed shut, or as shut as it could with a broken knob and lock. Smithy leaned to look past me, his wolfy side easing off. "Perhaps I will. I expect you at the station tomorrow as the sun rises. Oberfall is going to want to talk to you at length."

"I'll do my best."

"You will be there." He snapped his teeth at me, and his men tightened their circle around us.

I curled up one side of my mouth and let a single fang drop. "I will do my best, and you will have to be happy with that, my friend."

He took a step back, his face twitching with barely restrained emotions. "Fine."

I moved around him and the two girls followed. They slipped into the car on the passenger side, both fitting in the front seat. Their eyes flicked to me and then back to the SDMP members.

"Thanks," the dark-haired one said. "My name is Sandy. This is Beth."

"Girls. Nice to meet you. Let me give you the quick rundown. Merlin turned you into Greek monsters of some sort. It's what he did to me."

Beth started to cry, burying her face in her hands. "I knew something was going to go wrong. I just knew it."

Sandy wrapped her arms around her friend. "It will be okay. I promise." Her bright eyes met mine. I shrugged. "We're alive. That's got to be worth something."

Beth's shoulders shook as she sobbed. She spoke, but the words slurred between hiccups and tears. Where the hell was I going to take them? Where would they be safe from the Supe Squad, and who was I going to get to help me save Tad besides Officer Jensen . . . my thoughts trailed off with a single image of dark eyes rimmed in violet laughing at me. Remo.

See? You do need my help.

I drove to the safe house Dahlia had taken Tad and me to. Had it been only three days? It felt like I'd been a Drakaina for weeks, maybe even months. Not days.

I pulled into the driveway of the two-story house the vampires used for a place to crash within the city.

As I hustled the two girls in front of me, we entered the house. The place was quiet, and I could only hope that there were no vamps using it. Unless it was Dahlia. I checked the clock hanging on the wall. Eleven. It was dark until seven in the morning, which gave me eight hours if I was really going to do this thing. If I was really going to ask Remo for help.

A shudder slid through me that I tried to convince myself was sheer revulsion. Except that I remembered the kiss all too well and knew darn well revulsion wasn't on the list of emotions he invoked in me.

"You are a married woman. Even if the man you're married to is a cheating goat penis." I spoke softly, but Sandy turned her head.

"Who's a cheating goat penis?"

Heat curled up my neck. "My soon-to-be ex-husband."

Sandy smiled. "Sounds like my boyfriend. He was cheating on me too."

Beth sniffed. "And my fiancé. He cheated on me right before I was turned."

I frowned, thinking. That had to be a coincidence that all three of us were cheated on. Didn't it? Unless it fit into some sort of formula Merlin was looking for. I shook my head. No time for that.

"Look, you two will be . . . safe here." At least, safe from the SDMP.

"I don't like how you paused there," Sandy said.

"It's a safe house for vampires. I stayed here with a friend, and at least from those goons back there, you will be safe. That's the best I can do right now."

Footsteps echoed to me from the front porch. I lifted a hand to silence the two girls, and their mouths snapped shut in unison.

I tipped my head to one side, listening for a heartbeat. Nothing.

Vampire.

I crept to the door and peered through the peephole. Red hair filled the space. I jerked the door open and Dahlia fell in. I caught her, the scent of blood overwhelming me.

"Dahlia! What happened?"

"Rival gang from out east, they're making a push for territory and I got caught in the middle," she whispered. I dragged her into the room, a trail of blood trickling behind her. I couldn't see the wound, but I knew it had to be bad for there to be that much blood.

"Out of my way." Beth pushed me off her. "I'm a nurse."

Beth smoothed her short cropped blond hair back behind her ears and went to her knees beside Dahlia. "Where?"

"My side and thigh. They went for the big vein."

"The femoral," Beth murmured. "You're lucky to be alive."

"Manner of speaking," Dahlia whispered. "I just need some blood."

Beth grabbed the edges of her shirt and ripped a large strip off. Dahlia's side looked like it had been run through a table saw; ribbons of flesh flapped like open fish gills. The pulse of her life could be seen in the organs as they beat as slow as a watch with a dying battery. I swallowed hard, because the sight made my stomach roll.

With hunger.

I backed away. Or tried to. Dahlia grabbed hold of my wrist. "I know you don't have to. But please. I need your help."

Beth muttered as she tried to wrap Dahlia's side. "Whatever you're going to do, hurry it up, I can't stitch her up fast enough to stave off the blood loss."

I relaxed and let Dahlia draw my wrist to her mouth. She bore down with her teeth, but nothing happened. No pain for me. Well, this was—

"I can't break through your skin," Dahlia said. I looked down. My skin had torn, but not the scales underneath.

I frowned. "I don't know."

Dahlia's eyes rolled back in her head and she slumped. I grabbed her shoulders. "Dahlia!" I looked at Beth. "Do something!"

"I'm tying her leg off, she needs blood!"

I put my tongue to the roof of my mouth, brushing it against one of my fangs. The tip drew blood from my tongue. I was not about to give her a French kiss, but . . . I tipped my head back and flicked my left fang out, pushing it with my tongue. It didn't want to drop. Without a strong emotion behind my snaky side, it just didn't want to do anything.

Seconds passed as I shoved the fang forward far enough that I could catch it over my bottom lip. Using the tip, I opened up my wrist, cutting through skin and scale alike.

Blood welled up. Blood that sparkled with rainbow lights, as prismatic as my scales.

"Wow," Sandy or Beth said. I'm not sure which. I pressed my wrist to Dahlia's mouth.

"Please let this not be too late."

Beth took my arm and massaged it from the shoulder down. "The faster we can get the blood in her, the better."

Her tiny hands dug into my muscle hard enough to make me grimace. Strong hands for such a small girl. Of course, Beth was an epic monster.

Just like me.

Beneath my wrist, the pressure of Dahlia drawing on me on her own eased some of the tension, and I let out a breath.

Sandy stepped up beside us. "Her wounds are healing." Beth and I glanced at the same time. The gaping wounds in Dahlia's side were indeed healing. No, that wasn't accurate. Healed. The wounds were completely gone without even a scar to prove they'd been there.

I pulled my hand away from Dahlia's mouth. "You think that's enough?"

Dahlia let out a soft moan. "Oh my God. Alena, you taste amazing. An orgasm and fine wine with a hint of chocolate all rolled into a single drop."

I grimaced and tucked my wrist under my other arm. Beth grabbed it, took a piece of material from Dahlia's ripped clothes, and wrapped it around my wrist.

"Clean it at least twice a day and wrap it with clean cloth. You don't want an infection."

Dahlia sat up, her eyes brighter than the noonday sun, her hair glistening with life and vitality. "I feel . . . ten times better than when I was first turned."

Beth tightened the wrap and I flinched. "Ouch."

Her dark eyes flicked to mine, instantly filling with tears. "Sorry, I—"

I waved at her. "It's okay. I'm tougher than I look."

She laughed but it broke into tears, and I let out a sigh. With one arm I pulled her to my side. "You know, it's not so bad, I think."

Dahlia stared at me, her eyes wide and mouth slightly open as if she couldn't believe what I'd said. "Being a monster isn't so bad?"

"Not just any monster," I explained. "A mythological Greek monster that doesn't fit into any boxes the SDMP can check off on their forms."

Dahlia's mouth dropped farther and she spluttered. "What?"

"We'll talk about it later. I have a rescue to plan."

The sudden change of subject seemed to throw Dahlia as much as anything. "I'm sorry, who are you and what have you done with my friend?"

I laughed softly, but there was no real joy in it. "I ran a business for almost ten years. Like a general, my yaya always said. A general. So . . . I'm applying that to my life now. No more nice girl. Time for the general to make things happen."

Dahlia gave a slow grin and gave me a salute. "I'm with you, General Alena."

Beth grinned and Sandy gave me a funny look. "You don't look like a general. You look like an Amazonian supermodel."

"Dahlia. I . . . I need Remo's help."

Dahlia's eyes bugged out. "Why?"

I made myself stay standing straight and not slump. "Long story short, Achilles has my brother, and he's going to kill him the second I step into the stadium at CenturyLink Field."

The walkie-talkie took that moment to gasp to life, Officer Jensen's voice crackling over the airwaves. "Alena. We've got a problem."

I tugged the device off my waistband and pressed the button. "What is it?"

"We've got a huge number of unfriendlies here. Along with enough humans that the stadium is going to be full in a matter of half an hour. As in all seventy thousand seats." The squawk box hissed off.

I pressed my button again. "How many unfriendlies are we talking?"

There was silence for longer than a minute. Was he counting? Had he been caught?

It hissed to life. "Over a thousand."

My heart sank. "Any idea how these people showed up in time for the . . . show?"

"Hang on." The line hissed with empty white noise for a solid minute, the longest minute of my life, before he came back on.

"They've got flyers. Says it's a free show two thousand years in the making. And that two lucky people will win a million dollars each when the show concludes."

I closed my eyes. With a flyer like that, I was not surprised they filled the stadium. "Jensen, there is no money waiting for anyone. See if you can get people out of there. Quietly, though."

"Roger that. I'll check back if anything changes."

I put the walkie-talkie back over my waistband and put a hand to my head. "Dahlia, how fast are you?"

"Not fast enough to get through that many. I think you're right. You need help. More than I can give you."

"Darn it all to . . . to hell!" I snapped as I paced the room. There was no choice. I had to save Tad.

Even if it meant making a deal with the devil himself.

"Dahlia. Call Remo. Tell him I'm ready to take him up on his offer."

"Are you sure?"

I shook my head. "No. Not at all."

CHAPTER 14

Dahlia went to go find fresh clothes and, I assume, contact Remo. I continued to pace. Beth and Sandy sat beside each other on the couch. I glanced at them from time to time, seeing the overlay of birds on them here and there. They didn't look like songbirds, that was for sure.

"Alena, how long have you been . . . a monster?" Beth asked softly, her voice trembling. I was surprised at the shift in her demeanor. When Dahlia had needed help, Beth's training had kicked in and the timid woman had been washed away in what needed to be done. Maybe she was like me, stronger than she realized. That was a good thing, if I could get her to see her own abilities for the good they were.

"A few days." I kept up my pacing, feeling the snake in me coil and uncoil, agitated with the lack of real movement.

They exchanged a glance. Sandy cleared her throat. "How can you be sure we're what you say we are? Merlin saved us from the virus. Maybe you're just mad at him because he turned you into something you didn't want."

"He saved my life too." I snorted. "And now I can shift into a snake the size of a house. Not exactly what I asked for." Yet a part of me realized I'd made the mistake of not being more specific.

No. I was not going to take the blame for this. Dahlia stepped back into the room, her face grim and the phone in her hand. She held it out to me. "He'd like to talk to you."

I strode over and all but snatched the phone from her. "Hello?"

His deep bass rolled through the phone and over my skin. "Alena. Lovely to hear from you."

His voice did bad things, took my mind from the task at hand as it conjured up images of satiny soft sheets and body parts dipped in dark chocolate.

Time to cut to the chase. "I need your help."

"No proper hello? No thank you for answering the phone?" His soft rebuke held no real heat to it.

"My brother's life is on the line. I don't have time to be nice anymore." I had to focus to keep from snapping the phone in half.

"Well. That is a predicament, isn't it?"

"I . . ." I swallowed my pride and what was left of how I'd been raised. "I want your help to get him out."

"And what will you give me in return?"

Dahlia snatched the phone from me and put her hand over the mouthpiece. "Offer him blood. Your blood, for his help this time. Don't tie yourself to him."

I nodded and took the phone back. "A drink. On me."

He chuckled, low and deep, and the vibration did bad things to my mind-set. Something about him made me forget I was supposed to be repulsed by the vampire and the things he epitomized.

"While I appreciate the offer, it's not enough. I want you. All of you. I can get blood anywhere."

Dahlia shook her head and I took a slow breath. When my bakery clients balked at the cost of my goods, there was a surefire way to reel them in.

"I'll give you a taste test. To show you just how good it is."

He was quiet for a full ten seconds. "A taste test? Where are you?"

I handed the phone back to Dahlia. "Safe house number thirteen."

Of course it was.

She nodded several times. "She'll wait." A click of the button ended the connection, and I glanced at Dahlia.

"Do you think the blood will be enough?"

"Right now I'm sure of it. I think I could take him, if he tried to fight, Lena. I'm brand-new and he's over a thousand years old. I should never be able to take him. Your blood is a game changer."

Game changer . . .

"You mean because of the rival gang?"

"Yes. You could clinch Remo's victory. We were looking for info on them in the SDMP detachment the other day. We think the gang is working with them to wipe Remo and us out." Her eyes glittered. "You have the upper hand with these negotiations, remember that."

Beth and Sandy sat crouched on the couch, just like the birds they were, and a thought crossed my mind. "Do you have a computer here?" I asked Dahlia.

She took me upstairs to a room decked out in the newest gadgets, computers, and hardware, most of which I didn't recognize. "Here." She sat at the computer and flicked it on. The screen came to life, and Dahlia clicked on an Internet browser. "It's blocked from social media, but we can get information. What are you looking for?"

"Greek monsters. The two girls . . . the monster in me recognizes them, but I don't know what they are. Or what they're capable of."

"What does it matter?"

I sat down beside her in the only other chair in the room. "I think Merlin is turning people into Greek monsters to be killed by the heroes of old."

"What? That makes no sense."

I rubbed my hands on my thighs. "It does in a twisted sort of way. If Merlin turns people he thinks are weak willed, or weak in heart, into monsters, how easy are they to kill? Me and Beth and Sandy . . . he turned us because he didn't think we had it in us to embrace what he'd made us."

"But what would be the point? His clientele is based on referrals. There are other warlocks who can turn people; he would lose too much business." Dahlia sat facing me, her hands unmoving on the keyboard.

"Someone else hired him to do it, I think. Someone with a lot of money and power." Of course, I was assuming Hera had money.

"You know who it is?" Sandy asked from the doorway.

"Shit, I didn't hear them." Dahlia sucked in a quick breath. Neither had I. Good to know they could sneak up on even me.

"I think so"—I grimaced—"but I'm hoping I'm wrong."

"Because if you're right?" Beth's eyes were wide, the dark pupils blending into the dark of her iris.

"If I'm right, I'm not sure I can survive this." There it was, the words that had been rumbling through my head.

The four of us were quiet. I cleared my voice. "Let's see if we can figure out what you two are."

Dahlia moved aside and let me type. The search didn't take long. After making a few queries and searching one online encyclopedia article, I found a picture and description that fit.

I read it out loud. "Stymphalian birds."

"Keep going," Beth said.

"Well, it looks like you two are literally man-eating birds. You should have beaks of bronze and sharp metallic feathers you can launch at your enemies."

Sandy leaned forward for a better look. "Are you sure?"

I nodded. "So says the monster in me when I see the monsters in you."

Beth reached out and touched a name on the list of monsters, the picture beside it something I knew all too well. Drakaina. "At least we aren't that."

I couldn't help the laugh that burst out of me. "Well, it wasn't my choice either. But it's not so bad, it's come in handy."

Beth paled. "I'm sorry. I didn't realize . . ."

I waved at her. "Don't worry about it."

The click of a door opening froze all four of us. I motioned for Beth and Sandy to stay while Dahlia and I headed downstairs.

"You really are kind of a general once you stop being so worried about offending anyone." Dahlia kept pace with me down the stairs. I smiled. "Thanks."

We found Remo in the kitchen, leaning against the sink. He didn't fit in the room. Not his frame, the piercings in his chin, the tattoos curling across the bit of flesh I could see of his chest, or the heavy army boots he wore.

His smiled, showing off his fangs. "I came not for your blood. But that will be part of the package."

I drew in a breath. "Dahlia drank some of my blood earlier. To keep her from dying."

His eyebrows lifted ever so slightly. "Are you looking for my thanks? I have a hundred soldiers like her."

I put my hands on my hips, hoping that Dahlia was right about my blood. "I doubt that. Dahlia. Show him just how much my blood is worth."

She grinned. "With pleasure."

I blinked and she was on him, tackling him to the floor like a linebacker gone wild. She followed her body slam with a flurry of punches and kicks, and her teeth dug into the back of his neck while he tried to fight back. He might as well have been a small dog being mauled by a giant wolf even though he was twice her size. The fight was so one-sided as to be laughable.

She pinned him to his belly while holding both his hands with one of hers. "See, Remo? You should want her blood more than anything." He stared up at me. "This is not possible."

"It is. Now. I need help getting my brother out of the stadium. What I want from you is simple."

I reached out and took Dahlia's hand, pulling her off him and putting her behind me. Just in case he decided to lash out. He stood slowly, dusting off his clothes. But he held himself together. Perhaps the patience that came with a thousand years was finally showing.

"Simple? I doubt that. This deal will be done without witnesses."

"Not a good idea, Lena. He could fleece you later," Dahlia said. I kept my eyes locked on Remo's. He didn't move, hardly even breathed. Not that he needed to, being dead and all that.

"Dahlia, go and check on our guests. Please." What I didn't say was that we knew she would be able to hear from upstairs.

She sucked in a sharp breath but did as I asked and left the room.

He didn't close the distance between us, not the way I thought he would. Maybe I was a little disappointed.

I lifted my chin. "I need you and your vampires to get my brother out of the stadium. As soon as Achilles sees me, he'll kill my brother. I can't take the chance I won't make it to him in time."

Remo slid his fingers over the piercings in his chin, his dark eyes thoughtful. "How many men does this Achilles guy have?" He motioned for me to sit at the table.

I moved to the chair closest to me and sat down. "*The* Achilles, to be clear. And according to my reports, over a thousand."

Remo paused in midstep. "What do you mean, *the* Achilles?"

"The Greek hero. Come to save the world from monsters." I pointed at my chest. "From me and whatever other monsters Merlin dreams up."

He sat down across from me, the bruises and cuts from his tussle with Dahlia already fading. "Achilles is here to kill you?"

"Yes."

"Because you're a monster?" His lips twitched and I realized he didn't believe me.

I drew in a breath and let it out in a long low hiss, along with the lowering of my fangs. "Want to make something of it?"

His eyes snapped wide and he leaned back in his chair. He'd not want me in his bed now at least, now that he'd seen my fangs. More than a small part of me was hurt, and disappointed; if I was honest, I'd wanted him more than any other man I'd been around. Certainly more than Roger.

He reached across the table and scooped up one of my hands, pinning it between his. "Oh, you are an intriguing one. More than I realized."

"Are you going to help me or not?" I pulled my hand away while I tried to keep my lips from smiling, to stop the heat that flared between us. "And I'm married. Remember? So stop with the flirting; it will get you nowhere."

Grinning, he leaned back in his chair, stretching his long legs out so that he brushed up against my bare feet. A move like that shouldn't have held as much heat as what spread up my legs. I swallowed and tucked my feet back under my seat.

"I'll help you, for a month of feeding off you."

"*Too much!*" Dahlia yelled from upstairs.

"I know that!" I yelled back.

"Sorry!"

Remo laughed. "The supernatural world hasn't been this much fun in years. Two weeks of feeding, then."

"I'll give you two feedings from me," I said, folding my hands on the table. "And one taste test." I unwound the wrap from my wrist and tossed the saturated rag to him. My wrist wasn't healed up, and I pressed my fingers over it to stem the steady flow.

Remo lifted the rag over his head and let it drip into his mouth. Two drops fell and he lowered the rag. His eyes had a strange look to them I'd only ever seen in clients who'd fallen in love with my baking. I had him.

"A week of feeding," he said.

I lifted an eyebrow. "Two feedings. And not a drop more. Take it or leave it."

"What about your brother?"

I leaned back in my seat and smiled at him. "I heard something about a rival gang in town. I'm sure I can get them to help me."

"You are a shrewd negotiator." He grinned. "I can't wait until you get into trouble again. Consider the deal done." He held out his hand

and I placed mine in it. He closed down and pulled me across the table on my belly. I gasped, the wood surface slick enough I might as well have been on those satin sheets I'd imagined earlier. With a quick twist Remo spun me so my legs swung around. He grabbed my hips and sat me up so I faced him, his head now level with my chest.

"There, that's better." He lifted my wrist to his mouth, his eyes on mine as he licked along the wound. "I'm going to enjoy this, though I must admit I would have preferred to take it from your neck."

I jerked my head to one side, breaking his gaze as if it were a physical thing. "You have a time limit as far as I'm concerned. You can use it to play your games or feed."

He grunted and bent his head over my wrist. Unlike Dahlia, who'd been out cold, Remo was anything but. He latched onto my wrist as if his mouth were a suction cup, and the first drag he took . . . hurt. I closed my eyes and counted, knowing that Dahlia had had at best a minute of blood.

For Tad, I could do this. Even as with every second that passed, the pain increased, easily doubling. Sweat slid down my cheeks, neck, and arms. At fifty-eight I jerked my hand away from him. "Enough."

Remo barely moved except to let out a long whisper. "My God."

"Don't use his name here," I whispered. "Don't."

The vampire smiled as he tipped his head up. "Fine by me. He left me long ago and I do not miss his passing." His eyes sparked with a light burning hot from within, as if a fire burned behind them.

"Now we can go for Tad."

"I took a lot of blood from you. I think you should rest," Remo crooned, and his words made perfect sense. Of course I should rest. No, that wasn't right, I needed to get to Tad, to get him away from Achilles.

I blinked and glared at Remo. "Stop that."

His dark eyes widened ever so slightly, showing a hint of violet once more, and a smile curled his lips. "Stop what?"

"You know what I'm talking about. Stop trying to make me do what you want," I snapped. Though even I had to admit, the snap was more of a breathy whisper. I shook my head and slid off the table. My legs wobbled as I moved sideways to the counter. The granite was smooth under my hand, and I gripped it for all I was worth. A loud crack rent the air, the granite cracking under the pressure.

Remo cleared his throat. "I'll gather up my mob and head to the stadium. I'll wait for you across the street."

I nodded. "How long before you're there?"

"An hour."

One hour to get past the SDMP at the gate, and all the way to the stadium. This was going to be tight. Remo stood and stretched, his shirt pulling up, giving me a glimpse of pale belly and a thin line of dark hair that disappeared into the waistband of his jeans.

"Married, huh?"

I whipped my head up, but what could I say? "Looking isn't the same as touching. I'd have to be dead not to look."

He laughed. "I'll see you in an hour, Alena."

I closed my eyes as he passed by me, the smell of cinnamon and honey the only thing that told me he had moved. When it faded I opened my eyes. The room looked no different and yet . . . I was different. I'd made a deal with a devil: a devil I rather liked the look of.

"'I'd have to be dead not to look'? You realize that is rather ironic since most of the ass he taps is dead." Dahlia strode into the kitchen, Beth and Sandy trailing behind her.

I shrugged but couldn't meet her eyes.

"Wait, you don't really like him . . . do you?" Dahlia gasped. "Oh my God, you're hot for Remo."

"I am not hot for anyone. I'm married."

"You keep saying that," Dahlia snorted. "I don't think it matters anymore."

I frowned, hating that part of me agreed with her. "Whatever. We need to focus on getting Tad safe and making Achilles see I'm not the monster he thinks I am."

Dahlia shook her head and picked up the car keys from the counter. "You think you can convince him to simply back down from the fight?"

I nodded. "Why not? I've been able to convince other men to do what I want." The words popped out of me and I cringed. "Never mind, it will be up to me anyway."

"We're coming with you," Beth said. "If what you're saying is true, he'll come after us next, won't he?"

I bit my lower lip. "Yes, I think so. But that's only if he kills me."

"What's the chances of a hero, trained in the killing arts, with superhuman speed and a track record of 10–0, killing you, a brand-new monster with a dislike for ruffling feathers?" Dahlia glanced at the two girls. "No pun intended."

I slapped my hands on the table and leaned toward her. "I'm not leaving Tad. At the very least I'm getting him out of there. Do you understand me?" I didn't realize I was shouting until I stopped and the room echoed with my words.

Dahlia gave me a tight nod. "Got it, General Alena."

Beth and Sandy bobbed their heads in unison. "Understood."

"Then let's go. We're wasting time." I held my hand out to Dahlia and she dropped the keys into my palm.

They fell into step behind me.

"She really could be a general," Beth said.

Dahlia grunted. "Here I was thinking I'd be the one protecting her."

A flush of pride washed through me, and I knew in that moment I'd at least go out on a high note. Achilles would probably kill me, but I wouldn't go down without a fight. No, the dark night wouldn't claim me without a battle to remember.

CHAPTER 15

The gate at the Wall was open without a single SDMP member guarding it. Not one. And the Super Duper community was taking advantage of the lack of guards. A steady stream of Supes headed through the open gate. My first thought was the tracking chips they all had implanted.

"Why aren't they getting shocked?" I stared at them as they went through; not one Super Duper so much as twitched.

"Damn, I can't believe it worked!" Dahlia crowed. "That's part of what we did at the SDMP when we picked you and Tad up. We disabled the tracking chips."

I couldn't help showing my geek flag off. "How? What did you do, blow out the thermal exhaust port?"

"With a well-timed proton torpedo." She winked and leaned forward. "It's a lucky break for us, though. Don't slow down, just go."

I nodded and hit the horn with the heel of my hand. We got a few glances, but nobody hurried up. One werewolf flipped us the finger and a snarl. I pursed my lips. "Dang it all."

Dahlia hung out the window. "Everybody move or we'll call the SDMP on you!"

The way parted in front of us like an ocean splitting down the middle. I hit the gas and we sped forward.

Ten minutes later, the stadium could be seen in the distance, lit up like a game was being held.

I grabbed the walkie-talkie from my waist and pressed the button. "Jensen, what's going on?"

The static on the other end made my heart pick up speed. I spoke again. "Jensen, talk to me."

The click came from the other end and I breathed a sigh of relief. Until he spoke. It wasn't Jensen.

"Drakaina. Your minion is with me now. He and your brother for your life. Hurry, little monster, I'm losing patience," Achilles said.

"Don't hurt them! I'm coming."

"Hurry, little snake. Hurry. I'll give you ten minutes, not a single one more." He whispered the last word, and the walkie-talkie went dead in my hand. I threw it to the floor, focusing on the anger that built in my belly.

"You aren't really going to try to talk to him, are you?" Sandy asked from the backseat.

"Not anymore." I bit the words out, my fangs lowering and my skin itching. Not a good sign. Not at all.

We reached the stadium with only minutes to spare. I kicked my door open and the hinge snapped off. I didn't care. I fed the anger that burned, that made me forget everything I'd ever been taught. Remo stepped from the shadows. "Do you have a plan?"

The final pieces of what I saw happening if this went right came together in a flash, like the final ingredients to a masterpiece.

"Beth and Sandy will take you and Dahlia over the top right to Tad and Jensen. The rest of your vamps will be ready to help you out if necessary. As soon as you have them, I'll deal with Achilles."

Remo nodded. "You sure you can take him?"

"Right now? Yes." My whole body shivered, and I snapped my head to the side. I flicked my tongue out, tasting the air.

Beth cleared her throat. "But we've never shifted into our other forms."

"No time like the present." I turned and put a hand on her shoulder. "You're a nurse, right? Trained to save lives?"

The fear in her eyes faded, replaced by confidence. "Yes."

"This is the same thing. You'll be saving two lives. Just keep that in mind."

She drew her tiny body up under my hand and gave a nod. She took two steps back and closed her eyes. Sandy looked at her, then followed suit. Mist curled around them from their feet, all the way to the top of their heads, covering them completely. As it blew away, two birds stood in their place, easily six feet tall. Their feathers were black and gold, and their beaks were wicked long with tiny teeth inside the edge of them.

"Your wings don't look metallic, but the info said you can throw your feathers like daggers, so be careful," I said.

They bobbed their heads and clacked their beaks in unison.

Without a word they launched into the air, their wings giving off a vibration that trembled over my skin, calling to my snake. Calling on me to shift. I clenched my hands, digging my nails into my palms.

"Are you okay?" Dahlia put a hand on my shoulder and I shook her off.

"Just go. Get them out." I breathed the words out, knowing I didn't have much longer before the shift took me whether I wanted it to or not. From the corner of my eye I saw Remo and Dahlia leap into the air and grab hold of Sandy's and Beth's claws.

The four of them swept upward, silent as they climbed high into the dark night. From the shadows of the building, twenty-five of Remo's vampires ran toward the stadium, grinning like demons in the dark of the night.

I ran with them, the curl of the winter air on my skin cooling the need to shift. Movement helped keep it under control, apparently; would have been nice if Ernie had told me that.

The vamps stopped at the first door. Max was in the lead and he held up his hand, beckoning me forward. He pointed at a contraption woven around the handles.

"The doors are locked and linked to a trigger to explode if they're tampered with."

"Are you sure?"

"Used to be on the bomb squad. This is serious stuff; it'll take out the support walls and crush anyone in the tunnels as they try to leave."

We wouldn't even be able to get the humans out then.

I looked up at the side of the stadium. "Can you climb?"

He chuckled. "Of course. Can you?"

"Anything you can do, I can do better," I said.

With a grin he crouched, muscles bunching before he jumped, and the rest of the vampires followed his lead.

Just like that, it was a race with all of us leaping for handholds. A strange sense of nostalgia rolled over me, like we were kids on a playground. Maybe a rather large, deadly playground, but still the feeling was there. Like I'd shed all the rules and demands of being an adult, wife, or good girl.

I climbed as though I'd been doing it all my life: finding hand- and footholds with ease, leaping to the side where I had to, swinging off one hand even.

I couldn't stop grinning. My brother's life was in jeopardy, and for that matter so was mine. But I'd never felt so alive. Like I was finally a part of something that was important.

"I think she likes this." Max spoke over my head, but I didn't care. He was right.

Another few seconds and we were at the top of the stadium, hanging on by our fingertips. They all looked to me like I knew what was supposed to happen next. I wished I'd watched more of the action movies Roger liked so much.

"Pull up slow, stay on your bellies," I whispered.

They did as I asked, and I did the same. From our bellies, there wasn't much to see. I looked up to the sky, but there was no sign of Beth or Sandy. Then again, their dark feathers weren't going to show up well in the night.

"Stay here." I eased into a crouch, climbing over the cement barrier in front of us while still keeping as low as possible. The stadium opened up in front of me, the green grass churned to mud by a thousand pairs of hooves. Three-quarters of the stadium was full of humans, the hum and warble of their voices rising through the air at a low drone. In front of me, the stadium section was bare, without a single human sitting in the stands.

Jensen hadn't been exaggerating about the Bull Boys. There were easily a thousand of them. Some stood out, though, larger than their buddies. Bull Boys on steroids. At the center of the stadium was a huge platform with two stakes standing in the middle of it, a man tied to each. Tad was on the left, and Jensen on the right.

Ernie floated between them and Achilles paced the front of the platform, a microphone in one hand and a sword in the other. His voice echoed up to me perfectly. "Where is she?"

"She'll come. I'm sure of it," Ernie said. "But you'd better be careful, Achilles. She's stronger than we all thought she was going to be."

"Pah. Merlin handpicked her."

Handpicked . . .

"I mean, he even convinced her brother to infect her! And now they're both going to die." Achilles strutted across the platform, his hands spread out to the sides. He did a slow spin and brought the mic back to his mouth. "Am I not a hero? Have I ever failed in killing a monster? This Drakaina will be no different."

The humans clapped, but the sound died out almost as soon as it started. He was losing their attention.

They were used to monster-truck rallies, baseball games, and huge concerts. Not a man wearing a skirt talking to them about a monster they couldn't see.

I slid back to where the vamps waited. "Spread out close to the mud. If the bird girls can get Remo and Dahlia in and out, we may not even need you. Can any of you defuse the bomb on the doors?" I should have thought to ask that before.

Max nodded. "I can. I think."

"Do it. Otherwise when the fighting starts and the humans try to get out, there's going to be a real mess."

He nodded and slid back down the side of the stadium. I slipped back over the cement, keeping low but still watching Achilles. I spared a glance for the night sky. A flicker of bright wings caught my eye for a split second before they appeared, dropping from the sky in a breathtaking dive. Remo and Dahlia clung to their claws, legs swept straight back with the speed at which the four of them fell.

Achilles looked up, some instinct preserving him as the first feathers shot forward on a flick of one of the girls' wings. He dove to the side, right off the stadium and into the mud. The feathers rat-a-tat-tatted into the wooden platform like a machine gun.

"Stymphalian birds! They were just turned!" Ernie yelled. Remo and Dahlia dropped from the birds and ran to the two men at the stakes. Their movements were too fast to follow, but the ropes dropping were enough to know they were getting the job done.

The crowd went wild, cheering, and the Jumbotron came to life, projecting exactly what was happening in minute, horrifying detail.

Tad slumped into Dahlia's arms and Jensen into Remo's. I couldn't take my eyes from the scene as Achilles stood up, a sword in one hand and a shield in the other. With a roar he leapt to the stage and rushed them.

There was no way they'd make it away from him carrying the two men.

"*No!*" I screamed, and bolted down the stairs.

Achilles spun, saw me, and grinned. "There you are, Drakaina."

The crowd oohed, like they'd been prepped for me too.

I was halfway down, the people around me twisting in their seats. "I'm the one you want."

"I want all the monsters dead, fool. I care not what breed of evil they are, only that they end their lives on the tip of my sword." He whipped his sword hand around, the blade shining in the stadium lights, as it swept toward the one closest to him.

The crowd began to chant his name. "Achilles, Achilles, Achilles." He held up his hands, asking for more.

Tad's eyes lifted to mine as Achilles drove the blade through my brother's stomach and out his back. The crowd gasped, Achilles's name stilling on their lips as the moment stretched. I could not believe what I was seeing. It wasn't possible that Tad was run through.

"Alena. Run. Get away." His words were not loud, but I knew him. I knew his heart and how he would have fought for me. That even now, he would try to protect me.

"*Tad!*" I screamed his name, and the crowd nearby turned away from my grief-stricken cry. The cameras zoomed in closer on me, and I saw the smoke begin to curl around me.

The uncoiling of my snake ripped through me and carried with it a second scream that arched from my throat and into the night air, the stadium acoustics throwing it high and wide. Around me, the vamps slapped their hands over their ears and fell to the ground. The humans closest to me scrambled away, leaving a large swath of stadium below me wide open.

The mist wrapped up around me with the speed of a lighting strike, and in a split second I rose in the stadium, my coils moving me toward Achilles at top speed.

Ernie spun. "Alena! Don't let the rage take you, it's what he wants!"

I whipped my head toward him, hissing and flicking venom from my fangs. Ernie was not my friend, I knew that much. Just his being at Achilles's side was enough for me to consider him an enemy.

Behind me, the crowd cried out in fear, some of them calling on Achilles to save them from the monster. From me.

Achilles grinned, and the Bull Boys around him raised their weapons, roaring their challenge.

"Boys. Let's get her." He pointed his sword at me and I swung my tail forward, slamming it through the first row of Bull Boys as if they were bowling pins. I moved into the open space, swinging my head, biting through flesh and leather armor as if it were nothing. Screams rent the air, pulsing through my blood.

He'd killed Tad.

I'd failed my brother.

"Rope her!"

The first rope settled over my neck, strangling me. A hiss erupted out of me, and I snapped my mouth at the Bull Boys who held the end of the rope. But another woven rope settled over my mouth and clamped it shut. I whipped my tail forward again and tucked my head down into my coils, writhing for all I was worth. Mud and blood flung through the air as my multicolored scales glittered and flexed.

"She's wounded! Aim for it!"

Wounded? I wasn't wounded, what were they talking about?

"Alena, you idiot, you cut yourself?" Ernie screamed over the din. Was he on my side or not?

I couldn't answer him, even if my mouth weren't clamped shut. More ropes settled over me, pinning me to the ground despite my writhing. I looked for Tad, but he was gone, as were Jensen and the three girls.

Remo had stayed.

And my heart did a funny little thump as I watched him battle with Achilles, the crowd cheering once more. The two men were well matched, but Remo was bigger. Faster.

But Achilles was a hero, and I was beginning to understand that there was no beating a hero. That wasn't how the world worked.

The monsters didn't take first place. Not ever.

A sharp pain ripped up through my side, and the Bull Boys bellowed with nothing short of triumph. I twisted my head to see a spear sticking out of my side about ten feet down from my head. The wound I'd given myself to save Dahlia. They pushed the spear in farther and I groaned with pain. Laughing, they twisted the weapon like they were making meringue out of my innards, whipping it around faster and faster.

Ernie fluttered down to me, his face splattered with mud and several of his feathers bent. "Listen, you can still beat him. You have to. Do you understand?"

I tore my eyes from the men to look at Ernie. The Bull Boys tightened the ropes around my neck and I gasped for breath, the world darkening for a split second. Maybe that would be better. At least I wouldn't feel what they did to me if I was unconscious.

"You can't kill her, that's Achilles's job," Ernie barked. The stranglehold lessened, as did the pain in my side as they yanked the spear out.

Ernie was back to me, whispering, "Shift down, out of snake form, and take this." He held out a tiny arrow. "Use it on Achilles and no one has to die."

Except that Tad already had. I jerked my head to the side, managing to dislodge several of the bulls that held me, and smashed my head into Ernie. I sent him tumbling head over butt into the mud, where he lay on his back, not moving, but I still heard him. "Ahh, I thought I was wrong about you, Lena. I thought you would show them a different kind of monster."

His words stung, hitting home as no threat of violence could have. The anger left me in a rush, and I let the snake's desire to protect itself and its territory slide away from me. The mist wrapped around my form once more, and I fell to the mud, the snake gone, along with all my clothes.

The men, and a few women, in the crowd whistled and catcalled, a cacophony of noise I did my best to block out.

This was not a time to be prudish. I ran, clutching my now-mangled arm to my side, slipping through the mud and taking advantage of the Bull Boys' shock. I dropped to my knees beside Ernie. "I'm sorry. Give me the arrow." He pressed it into my hands, and I helped him out of the mud. "I thought you were on Hera's side."

"It's complicated," he muttered. "Go. Before Achilles does more damage."

I spun in the mud and started toward the platform. Whatever advantage I had was gone; the Bull Boys were back on me. But the mud wasn't any easier for them to maneuver in than it was for me. They'd reach for me and I'd flinch away, missed by an inch at best.

Like a game of horrible tackle football, we careened toward the platform. I'd catch glimpses of weapons, of Remo's face, of a set of horns as one of Achilles's minions charged. Twice I fell to my knees, and both times Bull Boys flew over me as they leapt and missed.

I'd swept around the platform twice before I realized there were no stairs, no easy way to get up to where Achilles stood. Clutching my mangled arm, I spun, put my back to the platform, and faced the Bull Boys.

A screech that resonated along my skin snapped every eye to the sky. The two Stymphalian birds swept in a perfect dive. I raised my good hand and one of them grabbed me, yanking me out of the mud with a squelching pop. "Drop me on the platform!"

She did a single loop while arrows and knives were thrown at us. I was hit twice, but they glanced off. My human skin tore, but the scales underneath protected me.

Thank God for that. Good grief, did I really just thank God I had scales?

Her claws clung to me as we circled, and then she dropped me right behind Remo. He leapt forward and into Achilles. They went down in a tangled heap. Remo was on top, his fist slamming into Achilles over and over, the power of my blood running through his veins. Achilles dodged several of the blows, which sent Remo's fist straight through the base of the platform. The second time it happened his fist seemed to stick for a split second. It was enough of an advantage for Achilles.

The hero pulled a shining silver blade from his side and drove it into Remo's neck. Remo slumped, his body limp as one hand rose to the blade in his neck.

"No!" I screamed the word, and Achilles grinned at me.

There was a gasp from the crowd and one woman cried out. They didn't want to see Remo go down any more than I did.

"Turn for me, monster." He grinned at me, and I clutched the tiny arrow in my hand.

There was nothing I could do for Remo if I was dead. "You want to fight me, then fight me. Leave the others out of it. Unless you're afraid?"

He circled around me, his sword flicking back and forth like a metronome. "Are you not enraged by the death of your brother?"

His words sparked the anger and I fought to breathe through it, the snake in me lashing with her tail and snapping her deadly fangs as she hissed. The sound rumbled out past my clenched lips, which only exaggerated it.

Achilles waved his sword at me. "Come then, let us see your snake again. Let this be a true battle between hero"—he gave me a mocking bow—"and monster."

The crowd in the stadium gave a low oohing gasp. I wiped the mud from my face, flicking it off my fingers. The arrow I clutched with my bad hand was tucked carefully against my side so it wouldn't prick me.

Without warning, he lunged, slamming his shield into my chest and throwing me across the platform. I slid on the wood, caught my hip, and tumbled off the edge. I caught the lip of the platform with my good hand, barely stopping my free fall.

"Just give up, Drakaina. I'll make it quick. Easy. Relatively pain-free. I have to make a bit of a show of it, otherwise the good people here"— Achilles stood over me. He lifted a foot and brought it down on my fingers. It didn't hurt, but he ground his heel, forcing my fingers to slowly release, one by one—"might be upset that they didn't get what they wanted."

The arrow began to slip.

I stared up into his dark eyes. "You're more of a monster than me, Achilles."

He threw back his head and laughed. "Oh, I don't think the people would agree. Would they?"

The crowd was silent as I hung there, fighting for everything I had. He'd wanted an audience, and he'd gotten it. Except the people here had no reason to be afraid of me. Not really. I'd not killed anyone. Achilles had killed Tad without provocation, and now Remo too.

He was the killer in their eyes, and I think we both knew it.

Achilles stepped away from me and lifted his hands to the crowd. "Does a monster not deserve to die? Would you rather I let her go? You saw what she can do, how big she is. How dangerous. There is no way to contain that. I will save you, because Hera wishes it. And you *will* worship her for the goddess she is."

The arrow slipped from my fingers, and with it my hope of resolving the situation peacefully fled. How was I going to end this now? How was I going to make him go away without killing him, or him killing me? I could see no way out.

A murmur began to build in the crowd; fear spilled from the humans and into the arena. I pulled myself back up onto the platform and crawled to where Remo lay. I touched his head, turning him so I could see his face. He gave me a wink, the wound in his neck gone already.

"I like the dirty look," the vamp said.

A hand clamped onto my shoulder and spun me around. I went with it, driving my good hand in a hard fist up into Achilles's family jewels. He gasped and his face went white, yellow, then green as his eyes rolled back in his head.

Remo sat up. "Tell me you held back."

"Not for a second." I wobbled to my feet. Achilles writhed on his back, tears streaming from his eyes. I bent and scooped up his fallen sword. "Remo, roll him to his belly."

"Whatever you say, boss." He smiled at me, slapped my ass as he walked by, then grabbed Achilles's feet. With a quick flip he had him on his belly. "Now what?"

"I'm just guessing here." I laid the sword across the back of Achilles's legs, right above the ankle. I took a deep breath. "Achilles, I don't want to kill you. But I think if you can't walk, you might be less of a problem." I pushed hard enough to cut through the tendons, but stopped at the bone. He screamed as the blood pumped out.

Remo's eyebrows shot up. "That's cold."

It took everything I had not to cringe from the criticism. "He had it coming. Besides, it's his myth, not mine. And I am not the monster he thinks I am."

I held the sword out to Remo. "Thanks. You didn't have to stay."

He wrapped an arm around my waist and pulled me against his side. "I'm one of the monsters too, Alena. Do you think he would have stopped with you?"

"So this was self-preservation?" I couldn't help but be a little hurt. After all, it was the first time any man had stood up for me. Don't blame me for wanting the white knight to at least *try* to save me.

I suddenly remembered I was naked, save for the mud, and my upbringing reminded me I was supposed to not show my bits to anyone but my husband. I clung to Remo. "Give me your shirt."

A slow chuckle rolled out of him. "Already trying to get me out of my clothes?"

The crowd laughed, and I closed my eyes. "Please don't make this day harder than it already is. Is it not bad enough that they killed Tad?"

Remo shook his head. "We don't know he's dead."

At our feet, Achilles rolled over. "It was a gut wound. If he's not dead, he will be."

"Shut up." Remo booted Achilles in the side, rolling him off the platform and into the mud.

"Here. You *are* distracting everyone."

Remo slowly pulled his T-shirt up and over his head. A low whisper of female appreciation rolled through the crowd. He smirked as he handed me the shirt. I pulled it on, his smell enveloping me. I kept my mouth shut to keep from flicking my tongue out and tasting the air around me more fully.

The vampire wrapped an arm around my waist and jumped off the platform. The Bull Boys shuffled their feet, but none tried to stop us. "What, you don't want to try to finish the job?" I bit the words out, a part of me wanting them to try. Just let them.

I'd snap them in half like two-day-old breadsticks.

One of Achilles's minions grunted. "We're cannon fodder. The rules are that when the hero goes down, we have to back off."

"Sounds about right," Remo said. He held me tight to his side, and while he didn't hurry, we weren't exactly going slowly as we made our exit.

"They aren't following us." I looked back. The Bull Boys were dismantling the platform, and one of them scooped up Achilles while he cried out that life wasn't fair.

A roll of thunder rent the air, and I tightened my hand on Remo. "Stop."

He turned as a woman appeared on the partially dismantled platform. Her silvery-white hair floated about her face as if a constant wind blew around her. She was tall and lithe, her body a perfect combination of slim and curved that her sheer dress gave credence to. Her blue-green eyes locked on mine. "We are not done, Drakaina."

I had no doubt who she was. "Hera. Leave my family and me alone."

Remo grunted. "Hera. You're shitting me."

"Your family will be the first to suffer for this." She snapped her fingers, and an explosion rocked the stadium. The humans screamed and Remo dropped us to the ground, curling his body around mine. I really didn't want to like him, but he kept doing things like this. Things that made me think he had potential.

Bad Alena. Bad. No playing with the vampires, you're a married woman.

I wanted to slap my inner voice and tell her to shut up. But she was right.

We stood and stared into the now-emptying stadium. So it wasn't the bombs going off? The humans filed out, and with the continued lack of explosions I guessed Max had managed to get the bombs defused. The big bang was just Hera making her exit. Score another one for our team.

Hera's words sank in as we walked. "She's going after my family; I have to get to them first." I pulled away from Remo and ran through the dark halls of the stadium, following the flickers of fresh air that took me to the main doors.

The rest of Remo's vampires waited for us outside, and they cheered when we appeared. I ignored them and ran for my car. I slid into the seat, my body shaking. Not with cold or adrenaline, but fear. Fear that I wouldn't make it to Tad in time. Maybe he was like the vamps, and I could give him blood and he would heal up. I could only hope.

I refused to pray.

Remo slid into the passenger seat. "Do you even know where he is?"

"I assumed the safe house. That's the only place Beth and Sandy would know to go." I put the car into gear and hit the pedal, my bare foot gripping the edge of it.

Remo was thrown back in his seat and he grunted. "Ease off, crazy woman."

I didn't look at him. As I kept my eyes locked on the road, all I could think about was making it to Tad in time.

Whether it was to say good-bye or help him, I didn't know. Either way, I needed to get to his side.

"You really love your brother, don't you?"

"You sound surprised." I spun the wheel and we drifted through a corner, barely losing speed, my seat belt the only thing holding me in.

Remo shifted in his seat, and the click of the seat belt made me smile for a split second. "Most siblings don't get on that well. Rivalry and all that."

We sped toward the gate at the Wall. The mass of supernaturals blocking the way was too much. I slammed on the brakes, and the car slid sideways as it lost traction on the slick road.

Remo reached across and took my hand. "Who taught you to drive like that?"

"Mario Andretti." I glanced at him and his wide eyes and realized he believed me. "Never mind, it was a joke. A bad one."

"I doubted you about Achilles, and that seemed far-fetched. Why not Mario Andretti? At least I know he exists," Remo said.

I laid on the horn as I leaned out the window. "Get out of my way!"

The crowd rumbled and grumbled but slowly shifted as I revved the engine. At a crawl, we crossed through the gate. As soon as the crowd was clear, I pressed the pedal to the floor and raced along the streets.

The safe house was lit up, every light blazing out through the windows. "Not a good sign. International distress sign for a vampire safe house," Remo said softly.

I leapt from the car and ran to the front door. Dahlia swung the door open. Her green eyes dripped with tears, several catching on her eyelashes like tiny diamonds.

# # # #

# #

"Lena." She choked on my name.

"Don't say anything." I stepped inside, bracing myself for what was coming. The place smelled of blood and something foul I couldn't place. My tongue flicked out without warning, and the scent solidified in my brain.

Viscera, punctured bowels. A gut wound, as Achilles had said. I let the smell pull me forward, to the kitchen. Tad lay on the table, a sheet covering him from the waist down. Beth leaned over him. "Stay with me, Tad. I've almost got you stitched up."

Sandy stood at his head, holding him. "Keep breathing." Her eyes flicked up as I entered the room. "Your sister is here."

He didn't move, and his skin was chalky and white. I stumbled to his side and pressed my hands against his chest. His heart beat slowly, and the rise and fall of the air in his lungs was sporadic. I looked to Beth. "How bad?"

She didn't lift her eyes, only kept on with her stitching. "Bad. We need a doctor, a blood transfusion. Painkillers, antibiotics. We need a hospital, Alena. And there is no such thing here. Supes don't need doctors, according to the world."

I closed my eyes. "We were the same blood type, before we were turned. Will that work now?"

"He's going to die if we don't give him something," Beth said. "Dahlia, you and Remo get in here."

The two vamps came to the door, and Beth fired off instructions like a surgeon. "Remo, clean up Alena's arm with whatever alcohol you have in the house. Dahlia, I saw a transfusion kit in the bathroom, grab it."

Remo took me by the hand and led me to the kitchen sink while Dahlia ran out of the room. "Why do you have a transfusion kit in the bathroom?"

"This is a safe house. Vamps sometimes come in so close to death that they can't take enough blood by mouth to survive. We keep the kit on hand."

The warm water sluiced off the blood and mud, showing the open wound in my wrist. It had begun to heal, though it was hardly needing to be reopened. Pain sliced through me as the water kissed the edges of it. I sucked in a sharp breath.

"The vodka is going to burn worse than the water." He turned and pulled the vodka out of the fridge and unscrewed the cap. "Ready?"

I nodded and he poured the alcohol over my arm. The pain of the water was nothing to the heat and sting of the high-proof booze. I closed my eyes and bit back the whimper. For Tad, I could do this.

"All done." Remo took me by the hand and led me back to the table. Dahlia already had one end of the IV hooked into Tad. She held the other to Remo. He took it and carefully threaded it into the open vein in my arm. A slight pinch and then he took the piece of clean cotton she offered.

He was incredibly gentle, and to say it surprised me was an understatement. "You're good at this."

"I should be. I was a doctor at one point."

Beth's head snapped up. "What? Why aren't you helping me, then?"

Remo's eyes met mine. "Because Tad is beyond any surgeon's help, even mine. His sister's blood will either save him or kill him. Supernaturals don't respond to traditional methods of healing."

Someone pushed a chair into the back of my knees, prompting me to sit down. Remo tightened his hold on me. "Don't sit. Stand, you need gravity to help you with the blood flow."

I stepped up onto the chair and looked down to my brother. My sparkling red blood flowed through the vinyl tube and into his arm. "How long before we know if it helps?"

Remo shrugged. "I'd guess not long."

The room was silent except for the steady thump of the hearts of those waiting with me, and the sporadic kick and thump of Tad's as it fought to keep going.

"Why aren't you still a doctor?" I asked, breaking the silence, needing someone to talk to distract me from my brother's slide into the darkness.

Remo cleared his throat. "There was a time I believed the world could be changed. That there was a way to help the humans and supernaturals come together. I was wrong."

Bitterness, and more than that, fatigue, flowed with his words.

I stared down at him. "You can't give up."

"Why, because you said so?" He arched an eyebrow. "You can't change this world, Alena. The humans are too many. The laws too unfair. The only thing that is certain is death. Even taxes can be evaded if you know what you're doing." He smirked at that last, but I didn't laugh.

"Tad isn't going to die."

My words were met with silence. I looked at each face around the table. Beth wouldn't meet my eyes. Sandy's were full of sadness, and Dahlia continued to cry. Tad's heart still beat, though. I straightened my shoulders. "Until his heart stops we are not giving up."

"What do you suggest, then?" Remo asked. "There are no healers here. We'd need a satyr for any real help."

I bit my lower lip, and the thought hit me like a boot to the head. "The fauns who were searching for Zeus! Damara was a satyr and she owes me!"

"Who?" Dahlia blinked up at me. My heart raced.

"Damara. A satyr Tad and I helped escape the SDMP. She said I could call on her if I had need."

"How are you going to do that?" Remo asked. "There is no way—"

"Hermes!" I hollered the messenger's name, not knowing if it would work. The others slapped their hands over their ears, and Tad gave a shudder even in his unconscious state.

"What the hell?" Remo snapped. "That is not how you—"

Hermes zipped in through the kitchen window and saluted me. "Drakaina, you have a message you need delivered?"

Remo's jaw dropped open, showing his fangs, but I didn't rub in the fact that calling for Hermes had indeed worked. "Damara, the satyr, can you find her?"

"Of course."

"I need her to come here. Tell her Alena needs her services as a healer."

He saluted and was gone in a flash of wings.

"Well, shit, you are just full of surprises, aren't you?" Remo muttered. I finally looked at him.

"I'm a woman. What did you expect, a Sunday drive?"

"No." He smiled. "But I didn't expect a trek through the jungle."

I tried to smile back, but the edges faltered and fell. Tad had to hold on, he had to.

I couldn't lose him again.

CHAPTER 16

An hour slipped by with no word from Hermes and no appearance of Damara. My blood dripped steadily into Tad, and his blood dripped steadily from his wounds no matter how Beth packed them.

"I'm sorry, I know I missed something but I can't find it."

I closed my eyes. "Thank you for trying. It's more than some people would do."

Remo grunted as if I'd slapped him. "Not subtle."

"Wasn't supposed to be," I murmured, swaying ever so slightly where I stood on the chair, a human IV bag.

Remo went to the sink and washed his hands. "Dahlia, pour the vodka for me."

She hurried to his side and did as he asked, dousing his hands with the alcohol.

He flicked his fingers once and then moved to Beth's side. He peered into the still-open wound. He reached in and touched a spot that seemed fine, but when he turned the piece of innards over, blood pulsed out. "Stitch this. He should stabilize."

Beth took the last of the catgut and went to work, stitching the final piece up. "I don't have enough to stitch him the rest of the way."

We all looked at each other, and I knew then that we'd lost Tad.

"Well, it's a good thing I do."

I whipped my head around to see the petite blond satyr step into the room. "You made it. Thank you for coming."

She didn't look at me, her eyes locking on Tad's wounds. "I gave you my word I'd help you if you called on me. Hermes made it clear your brother was wounded badly and needed a healer's touch." Damara hurried to Tad's side and peered into his stomach. "Healing up a supernatural isn't like a human. On one hand harder and the other hand easier. A human would have never survived this long." She dug into her bag and laid a few things out on Tad's chest. "And yet if he'd been human you could have taken him to the hospital."

Her tiny hands moved like butterflies, lighting on things from her bag, herbs and pieces of bark, and then fluttering over the wound. "Whoever stitched him up saved him. The blood was a good idea too."

She yanked the IV out of his arm. "But I need you all out now. I work alone."

Beth held her ground. "I'm a nurse. If I'm going to live in this world, I want to be able to help still."

"Fine." Damara waved a hand absently at her. "Stay. But the rest, out."

Dahlia touched Tad on the cheek as she went by, and Sandy followed her lead. Remo held a hand up to me and helped me down. I stumbled and he caught me.

"How long since you slept?"

I blinked up at him, as I counted back. "I haven't."

His eyes shot up. "Since you've been turned?"

I shook my head. "No, I haven't had time."

He hustled me out of the room, through the living area, and up the stairs to the second floor. "Shower. Clean clothes. Then sleep." He all but shoved me into the bathroom.

The word *sleep* resonated through me, and my movements became sluggish as if I were drugged. I flicked on the hot water and stepped into the heavy flow. The shower didn't perk me up but instead seemed to drug me further, slowing my movements to a crawl. With the mud, blood, and sweat from the last few days washed off my body, I wrapped myself in a towel and stepped out of the bathroom. Immediately across from me was a bedroom, the sheets turned down on the bed. I dropped the towel and climbed under the blankets. The sheets were soft and the mattress seemed to suck me down into it in a welcoming embrace. I breathed out a sigh and closed my eyes, and sleep claimed me.

A soft rumble in my ear woke me and I rolled into the deep bass, my nose leading me. I buried my face against the juncture of neck and chest and breathed in his smell. Roger had never smelled so good. Cinnamon and honey . . . my mouth watered with wanting to taste the combination.

I jerked upright, the sheets falling to my waist. Remo grinned up at me. "That's a good look for you."

I yanked the sheets up, or tried to. He lay on top of the blankets, effectively keeping me from covering up. I slid back down enough that I could at least cover my chest.

"What time is it?"

"Midnight."

"That's not possible, it was after midnight when . . . I slept that long?"

He nodded. "Almost twenty-four hours. Even supernaturals need to sleep. Especially those who are freshly turned. The fact that you stayed awake as long as you did is surprising."

A tremor started in my belly and spilled upward. "Tad. Did he . . . ?"

Remo gave me a wink. "Remind me never to bet against you."

Alive, Tad was alive? "Really?"

He nodded. "Really."

I leapt from the bed, no longer caring that I was naked as I streaked down the stairs and ran into the kitchen.

Tad wasn't there. I spun around. "Where is he?"

"Sis?" Tad called, and I turned again to see him on the couch in the living room I'd just streaked through. Dahlia sat next to him, and Damara was at his feet, her bag open along with her mouth. Beth and Sandy were nowhere to be seen, but when I listened, I could hear their hearts beating in tandem upstairs. I grinned.

"Tad, you're okay!"

"Can you do something for me?" He grimaced and rolled his eyes up to the ceiling.

"Of course, anything." I took a step toward him and he put up his hand.

"Can you go put some clothes on?"

I laughed. "Tad, you think this is bad, you should see me covered in scales and blood."

He peeked at me with one eye. "Do I even want to know?"

Still laughing, I shook my head. "Maybe. But I think I'll wait till Yaya gets inside before we talk about that."

"Yaya's here?"

I nodded and headed for the stairs, Yaya's heartbeat calling to me from the other side of the door, as familiar to me as Tad's. I paused and held it open. "Hey, Yaya."

She smiled up at me. "My beautiful girl. Go put some clothes on, you make my skin twitch and shiver just looking at you."

Smiling, I went upstairs. The closet of clothes offered up a variety of things, and I took my time picking through. Now that we'd stopped Achilles and saved Tad, and Yaya was out of the hospital, the weight of responsibility dusted off my shoulders. I took my time looking through the variety of materials and choices. I steered clear of the longer skirts and thick winter sweaters. The cold didn't bother me, no need to pretend I was something I wasn't. Finally I settled on the everyday, and yet even that wasn't quite right.

I slid on a pair of jeans and a long-sleeved lace top. The lace played peekaboo with the skin across my middle, the pattern on it mimicking the scales that lay hidden another layer below. I liked the look. For the first time since I was a little girl, I felt like . . . me. Like this was the Alena I was always meant to be.

I brushed through my hair and stared at the mirror. Attached to it was a note from Remo.

You know where I am.

"Cocky," I whispered, my mouth stumbling over the almost-naughty word. Yet I still smiled.

I was halfway down the stairs when trouble flew in through the door. Ernie grimaced up at me and my smile slid.

"I don't think you should be here, cherub." My smile slipped further until I was frowning. "I don't know whose side you're on."

He let out a long sigh. "It's complicated. I'm on your side, but the people I deal with, they aren't exactly stable. You saw Hera. Achilles. Even Zeus. You think keeping my head attached to my body has been an easy thing all these years? You have to look like you support them all, while making sure they all think you only support the one you're dealing with."

His explanation didn't make me feel any better. But for the moment, it would have to do.

"Fine. But don't tell me we have more problems. I've had my share for the year."

"Oh, *we* don't have problems. But you do. You most certainly do."

I slid to my bum on the stairs. "Tell me."

Ernie flitted to my side and sat beside me. "Achilles is dealt with; that was a slick move cutting his tendons. But Hera is far from done. She's raising another hero to take you and the bird girls out. Someone even stronger than Achilles."

"Who?" I whispered.

"The slayer of the Minotaur. He's smarter than Achilles and is a demigod to boot." Ernie paused, and I let out a breath.

"You mean that Achilles was just the warm-up act?"

"Exactly. Hera is pulling out the big guns now. Theseus will not go down as easy as Achilles. Not by a long shot." Ernie placed a hand on my knee. "And Zeus is nowhere to be found."

"You mean he's been godnapped?" Tad barked out from the living room.

Ernie shook his head. "No, I mean he's gone into hiding. He won't be any help against Hera and Theseus."

The smile and laughter that had been so light on my shoulders faded. "Then I will face Theseus without Zeus. Not that he was much help this time around."

"Not without me," Dahlia said. I smiled at her, the weight on me easing a little.

"Or me," Sandy and Beth said together.

Yaya winked at me and made a shooting motion with one hand. "Or me. We will stand together in this, little snake. Just like a family should."

I stood up. "Well, until Theseus shows up at the door, there's no point in worrying."

"What are you going to do?" Damara stood and faced me.

"I'm going to bake something. Maybe add a little venom to it and have it delivered to Hera. What do you say, Ernie? Think she would like some venom in her vanilla cupcakes?"

Ernie laughed and flipped over backward. "Oh, I think she would love them."

Though my smile was not as big, the weight on my shoulders wasn't either. I wasn't facing this alone. And maybe, just maybe, I could find a way to make it in this life as a monster.

ACKNOWLEDGMENTS

I'd like to thank all those who helped bring this piece to publication. First thanks go to Adrienne Lombardo, who saw the potential in Alena to be a character readers would root for and has gone to bat for Alena more than once in this process. I would also be remiss if I didn't mention Tegan Tigani, my developmental editor. She drew depth and story layers out of this book that I don't think would have otherwise happened. ☺ As always I need to thank my wonderful husband (who still hasn't read a thing I've written, and I doubt he ever will unless I can knock out a western). He still cheers me on even though I know his eyes glaze over when I launch into telling him about a new story idea. My little man (Little T) is too young to know his mama's a writer, but even so he inspires me every day. I thank those who have encouraged me, most especially those who were there at the beginning: my friends Lux, Katie, Carmen, Eilish, and Dmytry (San Francisco and Pillow Gate shall be a memory I cherish always, ha-ha!). And thanks to Denise for reading a rather rough draft—that is a real friend who can read something that needs editing and still see it for what it could be. Last but not least, thank you, Lysa, for your support, long phone calls, and sometimes longer texts. Your friendship and shoulder have made the last few years more than bearable as well as more than a little crazy.

They've helped make them outstanding.

ABOUT THE AUTHOR

Shannon Mayer lives in the southwestern tip of Canada with her husband, dog, cats, horse, and cows. When not writing she spends her time staring at immense amounts of rain, herding old people (similar to herding cats), and attempting to stay out of trouble. Especially that last is difficult for her.

She is the *USA Today* bestselling author of the Rylee Adamson Novels, the Elemental Series, the Nevermore Trilogy, A Celtic Legacy series, and several contemporary romances.

To learn more about Shannon and her books, go to www.shannonmayer.com.

Sign up for Shannon Mayer's Newsletter:
http://www.shannonmayer.com/tut8